PENGUIN ENGLISH LIBRARY

# The Cop and the Anthem

O. Henry (1862–1910) had a short but colourful life. Born William Porter in Greensboro, North Carolina, he initially worked as a pharmacist before moving into journalism. In 1896 he was arrested for embezzling funds while working as a bookkeeper for a bank. In a moment of madness, he absconded on his way to the courthouse before his trial and fled to Honduras for six months. He returned to face trial after learning that his wife was dying of tuberculosis and served three years in jail. While in prison, he adopted the pen name O. Henry, and after his release he found great fame and popularity as a short story writer.

T0322322

# The Cop and the Anthem and Other Stories

## O. HENRY

•••

PENGUIN ENGLISH
LIBRARY

# PENGUIN BOOKS

UK | USA | Canada | Ireland | Australia
India | New Zealand | South Africa

Penguin Books is part of the Penguin Random House group of companies
whose addresses can be found at global.penguinrandomhouse.com.

This selection first published in the Penguin English Library 2020

I

Front cover illustration: Coralie Bickford-Smith

Set in 11/13 pt Dante MT Std
Typeset by Jouve (UK), Milton Keynes
Printed and bound in Great Britain by Clays Ltd, Elcograf S.p.A.

A CIP catalogue record for this book is available from the British Library

ISBN: 978-0-241-44746-8

# Contents

# Contents

# The Cop and the Anthem

On his bench in Madison Square Soapy moved uneasily. When wild geese honk high of nights, and when women without sealskin coats grow kind to their husbands, and when Soapy moves uneasily on his bench in the park, you may know that winter is near at hand.

A dead leaf fell in Soapy's lap. That was Jack Frost's card. Jack is kind to the regular denizens of Madison Square, and gives fair warning of his annual call. At the corners of four streets he hands his pasteboard to the North Wind, footman of the mansion of All Outdoors, so that the inhabitants thereof may make ready.

Soapy's mind became cognizant of the fact that the time had come for him to resolve himself into a singular Committee of Ways and Means to provide against the coming rigor. And therefore he moved uneasily on his bench.

The hibernatorial ambitions of Soapy were not of the highest. In them were no considerations of Mediterranean cruises, of soporific Southern skies or drifting in the Vesuvian Bay. Three months on the Island was what his soul craved. Three months of assured board and bed and congenial company, safe from Boreas and bluecoats, seemed to Soapy the essence of things desirable.

For years the hospitable Blackwell's had been his winter quarters. Just as his more fortunate fellow New Yorkers had bought their tickets to Palm Beach and the Riviera each winter, so Soapy had made his humble arrangements for his annual hegira to the Island. And now the time was come. On the previous night three Sabbath newspapers, distributed beneath his coat, about his ankles and over his lap, had failed to repulse the cold as he slept on his bench near the spurting fountain in the ancient square. So the Island loomed big and timely in Soapy's mind. He scorned the provisions made in the name of charity for the city's dependants. In Soapy's opinion the Law was more benign than Philanthropy. There was an endless round of institutions, municipal and elee-mosynary, on which he might set out and receive lodging and food accordant with the simple life. But to one of Soapy's proud spirit the gifts of charity are encumbered. If not in coin you must pay in humiliation of spirit for every benefit received at the hands of philanthropy. As Caesar had his Brutus, every bed of charity must have its toll of a bath, every loaf of bread its compensation of a private and personal inquisition. Wherefore it is better to be a guest of the law, which, though conducted by rules, does not meddle unduly with a gentleman's private affairs.

Soapy, having decided to go to the Island, at once set about accomplishing his desire. There were many easy ways of doing this. The pleasantest was to dine luxuriously at some expensive restaurant; and then, after declaring insolvency, be handed over quietly and without uproar to a policeman. An accommodating magistrate would do the rest.

Soapy left his bench and strolled out of the square and across the level sea of asphalt, where Broadway and Fifth Avenue flow together. Up Broadway he turned, and halted at a glittering café, where are gathered together nightly the choicest products of the grape, the silkworm, and the protoplasm.

Soapy had confidence in himself from the lowest button of his vest upward. He was shaven, and his coat was decent and his neat black, ready-tied four-in-hand had been presented to him by a lady missionary on Thanksgiving Day. If he could reach a table in the restaurant unsuspected success would be his. The portion of him that would show above the table would raise no doubt in the wait-er's mind. A roasted mallard duck, thought Soapy, would be about the thing – with a bottle of Chablis, and then Camembert, a demi-tasse and a cigar. One dollar for the cigar would be enough. The total would not be so high as to call forth any supreme manifest-ation of revenge from the café management; and yet the meat would leave him filled and happy for the journey to his winter refuge.

But as Soapy set foot inside the restaurant door the head waiter's eye fell upon his frayed trousers and decadent shoes. Strong and ready hands turned him about and conveyed him in silence and haste to the sidewalk and averted the ignoble fate of the menaced mallard.

Soapy turned off Broadway. It seemed that his route to the coveted Island was not to be an epicurean one. Some other way of entering limbo must be thought of.

At a corner of Sixth Avenue electric lights and cunningly displayed wares behind plate-glass made a shop window conspicuous. Soapy took a cobblestone and dashed it through the glass. People came running around the corner, a policeman in the lead. Soapy stood still, with his hands in his pockets, and smiled at the sight of brass buttons.

'Where's the man that done that?' inquired the officer, excitedly.

'Don't you figure out that I might have had something to do with it?' said Soapy, not without sarcasm, but friendly, as one greets good fortune.

The policeman's mind refused to accept Soapy even as a clue. Men who smash windows do not remain to parley with the law's minions. They take to their heels. The policeman saw a man half-way down the block running to catch a car. With drawn club he joined in the pursuit. Soapy, with disgust in his heart, loafed along, twice unsuccessful.

On the opposite side of the street was a restaurant of no great pretensions. It catered to large appetites and modest purses. Its crockery and atmosphere were thick; its soup and napery thin. Into this place Soapy took his accusive shoes and telltale trousers without challenge. At a table he sat and consumed beefsteak, flapjacks, doughnuts and pie. And then to the waiter he betrayed the fact that the minutest coin and himself were strangers.

'Now, get busy and call a cop,' said Soapy. 'And don't keep a gentleman waiting.'

'No cop for youse,' said the waiter, with a voice like butter cakes and an eye like the cherry in a Manhattan cocktail. 'Hey, Con!'

Neatly upon his left ear on the callous pavement two waiters pitched Soapy. He arose joint by joint, as a carpenter's rule opens, and beat the dust from his clothes. Arrest seemed but a rosy dream. The Island seemed very far away. A policeman who stood before a drug store two doors away laughed and walked down the street.

Five blocks Soapy traveled before his courage permitted him to woo capture again. This time the opportunity presented what he fatuously termed to himself a 'cinch.' A young woman of a modest and pleasing guise was standing before a shop window gazing with sprightly interest at its display of shaving mugs and inkstands, and two yards from the window a large policeman of severe demeanor leaned against a water plug.

It was Soapy's design to assume the rôle of the despicable and execrated 'masher.' The refined and elegant appearance of his victim and the contiguity of the conscientious cop encouraged him to believe that he would soon feel the pleasant official clutch upon his arm that would insure his winter quarters on the right little, tight little isle.

Soapy straightened the lady missionary's ready-made tie, dragged his shrinking cuffs into the open, set his hat at a killing cant and sidled toward the young woman. He made eyes at her, was taken with sudden coughs and 'hems,' smiled, smirked and went brazenly through the impudent and contemptible litany of the 'masher.' With half an eye Soapy saw that the policeman was watching him fixedly. The young woman moved away a few steps, and again bestowed her absorbed attention upon the shaving mugs. Soapy followed, boldly stepping to her side, raised his hat and said:

'Ah there, Bedelia! Don't you want to come and play in my yard?'

The policeman was still looking. The persecuted young woman had but to beckon a finger and Soapy would be practically en route for his insular haven. Already he imagined he could feel the cozy warmth of the stationhouse. The young woman faced him and, stretching out a hand, caught Soapy's coat sleeve.

'Sure, Mike,' she said, joyfully, 'if you'll blow me to a pail of suds. I'd have spoke to you sooner, but the cop was watching.'

With the young woman playing the clinging ivy to his oak Soapy walked past the policeman overcome with gloom. He seemed doomed to liberty.

At the next corner he shook off his companion and ran. He halted in the district where by night are found the lightest streets, hearts, vows and librettos. Women in furs and men in greatcoats moved gaily in the wintry air. A sudden fear seized Soapy that some dreadful enchantment had rendered him immune to arrest. The thought brought a little of panic upon it, and when he came upon another policeman lounging grandly in front of a transplendent theater he caught at the immediate straw of 'disorderly conduct.'

On the sidewalk Soapy began to yell drunken gibberish at the top of his harsh voice. He danced, howled, raved, and otherwise distributed the welkin.

The policeman twirled his club, turned his back to Soapy and remarked to a citizen:

' 'Tis one of them Yale lads celebratin' the goose egg they give to the Hartford College. Noisy; but no harm. We've instructions to lave them be.'

Disconsolate, Soapy ceased his unavailing racket. Would never a policeman lay hands on him? In his fancy the Island seemed an unattainable Arcadia. He buttoned his thin coat against the chilling wind.

In a cigar store he saw a well-dressed man lighting a cigar at a swinging light. His silk umbrella he had set by the door on entering. Soapy stepped inside, secured the umbrella and sauntered off with it slowly. The man at the cigar light followed hastily.

'My umbrella,' he said, sternly.

'Oh, is it?' sneered Soapy, adding insult to petit larceny. 'Well, why don't you call a policeman? I took it. Your umbrella! Why don't you call a cop? There stands one on the corner.'

The umbrella owner slowed his steps. Soapy did likewise, with a presentiment that luck would again run against him. The policeman looked at the two curiously.

'Of course,' said the umbrella man – 'that is – well, you know how these mistakes occur – I – if it's your umbrella I hope you'll excuse me – I picked it up this morning in a restaurant – If you recognize it as yours, why – I hope you'll –'

'Of course it's mine,' said Soapy, viciously.

The ex-umbrella man retreated. The policeman hurried to assist a tall blonde in an opera cloak across the street in front of a street car that was approaching two blocks away.

Soapy walked eastward through a street damaged by improvements. He hurled the umbrella wrathfully into an excavation. He muttered against the men who wear helmets and carry clubs. Because he wanted to fall into their clutches, they seemed to regard him as a king who could do no wrong.

At length Soapy reached one of the avenues to the east where the glitter and turmoil was but faint. He set his face down this toward Madison Square, for the homing instinct survives even when the home is a park bench.

But on an unusually quiet corner Soapy came to a standstill. Here was an old church, quaint and rambling and gabled. Through one violet-stained window a soft light glowed, where, no doubt, the organist loitered over the keys, making sure of his mastery of the coming Sabbath anthem. For there drifted out to Soapy's ears sweet music that caught and held him transfixed against the convolutions of the iron fence.

The moon was above, lustrous and serene; vehicles and pedestrians were few; sparrows twittered sleepily in the eaves – for a little while the scene might have been a country church-yard. And the anthem that the organist played cemented Soapy to the iron fence, for he had known it well in the days when his life contained such things as mothers and roses and ambitions and friends and immaculate thoughts and collars.

The conjunction of Soapy's receptive state of mind and the influences about the old church wrought a sudden and wonderful change in his soul. He viewed with swift horror the pit into which he had tumbled, the degraded days, unworthy desires, dead hopes, wrecked faculties and base motives that made up his existence.

And also in a moment his heart responded thrillingly to this novel mood. An instantaneous and strong impulse moved him to battle with his desperate fate. He would pull himself out of the mire; he would make a man of himself again; he would conquer the evil that had taken possession of him. There was time; he was comparatively young yet: he would resurrect his old eager ambitions and pursue them without faltering. Those solemn but sweet organ notes had set up a revolution in him. To-morrow he would go into the roaring downtown district and find work. A fur importer had once offered him a place as driver. He would find him to-morrow and ask for the position. He would be somebody in the world. He would –

Soapy felt a hand laid on his arm. He looked quickly around into the broad face of a policeman.

'What are you doin' here?' asked the officer.

'Nothin',' said Soapy.

'Then come along,' said the policeman.

'Three months on the Island,' said the Magistrate in the Police Court the next morning.

# The Gift of the Magi

One dollar and eighty-seven cents. That was all. And sixty cents of it was in pennies. Pennies saved one and two at a time by bull-dozing the grocer and the vegetable man and the butcher until one's cheeks burned with the silent imputation of parsimony that such close dealing implied. Three times Della counted it. One dollar and eighty-seven cents. And the next day would be Christmas.

There was clearly nothing to do but flop down on the shabby little couch and howl. So Della did it. Which instigates the moral reflection that life is made up of sobs, sniffles, and smiles, with sniffles predominating.

While the mistress of the home is gradually subsiding from the first stage to the second, take a look at the home. A furnished flat at $8 per week. It did not exactly beggar description, but it certainly had that word on the lookout for the mendicancy squad.

In the vestibule below was a letter-box into which no letter would go, and an electric button from which no mortal finger could coax a ring. Also appertaining thereunto was a card bearing the name 'Mr James Dillingham Young.'

The 'Dillingham' had been flung to the breeze during a former period of prosperity when its possessor was being paid $30 per week. Now, when the income was shrunk to $20, the letters of 'Dillingham' looked blurred, as though they were thinking ser-iously of contracting to a modest and unassuming D. But whenever Mr James Dillingham Young came home and reached his flat above he was called 'Jim' and greatly hugged by Mrs James Dillingham Young, already introduced to you as Della. Which is all very good.

Della finished her cry and attended to her cheeks with the

powder rag. She stood by the window and looked out dully at a gray cat walking a gray fence in a gray backyard. To-morrow would be Christmas Day and she had only $1.87 with which to buy Jim a present. She had been saving every penny she could for months, with this result. Twenty dollars a week doesn't go far. Expenses had been greater than she had calculated. They always are. Only $1.87 to buy a present for Jim. Her Jim. Many a happy hour she had spent planning for something nice for him. Something fine and rare and sterling – something just a little bit near to being worthy of the honor of being owned by Jim.

There was a pier-glass between the windows of the room. Perhaps you have seen a pier-glass in an $8 flat. A very thin and very agile person may, by observing his reflection in a rapid sequence of longitudinal strips, obtain a fairly accurate conception of his looks. Della, being slender, had mastered the art.

Suddenly she whirled from the window and stood before the glass. Her eyes were shining brilliantly, but her face had lost its color within twenty seconds. Rapidly she pulled down her hair and let it fall to its full length.

Now, there were two possessions of the James Dillingham Youngs in which they both took a mighty pride. One was Jim's gold watch that had been his father's and his grandfather's. The other was Della's hair. Had the Queen of Sheba lived in the flat across the airshaft, Della would have let her hair hang out the window some day to dry just to depreciate Her Majesty's jewels and gifts. Had King Solomon been the janitor, with all his treasures piled up in the basement, Jim would have pulled out his watch every time he passed, just to see him pluck at his beard from envy.

So now Della's beautiful hair fell about her rippling and shining like a cascade of brown waters. It reached below her knee and made itself almost a garment for her. And then she did it up again nervously and quickly. Once she faltered for a minute and stood still while a tear or two splashed on the worn red carpet.

On went her old brown jacket; on went her old brown hat. With a whirl of skirts and with the brilliant sparkle still in her eyes, she fluttered out the door and down the stairs to the street.

Where she stopped the sign read: 'Mme. Sofronie. Hair Goods of All Kinds.' One flight up Della ran, and collected herself, panting. Madame, large, too white, chilly, hardly looked the 'Sofronie.'

'Will you buy my hair?' asked Della.

'I buy hair,' said Madame. 'Take yer hat off let's have a sight at the looks of it.'

Down rippled the brown cascade.

'Twenty dollars,' said Madame, lifting the mass with a practiced hand.

'Give it to me quick,' said Della.

Oh, and the next two hours tripped by on rosy wings. Forget the hashed metaphor. She was ransacking the stores for Jim's present.

She found it at last. It surely had been made for Jim and no one else. There was no other like it in any of the stores, and she had turned all of them inside out. It was a platinum fob chain simple and chaste in design, properly proclaiming its value by substance alone and not by meretricious ornamentation – as all good things should do. It was even worthy of The Watch. As soon as she saw it she knew that it must be Jim's. It was like him. Quietness and value – the description applied to both. Twenty-one dollars they took from her for it, and she hurried home with the 87 cents. With that chain on his watch Jim might be properly anxious about the time in any company. Grand as the watch was, he sometimes looked at it on the sly on account of the old leather strap that he used in place of a chain.

When Della reached home her intoxication gave way a little to prudence and reason. She got out her curling irons and lighted the gas and went to work repairing the ravages made by generosity added to love. Which is always a tremendous task, dear friends – a mammoth task.

Within forty minutes her head was covered with tiny, close-lying curls that made her look wonderfully like a truant schoolboy. She looked at her reflection in the mirror long, carefully, and critically.

'If Jim doesn't kill me,' she said to herself, 'before he takes a second look at me, he'll say I look like a Coney Island chorus girl. But what could I do – oh! what could I do with a dollar and eighty-seven cents?'

At 7 o'clock the coffee was made and the frying-pan was on the back of the stove hot and ready to cook the chops.

Jim was never late. Della doubled the fob chain in her hand and sat on the corner of the table near the door that he always entered. Then she heard his step on the stair away down on the first flight, and she turned white for just a moment. She had a habit of saying little silent prayers about the simplest everyday things, and now she whispered: 'Please God, make him think I am still pretty.'

The door opened and Jim stepped in and closed it. He looked thin and very serious. Poor fellow, he was only twenty-two – and to be burdened with a family! He needed a new overcoat and he was without gloves.

Jim stepped inside the door, as immovable as a setter at the scent of quail. His eyes were fixed upon Della, and there was an expression in them that she could not read, and it terrified her. It was not anger, nor surprise, nor disapproval, nor horror, nor any of the sentiments that she had been prepared for. He simply stared at her fixedly with that peculiar expression on his face.

Della wriggled off the table and went for him.

'Jim, darling,' she cried, 'don't look at me that way. I had my hair cut off and sold it because I couldn't have lived through Christmas without giving you a present. It'll grow out again – you won't mind, will you? I just had to do it. My hair grows awfully fast. Say "Merry Christmas!" Jim, and let's be happy. You don't know what a nice – what a beautiful, nice gift I've got for you.'

'You've cut off your hair?' asked Jim, laboriously, as if he had not arrived at that patent fact yet even after the hardest mental labor.

'Cut it off and sold it,' said Della. 'Don't you like me just as well, anyhow? I'm me without my hair, ain't I?'

Jim looked about the room curiously.

'You say your hair is gone?' he said, with an air almost of idiocy.

'You needn't look for it,' said Della. 'It's sold, I tell you – sold and gone, too. It's Christmas Eve, boy. Be good to me, for it went for you. Maybe the hairs on my head were numbered,' she went on with a sudden serious sweetness, 'but nobody could ever count my love for you. Shall I put the chops on, Jim?'

Out of his trance Jim seemed quickly to wake. He enfolded his Della. For ten seconds let us regard with discreet scrutiny some inconsequential object in the other direction. Eight dollars a week or a million a year – what is the difference? A mathematician or a wit would give you the wrong answer. The magi brought valuable gifts, but that was not among them. This dark assertion will be illuminated later on.

Jim drew a package from his overcoat pocket and threw it upon the table.

'Don't make any mistake, Dell,' he said, 'about me. I don't think there's anything in the way of a haircut or a shave or a shampoo that could make me like my girl any less. But if you'll unwrap that package you may see why you had me going a while at first.'

White fingers and nimble tore at the string and paper. And then an ecstatic scream of joy; and then, alas! a quick feminine change to hysterical tears and wails, necessitating the immediate employment of all the comforting powers of the lord of the flat.

For there lay The Combs – the set of combs, side and back, that Della had worshipped for long in a Broadway window. Beautiful combs, pure tortoise shell, with jeweled rims – just the shade to wear in the beautiful vanished hair. They were expensive combs, she knew, and her heart had simply craved and yearned over them without the least hope of possession. And now, they were hers, but the tresses that should have adorned the coveted adornments were gone.

But she hugged them to her bosom, and at length she was able to look up with dim eyes and a smile and say: 'My hair grows so fast, Jim!'

And then Della leaped up like a little singed cat and cried, 'Oh, oh!'

Jim had not yet seen his beautiful present. She held it out to him eagerly upon her open palm. The dull precious metal seemed to flash with a reflection of her bright and ardent spirit.

'Isn't it a dandy, Jim? I hunted all over town to find it. You'll have to look at the time a hundred times a day now. Give me your watch. I want to see how it looks on it.'

Instead of obeying, Jim tumbled down on the couch and put his hands under the back of his head and smiled.

'Dell,' said he, 'let's put our Christmas presents away and keep 'em a while. They're too nice to use just at present. I sold the watch to get the money to buy your combs. And now suppose you put the chops on.'

The magi, as you know, were wise men – wonderfully wise men – who brought gifts to the Babe in the manger. They invented the art of giving Christmas presents. Being wise, their gifts were no doubt wise ones, possibly bearing the privilege of exchange in case of duplication. And here I have lamely related to you the uneventful chronicle of two foolish children in a flat who most unwisely sacrificed for each other the greatest treasures of their house. But in a last word to the wise of these days let it be said that of all who give gifts these two were the wisest. Of all who give and receive gifts, such as they are wisest. Everywhere they are wisest. They are the magi.

# The Love-Philtre of Ikey Schoenstein

The Blue Light Drug Store is downtown, between the Bowery and First Avenue, where the distance between the two streets is the shortest. The Blue Light does not consider that pharmacy is a thing of bric-à-brac, scent and ice-cream soda. If you ask it for pain-killer it will not give you a bonbon.

The Blue Light scorns the labor-saving arts of modern pharmacy. It macerates its opium and percolates its own laudanum and paregoric. To this day pills are made behind its tall prescription desk – pills rolled out on its own pill-tile, divided with a spatula, rolled with the finger and thumb, dusted with calcined magnesia and delivered in little round pasteboard pill-boxes. The store is on a corner about which coveys of ragged-plumed, hilarious children play and become candidates for the cough drops and soothing syrups that wait for them inside.

Ikey Schoenstein was the night clerk of the Blue Light and the friend of his customers. Thus it is on the East Side, where the heart of pharmacy is not glacé. There, as it should be, the druggist is a counsellor, a confessor, an adviser, an able and willing missionary and mentor whose learning is respected, whose occult wisdom is venerated and whose medicine is often poured, untasted, into the gutter. Therefore Ikey's corniform, be-spectacled nose and narrow, knowledge-bowed figure was well known in the vicinity of the Blue Light, and his advice and notice were much desired.

Ikey roomed and breakfasted at Mrs Riddle's two squares away. Mrs Riddle had a daughter named Rosy. The circumlocution has been in vain – you must have guessed it – Ikey adored Rosy. She tinctured all his thoughts; she was the compound extract of all that was chemically pure and official – the dispensary contained nothing equal to her. But Ikey was timid, and his hopes remained insoluble in the menstruum of his backwardness and fears. Behind his counter he was a superior being, calmly conscious of special knowledge and worth; outside he was a weak-kneed, purblind, motorman-cursed rambler, with ill-fitting clothes stained with chemicals and smelling of socotrine aloes and valerianate of ammonia.

The fly in Ikey's ointment (thrice welcome, pat trope!) was Chunk McGowan.

Mr McGowan was also striving to catch the bright smiles tossed about by Rosy. But he was no out-fielder as Ikey was; he picked them off the bat. At the same time he was Ikey's friend and customer, and often dropped in at the Blue Light Drug Store to have a bruise painted with iodine or get a cut rubber-plastered after a pleasant evening spent along the Bowery.

One afternoon McGowan drifted in in his silent, easy way, and sat, comely, smooth-faced, hard, indomitable, good-natured, upon a stool.

'Ikey,' said he, when his friend had fetched his mortar and sat opposite, grinding gum benzoin to a powder, 'get busy with your ear. It's drugs for me if you've got the line I need.'

Ikey scanned the countenance of Mr McGowan for the usual evidence of conflict, but found none.

'Take your coat off,' he ordered. 'I guess already that you have been stuck in the ribs with a knife. I have many times told you those Dagoes would do you up.'

Mr McGowan smiled. 'Not them,' he said. 'Not any Dagoes. But you've located the diagnosis all right enough – it's under my coat, near the ribs. Say! Ikey – Rosy and me are goin' to run away and get married to-night.'

Ikey's left forefinger was doubled over the edge of the mortar, holding it steady. He gave it a wild rap with the pestle, but felt it not. Meanwhile Mr McGowan's smile faded to a look of perplexed gloom.

'That is,' he continued, 'if she keeps in the notion until the time comes. We've been layin' pipes for the gateway for two weeks. One day she says she will; the same evenin' she says nixy. We've agreed on to-night, and Rosy's stuck to the affirmative this time for two whole days. But it's five hours yet till the time, and I'm afraid she'll stand me up when it comes to the scratch.'

'You said you wanted drugs,' remarked Ikey.

Mr McGowan looked ill at ease and harassed – a condition opposed to his usual line of demeanor. He made a patent-medicine almanac into a roll and fitted it with unprofitable carefulness about his finger.

'I wouldn't have this double handicap make a false start to-night for a million,' he said. 'I've got a little flat up in Harlem all ready, with chrysanthemums on the table and a kettle ready to boil. And I've engaged a pulpit pounder to be ready at his house for us at 9:30. It's got to come off. And if Rosy don't change her mind again!' – Mr McGowan ceased, a prey to his doubts.

'I don't see then yet,' said Ikey, shortly, 'what makes it that you talk of drugs, or what I can be doing about it.'

'Old man Riddle don't like me a little bit,' went on the uneasy suitor, bent upon marshalling his arguments. 'For a week he hasn't let Rosy step outside the door with me. If it wasn't for losin' a boarder they'd have bounced me long ago. I'm makin' $ dollar; 20 a week and she'll never regret flyin' the coop with Chunk McGowan.'

'You will excuse me, Chunk,' said Ikey. 'I must make a prescription that is to be called for soon.'

'Say,' said McGowan, looking up suddenly, 'say, Ikey, ain't there a drug of some kind – some kind of powders that'll make a girl like you better if you give 'em to her?'

Ikey's lip beneath his nose curled with the scorn of superior enlightenment; but before he could answer, McGowan continued:

'Tim Lacy told me he got some once from a croaker uptown and fed 'em to his girl in soda water. From the very first dose he

16

was ace-high and everybody else looked like thirty cents to her. They was married in less than two weeks.'

Strong and simple was Chunk McGowan. A better reader of men than Ikey was could have seen that his tough frame was strung upon fine wires. Like a good general who was about to invade the enemy's territory he was seeking to guard every point against possible failure.

'I thought,' went on Chunk, hopefully, 'that if I had one of them powders to give Rosy when I see her at supper to-night it might brace her up and keep her from reneging on the proposition to skip. I guess she don't need a mule team to drag her away, but women are better at coaching than they are at running bases. If the stuff'll work just for a couple of hours it'll do the trick.'

'When is this foolishness of running away to be happening?' asked Ikey

'Nine o'clock,' said Mr McGowan. 'Supper's at seven. At eight Rosy goes to bed with a headache, at nine old Parvenzano lets me through to his backyard, where there's a board off Riddle's fence, next door. I go under her window and help her down the fire-escape. We've got to make it early on the preacher's account. It's all dead easy if Rosy don't balk when the flag drops. Can you fix me one of them powders, Ikey?'

Ikey Schoenstein rubbed his nose slowly.

'Chunk,' said he, 'it is of drugs of that nature that pharmaceutists must have much carefulness. To you alone of my acquaintance would I intrust a powder like that. But for you I shall make it, and you shall see how it makes Rosy to think of you.'

Ikey went behind the prescription desk. There he crushed to a powder two soluble tablets, each containing a quarter of a grain of morphia. To them he added a little sugar of milk to increase the bulk, and folded the mixture neatly in a white paper. Taken by an adult this powder would insure several hours of heavy slumber without danger to the sleeper. This he handed to Chunk

McGowan, telling him to administer it in a liquid if possible, and received the hearty thanks of the backyard Lochinvar.

The subtlety of Ikey's action becomes apparent upon recital of his subsequent move. He sent a messenger for Mr Riddle and disclosed the plans of Mr McGowan for eloping with Rosy. Mr Riddle was a stout man, brick-dusty of complexion and sudden in action.

'Much obliged,' he said, briefly, to Ikey. 'The lazy Irish loafer! My own room's just above Rosy's. I'll just go up there myself after supper and load the shot-gun and wait. If he comes in my backyard he'll go away in a ambulance instead of a bridal chaise.'

With Rosy held in the clutches of Morpheus for many hours' deep slumber, and the blood-thirsty parent waiting, armed and forewarned, Ikey felt that his rival was close, indeed, upon discomfiture.

All night in the Blue Light Drug Store he waited at his duties for chance news of the tragedy, but none came.

At eight o'clock in the morning the day clerk arrived and Ikey started hurriedly for Mrs Riddle's to learn the outcome. And, lo! as he stepped out of the store who but Chunk McGowan sprang from a passing street car and grasped his hand – Chunk McGowan with a victor's smile and flushed with joy.

'Pulled it off,' said Chunk with Elysium in his grin. 'Rosy hit the fire-escape on time to a second, and we was under the wire at the Reverend's at 9:30¼. She's up at the flat – she cooked eggs this mornin' in a blue kimono – Lord! how lucky I am! You must pace up some day, Ikey, and feed with us. I've got a job down near the bridge, and that's where I'm heading for now.'

'The – the – powder?' stammered Ikey.

'Oh, that stuff you gave me!' said Chunk, broadening his grin; 'well, it was this way. I sat down at the supper table last night at Riddle's, and I looked at Rosy, and I says to myself, "Chunk, if you get the girl get her on the square – don't try any hocus-pocus with a thoroughbred like her." And I keeps the paper you give me in my pocket. And then my lamps fall on another party present, who, I says to myself, is failin' in a proper affection toward his comin' son-in-law, so I watches my chance and dumps that powder in old man Riddle's coffee – see?'

# Springtime à la Carte

It was a day in March.

Never, never begin a story this way when you write one. No opening could possibly be worse. It is unimaginative, flat, dry, and likely to consist of mere wind. But in this instance it is allowable. For the following paragraph, which should have inaugurated the narrative, is too wildly extravagant and preposterous to be flaunted in the face of the reader without preparation.

Sarah was crying over her bill of fare.

Think of a New York girl shedding tears on the menu card!

To account for this you will be allowed to guess that the lobsters were all out, or that she had sworn ice-cream off during Lent, or that she had ordered onions, or that she had just come from a Hackett matinée. And then, all these theories being wrong, you will please let the story proceed.

The gentleman who announced that the world was an oyster which he with his sword would open made a larger hit than he deserved. It is not difficult to open an oyster with a sword. But did you ever notice anyone try to open the terrestrial bivalve with a typewriter? Like to wait for a dozen raw opened that way?

Sarah had managed to pry apart the shells with her unhandy weapon far enough to nibble a wee bit at the cold and clammy world within. She knew no more shorthand than if she had been a graduate in stenography just let slip upon the world by a business college. So, not being able to stenog, she could not enter that bright galaxy of office talent. She was a freelance typewriter and canvassed for odd jobs of copying.

The most brilliant and crowning feat of Sarah's battle with the world was the deal she made with Schulenberg's Home

Restaurant. The restaurant was next door to the old red brick in which she hall-roomed. One evening after dining at Schulenberg's 40-cent, five-course *table d'hôte* (served as fast as you throw the five baseballs at the colored gentleman's head) Sarah took away with her the bill of fare. It was written in an almost unreadable script neither English nor German, and so arranged that if you were not careful you began with a toothpick and rice pudding and ended with soup and the day of the week.

The next day Sarah showed Schulenberg a neat card on which the menu was beautifully typewritten with the viands temptingly marshaled under their right and proper heads from 'hors d'œuvre' to 'not responsible for over-coats and umbrellas.'

Schulenberg became a naturalized citizen on the spot. Before Sarah left him she had him willingly committed to an agreement. She was to furnish typewritten bills of fare for the twenty-one tables in the restaurant – a new bill for each day's dinner, and new ones for breakfast and lunch as often as changes occurred in the food or as neatness required.

In return for this Schulenberg was to send three meals per diem to Sarah's hall room by a waiter – an obsequious one if possible – and furnish her each afternoon with a pencil draft of what Fate had in store for Schulenberg's customers on the morrow.

Mutual satisfaction resulted from the agreement. Schulenberg's patrons now knew what the food they ate was called even if its nature sometimes puzzled them. And Sarah had food during a cold, dull winter, which was the main thing with her.

And then the almanac lied, and said that spring had come. Spring comes when it comes. The frozen snows of January still lay like adamant in the cross-town streets. The hand-organs still played 'In the Good Old Summertime,' with their December vivacity and expression. Men began to make thirty-day notes to buy Easter dresses. Janitors shut off steam. And when these things happen one may know that the city is still in the clutches of winter.

One afternoon Sarah shivered in her elegant hall bedroom;

'house heated; scrupulously clean; conveniences; seen to be appreciated.' She had no work to do except Schulenberg's menu cards. Sarah sat in her squeaky willow rocker, and looked out the window. The calendar on the wall kept crying to her: 'Springtime is here, Sarah – springtime is here, I tell you. Look at me, Sarah, my figures show it. You've got a neat figure yourself, Sarah – a – nice springtime figure – why do you look out the window so sadly?'

Sarah's room was at the back of the house. Looking out the window she could see the windowless rear brick wall of the box factory on the next street. But the wall was clearest crystal; and Sarah was looking down a grassy lane shaded with cherry trees and elms and bordered with raspberry bushes and Cherokee roses.

Spring's real harbingers are too subtle for the eye and ear. Some must have the flowering crocus, the wood-starring dogwood, the voice of bluebird – even so gross a reminder as the farewell handshake of the retiring buckwheat and oyster before they can welcome the Lady in Green to their dull bosoms. But to old earth's choicest kind there come straight, sweet messages from his newest bride, telling them they shall be no stepchildren unless they choose to be.

On the previous summer Sarah had gone into the country and loved a farmer.

(In writing your story never hark back thus. It is bad art, and cripples interest. Let it march, march.)

Sarah stayed two weeks at Sunnybrook Farm. There she learned to love old Farmer Franklin's son Walter. Farmers have been loved and wedded and turned out to grass in less time. But young Walter Franklin was a modern agriculturist. He had a telephone in his cow house, and he could figure up exactly what effect next year's Canada wheat crop would have on potatoes planted in the dark of the moon.

It was in this shaded and raspberried lane that Walter had wooed and won her. And together they had sat and woven a crown of dandelions for her hair. He had immoderately praised the effect of the yellow blossoms against her brown tresses; and she had left the chaplet there, and walked back to the house swinging her straw sailor in her hands.

They were to marry in the spring – at the very first signs of spring, Walter said. And Sarah came back to the city to pound her typewriter.

A knock at the door dispelled Sarah's visions of that happy day. A waiter had brought the rough pencil draft of the Home Restaurant's next day fare in old Schulenberg's angular hand.

Sarah sat down to her typewriter and slipped a card between the rollers. She was a nimble worker. Generally in an hour and a half the twenty-one menu cards were written and ready.

To-day there were more changes on the bill of fare than usual. The soups were lighter; pork was eliminated from the entrées, figuring only with Russian turnips among the roasts. The gracious spirit of spring pervaded the entire menu. Lamb, that lately capered on the greening hillsides, was becoming exploited with the sauce that commemorated its gambols. The song of the oyster, though not silenced, was *dimuendo con amore*. The frying-pan seemed to be held, inactive, behind the beneficent bars of the broiler. The pie list swelled; the richer puddings had vanished; the sausage, with his drapery wrapped about him, barely lingered in a pleasant thanatopsis with the buckwheats and the sweet but doomed maple.

Sarah's fingers danced like midgets above a summer stream. Down through the courses she worked, giving each item its position according to its length with an accurate eye.

Just above the desserts came the list of vegetables. Carrots and peas, asparagus on toast, the perennial tomatoes and corn and succotash, lima beans, cabbage – and then –

Sarah was crying over her bill of fare. Tears from the depths of some divine despair rose in her heart and gathered to her eyes. Down went her head on the little typewriter stand; and the keyboard rattled a dry accompaniment to her moist sobs.

For she had received no letter from Walter in two weeks, and the next item on the bill of fare was dandelions – dandelions, with whose golden blooms Walter had crowned her his queen of love and future bride – dandelions, the harbingers of spring, her sorrow's crown of sorrow – reminder of her happiest days.

Madam, I dare you to smile until you suffer this test: Let the Marechal Niel roses that Percy brought you on the night you gave him your heart be served as a salad with French dressing before your eyes at a Schulenberg *table d'hôte*. Had Juliet so seen her love tokens dishonored the sooner would she have sought the lethean herbs of the good apothecary.

But what witch is Spring! Into the great cold city of stone and iron a message had to be sent. There was none to convey it but the little hardy courier of the fields with his rough green coat and modest air. He is a true soldier of fortune, this *dent-de-lion* – this lion's tooth, as the French chefs call him. Flowered, he will assist at love-making, wreathed in my lady's nut-brown hair; young and callow and unblossomed, he goes into the boiling pot and delivers the word of his sovereign mistress.

By and by Sarah forced back her tears. The cards must be written. But, still in a faint, golden glow from her dandelion dream, she fingered the typewriter keys absently for a little while, with her mind and heart in the meadow lane with her young farmer. But soon she came swiftly back to the rockbound lanes of Manhattan, and the typewriter began to rattle and jump like a strike-breaker's motor car.

At 6 o'clock the waiter brought her dinner and carried away the typewritten bill of fare. When Sarah ate she set aside, with a sigh, the dish of dandelions with its crowning ovarious accompaniment. As this dark mass had been transformed from a bright and love-indorsed flower to be an ignominious vegetable, so had her summer hopes wilted and perished. Love may, as Shakespeare said, feed on itself: but Sarah could not bring herself to eat the dandelions that had graced, as ornaments, the first spiritual banquet of her heart's true affection.

At 7:30 the couple in the next room began to quarrel: the man in the room above sought for A on his flute; the gas went a little lower; three coal wagons started to unload – the only sound of which the phonograph is jealous; cats on the back fences slowly retreated toward Mukden. By these signs Sarah knew that it was time for her to read. She got out 'The Cloister and the Hearth,' the best non-selling book of the month, settled her feet on her trunk, and began to wander with Gerard.

The front door bell rang. The landlady answered it. Sarah left Gerard and Denys treed by a bear and listened. Oh, yes; you would, just as she did!

And then a strong voice was heard in the hall below, and Sarah jumped for her door, leaving the book on the floor and the first round easily the bear's.

You have guessed it. She reached the top of the stairs just as her farmer came up, three at a jump, and reaped and garnered her, with nothing left for the gleaners.

'Why haven't you written – oh, why?' cried Sarah.

'New York is a pretty large town,' said Walter Franklin. 'I came in a week ago to your old address. I found that you went away on a Thursday. That consoled some; it eliminated the possible Friday bad luck. But it didn't prevent my hunting for you with police and otherwise ever since!'

'I wrote!' said Sarah, vehemently.

'Never got it!'

'Then how did you find me?'

The young farmer smiled a springtime smile.

'I dropped into that Home Restaurant next door this evening,' said he. 'I don't care who knows it; I like a dish of some kind of greens at this time of the year. I ran my eye down that nice type-written bill of fare looking for something in that line. When I got below cabbage I turned my chair over and hollered for the proprietor. He told me where you lived.'

'I remember,' sighed Sarah, happily. 'That was dandelions below cabbage.'

'I'd know that cranky capital W 'way above the line that your typewriter makes anywhere in the world,' said Franklin.

'Why, there's no W in dandelions,' said Sarah in surprise.

The young man drew the bill of fare from his pocket and pointed to a line.

Sarah recognized the first card she had typewritten that afternoon. There was still the rayed splotch in the upper right-hand corner where a tear had fallen. But over the spot where one should have read the name of the meadow plant, the clinging memory of their golden blossoms had allowed her fingers to strike strange keys.

Between the red cabbage and the stuffed green peppers was the item:

'DEAREST WALTER, WITH HARD-BOILED EGG.'

# An Unfinished Story

We no longer groan and heap ashes upon our heads when the flames of Tophet are mentioned. For, even the preachers have begun to tell us that God is radium, or ether or some scientific compound, and that the worst we wicked ones may expect is a chemical reaction. This is a pleasing hypothesis; but there lingers yet some of the old, goodly terror of orthodoxy.

There are but two subjects upon which one may discourse with a free imagination, and without the possibility of being controverted. You may talk of your dreams; and you may tell what you heard a parrot say. Both Morpheus and the bird are incompetent witnesses; and your listener dare not attack your recital. The baseless fabric of a vision, then, shall furnish my theme – chosen with apologies and regrets instead of the more limited field of pretty Polly's small talk.

I had a dream that was so far removed from the higher criticism that it had to do with the ancient, respectable, and lamented bar-of-judgment theory.

Gabriel had played his trump; and those of us who could not follow suit were arraigned for examination. I noticed at one side a gathering of professional bondsmen in solemn black and collars that buttoned behind; but it seemed there was some trouble about their real estate titles; and they did not appear to be getting any of us out.

A fly cop – an angel policeman – flew over to me and took me by the left wing. Near at hand was a group of very prosperous-looking spirits arraigned for judgment.

'Do you belong with that bunch?' the policeman asked.

'Who are they?' was my answer.

'Why,' said he, 'they are – '

But this irrelevant stuff is taking up space that the story should occupy.

Dulcie worked in a department store. She sold Hamburg edging, or stuffed peppers, or automobiles, or other little trinkets such as they keep in department stores. Of what she earned, Dulcie received six dollars per week. The remainder was credited to her and debited to somebody else's account in the ledger kept by G—— Oh, primal energy, you say, Reverend Doctor – Well, then, in the Ledger of Primal Energy.

During her first year in the store, Dulcie was paid five dollars per week. It would be instructive to know how she lived on that amount. Don't care? Very well; probably you are interested in larger amounts. Six dollars is a larger amount. I will tell you how she lived on six dollars per week.

One afternoon at six, when Dulcie was sticking her hat pin within an eighth of an inch of her *medulla oblongata*, she said to her chum, Sadie – the girl that waits on you with her left side:

'Say, Sade, I made a date for dinner this evening with Piggy.'

'You never did!' exclaimed Sadie, admiringly. 'Well, ain't you the lucky one? Piggy's an awful swell; and he always takes a girl to swell places. He took Blanche up to the Hoffman House one evening, where they have swell music, and you see a lot of swells. You'll have a swell time, Dulce.'

Dulcie hurried homeward. Her eyes were shining, and her cheeks showed the delicate pink of life's – real life's – approaching dawn. It was Friday; and she had fifty cents left of her week's wages.

The streets were filled with the rush-hour floods of people. The electric lights of Broadway were glowing – calling moths from miles, from leagues, from hundreds of leagues out of darkness around to come in and attend the singeing school. Men in accurate clothes, with faces like those carved on cherry stones by the old salts in sailors' homes, turned and stared at Dulcie as she sped, unheeding, past them. Manhattan, the night-blooming cereus, was beginning to unfold its dead-white, heavy-odored petals.

Dulcie stopped in a store where goods were cheap and bought an imitation lace collar with her fifty cents. That money was to have been spent otherwise – fifteen cents for supper, ten cents for breakfast, ten cents for lunch. Another dime was to be added to her small store of savings; and five cents was to be squandered for licorice drops – the kind that made your cheek look like the tooth-ache, and last as long. The licorice was an extravagance – almost a carouse – but what is life without pleasures?

Dulcie lived in a furnished room. There is this difference between a furnished room and a boarding-house. In a furnished room, other people do not know it when you go hungry.

Dulcie went up to her room – the third-floor-back in a West Side brownstone-front. She lit the gas. Scientists tell us that the diamond is the hardest substance known. Their mistake. Land-ladies know of a compound beside which the diamond is as putty. They pack it in the tips of gas-burners; and one may stand on a chair and dig at it in vain until one's fingers are pink and bruised. A hairpin will not remove it; therefore let us call it immovable.

So Dulcie lit the gas. In its one-fourth-candle-power glow we will observe the room.

Couch-bed, dresser, table, washstand, chair – of this much the landlady was guilty. The rest was Dulcie's. On the dresser were her treasures – a gilt china vase presented to her by Sadie, a calendar issued by a pickle works, a book on the divination of dreams, some rice powder in a glass dish, and a cluster of artificial cherries tied with a pink ribbon.

Against the wrinkly mirror stood pictures of General Kitchener, William Muldoon, the Duchess of Marlborough, and Benvenuto Cellini. Against one wall was a plaster of Paris plaque of an O'Callahan in a Roman helmet. Near it was a violent oleograph of a lemon-colored child assaulting an inflammatory butterfly. This was Dulcie's final judgment in art; but it had never been upset. Her rest had never been disturbed by whispers of stolen copes; no critic had elevated his eyebrows at her infantile entomologist.

Piggy was to call for her at seven. While she swiftly makes ready, let us discreetly face the other way and gossip.

For the room, Dulcie paid two dollars per week. On week-days her breakfast cost ten cents; she made coffee and cooked an egg over the gaslight while she was dressing. On Sunday mornings she feasted royally on veal chops and pineapple fritters at 'Billy's' restaurant, at a cost of twenty-five cents – and tipped the waitress ten cents. New York presents so many temptations for one to run into extravagance. She had her lunches in the department-store restaurant at a cost of sixty cents for the week; dinners were $1.05. The evening papers – show me a New Yorker going without his daily paper! – came to six cents; and two Sunday papers – one for the personal column and the other to read – were ten cents. The total amounts to $4.76. Now, one has to buy clothes, and –

I give it up. I hear of wonderful bargains in fabrics, and of miracles performed with needle and thread; but I am in doubt. I hold my pen poised in vain when I would add to Dulcie's life some of those joys that belong to woman by virtue of all the unwritten, sacred, natural, inactive ordinances of the equity of heaven. Twice she had been to Coney Island and had ridden the hobby-horses. 'Tis a weary thing to count your pleasures by summers instead of by hours.

Piggy needs but a word. When the girls named him, an undeserving stigma was cast upon the noble family of swine. The words-of-three-letters lesson in the old blue spelling book begins with Piggy's biography. He was fat; he had the soul of a rat, the habits of a bat, and the magnanimity of a cat . . . He wore expensive clothes; and was a connoisseur in starvation. He could look at a shop-girl and tell you to an hour how long it had been since she had eaten anything more nourishing than marshmallows and tea. He hung about the shopping districts, and prowled around in department stores with his invitations to dinner. Men who escort dogs upon the streets at the end of a string look down upon him. He is a type; I can dwell upon him no longer; my pen is not the kind intended for him; I am no carpenter.

At ten minutes to seven Dulcie was ready. She looked at herself in the wrinkly mirror. The reflection was satisfactory. The dark blue dress, fitting without a wrinkle, the hat with its jaunty black feather, the but-slightly-soiled gloves – all representing self-denial, even of food itself – were vastly becoming.

Dulcie forgot everything else for a moment except that she was beautiful, and that life was about to lift a corner of its mysterious veil for her to observe its wonders. No gentleman had ever asked her out before. Now she was going for a brief moment into the glitter and exalted show.

The girls said that Piggy was a 'spender.' There would be a grand dinner, and music, and splendidly dressed ladies to look at and things to eat that strangely twisted the girls' laws when they tried to tell about them. No doubt she would be asked out again.

There was a blue pongee suit in a window that she knew – by saving twenty cents a week instead of ten in – let's see – Oh, it would run into years! But there was a second-hand store in Seventh Avenue where –

Somebody knocked at the door. Dulcie opened it. The landlady stood there with a spurious smile, sniffing for cooking by stolen gas.

'A gentleman's downstairs to see you,' she said. 'Name is Mr Wiggins.'

By such epithet was Piggy known to unfortunate ones who had to take him seriously.

Dulcie turned to the dresser to get her handkerchief; and then she stopped still, and bit her underlip hard. While looking in her mirror she had seen fairyland and herself, a princess, just awakening from a long slumber. She had forgotten one that was watching her with sad, beautiful, stern eyes – the only one there was to approve or condemn what she did. Straight and slender and tall, with a look of sorrowful reproach on his handsome, melancholy face, General Kitchener fixed his wonderful eyes on her out of his gilt photograph frame on the dresser.

Dulcie turned like an automatic doll to the landlady.

'Tell him I can't go,' she said, dully. 'Tell him I'm sick, or something. Tell him I'm not going out.'

After the door was closed and locked, Dulcie fell upon her bed, crushing her black tip, and cried for ten minutes. General Kitchener was her only friend. He was Dulcie's ideal of a gallant knight. He looked as if he might have a secret sorrow, and his wonderful moustache was a dream, and she was a little afraid of that stern yet tender look in his eyes. She used to have little fancies that he would call at the house sometime, and ask for her, with his sword clanking against his high boots. Once, when a boy was rattling a piece of chain against a lamp post she had opened the window and looked out. But there was no use. She knew that General Kitchener was away over in Japan, leading his army against the savage Turks; and he would never step out of his gilt frame for her. Yet one look from him had vanquished Piggy that night. Yes, for that night.

When her cry was over Dulcie got up and took off her best dress, and put on her old blue kimono. She wanted no dinner. She sang two verses of 'Sammy.' Then she became intensely interested in a little red speck on the side of her nose. And after that was attended to, she drew up a chair to the rickety table, and told her fortune with an old deck of cards.

'The horrid, impudent thing!' she said aloud. 'And I never gave him a word or a look to make him think it!'

At nine o'clock Dulcie took a tin box of crackers and a little pot of raspberry jam out of her trunk and had a feast. She offered General Kitchener some jam on a cracker; but he only looked at her as the sphinx would have looked at a butterfly – if there are butterflies in the desert.

'Don't eat if you don't want to,' said Dulcie. 'And don't put on so many airs and scold so with your eyes. I wonder if you'd be so superior and snippy if you had to live on six dollars a week.'

It was not a good sign for Dulcie to be rude to General Kitchener. And then she turned Benvenuto Cellini face downward with a severe gesture. But that was not inexcusable; for she had always thought he was Henry VIII, and she did not approve of him.

At half-past nine Dulcie took a last look at the pictures on the dresser, turned out the light and skipped into bed. It's an awful thing to go to bed with a good-night look at General Kitchener, William Muldoon, the Duchess of Marlborough, and Benvenuto Cellini.

This story doesn't really get anywhere at all. The rest of it comes later – sometime when Piggy asks Dulcie again to dine with him, and she is feeling lonelier than usual, and General Kitchener happens to be looking the other way; and then –

As I said before, I dreamed that I was standing near a crowd of prosperous-looking angels, and a policeman took me by the wing and asked if I belonged with them.

'Who are they?' I asked.

'Why,' said he, 'they are the men who hired working-girls, and paid 'em five or six dollars a week to live on. Are you one of the bunch?'

'Not on your immortality,' said I. 'I'm only a fellow that set fire to an orphan asylum, and murdered a blind man for his pennies.'

# The Furnished Room

Restless, shifting, fugacious as time itself is a certain vast bulk of the population of the red brick district of the lower West Side. Homeless, they have a hundred homes. They flit from furnished room to furnished room, transients forever – transients in abode, transients in heart and mind. They sing 'Home, Sweet Home' in ragtime; they carry their *lares et penates* in a bandbox; their vine is entwined about a picture hat; a rubber plant is their fig tree.

Hence the houses of this district, having had a thousand dwellers, should have a thousand tales to tell, mostly dull ones, no doubt; but it would be strange if there could not be found a ghost or two in the wake of all these vagrant guests.

One evening after dark a young man prowled among these crumbling red mansions, ringing their bells. At the twelfth he rested his lean hand-baggage upon the step and wiped the dust from his hatband and forehead. The bell sounded faint and far away in some remote, hollow depths.

To the door of this, the twelfth house whose bell he had rung, came a housekeeper who made him think of an un-wholesome, surfeited worm that had eaten its nut to a hollow shell and now sought to fill the vacancy with edible lodgers.

He asked if there was a room to let.

'Come in,' said the housekeeper. Her voice came from her throat; her throat seemed lined with fur. 'I have the third-floor-back, vacant since a week back. Should you wish to look at it?'

The young man followed her up the stairs. A faint light from no particular source mitigated the shadows of the halls. They trod noiselessly upon a stair carpet that its own loom would have forsworn. It seemed to have become vegetable; to have degenerated in that rank, sunless air to lush lichen or spreading moss that grew in patches to the staircase and was viscid under the foot like organic matter. At each turn of the stairs were vacant niches in the wall. Perhaps plants had once been set within them. If so they had died in that foul and tainted air. It may be that statues of the saints had stood there, but it was not difficult to conceive that imps and devils had dragged them forth in the darkness and down to the unholy depths of some furnished pit below.

'This is the room,' said the housekeeper, from her furry throat. 'It's a nice room. It ain't often vacant. I had some most elegant people in it last summer – no trouble at all, and paid in advance to the minute. The water's at the end of the hall. Sprowls and Mooney kept it three months. They done a vaudeville sketch. Miss B'retta Sprowls – you may have heard of her – Oh, that was just the stage names – right there over the dresser is where the marriage certificate hung, framed. The gas is here, and you see there is plenty of closet room. It's a room everybody likes. It never stays idle long.'

'Do you have many theatrical people rooming here?' asked the young man.

'They comes and goes. A good proportion of my lodgers is connected with the theaters. Yes, sir, this is the theatrical district. Actor people never stays long anywhere. I get my share. Yes, they comes and they goes.'

He engaged the room, paying for a week in advance. He was tired, he said, and would take possession at once. He counted out the money. The room had been made ready, she said, even to towels and water. As the housekeeper moved away he put, for the thousandth time, the question that he carried at the end of his tongue.

'A young girl – Miss Vashner – Miss Eloise Vashner – do you remember such a one among your lodgers? She would be singing on the stage, most likely. A fair girl, of medium height and slender, with reddish, gold hair and a dark mole near her left eyebrow.'

'No, I don't remember the name. Them stage people has names they change as often as their rooms. They comes and they goes. No, I don't call that one to mind.'

No. Always no. Five months of ceaseless interrogation and the inevitable negative. So much time spent by day in questioning managers, agents, schools and choruses; by night among the audiences of theatres from all-star casts down to music halls so low that he dreaded to find what he most hoped for. He who had loved her best had tried to find her. He was sure that since her disappearance from home this great, water-girt city held her somewhere, but it was like a monstrous quicksand, shifting its particles constantly, with no foundation, its upper granules of to-day buried to-morrow in ooze and slime.

The furnished room received its latest guest with a first glow of pseudo-hospitality, a hectic, haggard, perfunctory welcome like the specious smile of a demirep. The sophistical comfort came in reflected gleams from the decayed furniture, the ragged brocade upholstery of a couch and two chairs, a foot-wide cheap pier glass between the two windows, from one or two gilt picture frames and a brass bedstead in a corner.

The guest reclined, inert, upon a chair, while the room, confused in speech as though it were an apartment in Babel, tried to discourse to him of its divers tenantry.

A polychromatic rug like some brilliant-flowered, rectangular, tropical islet lay surrounded by a billowy sea of soiled matting. Upon the gay-papered wall were those pictures that pursue the homeless one from house to house – The Huguenot Lovers, The First Quarrel. The Wedding Breakfast, Psyche at the Fountain. The mantel's chastely severe outline was ingloriously veiled behind some pert drapery drawn rakishly askew like the sashes of the Amazonian ballet. Upon it was some desolate jetsam cast aside by the room's marooned when a lucky sail had borne them to a fresh port – a trifling vase or two, pictures of actresses, a medicine bottle, some stray cards out of a deck.

One by one, as the characters of a cryptograph became explicit, the little signs left by the furnished room's procession of guests developed a significance. The threadbare space in the rug in front of the dresser told that lovely women had marched in the throng. The tiny fingerprints on the wall spoke of little prisoners trying to feel their way to sun and air. A splattered stain, raying like the shadow of a bursting bomb, witnessed where a hurled glass or bottle had splintered with its contents against the wall. Across the pier glass had been scrawled with a diamond in staggering letters the name 'Marie.' It seemed that the succession of dwellers in the furnished room had turned in fury – perhaps tempted beyond forbearance by its garish coldness – and wreaked upon it their passions. The furniture was chipped and bruised; the couch, distorted by bursting the stress of some grotesque convulsion. Some more potent upheaval had cloven a great slice from the marble mantel. Each plank in the floor owned its particular cant and shriek as from a separate and individual agony. It seemed incredible that all this malice and injury had been wrought upon the room by those who had called it for a time their home; and yet it may have been the cheated home instinct surviving blindly, the resentful rage at false household gods that had kindled their wrath. A hut that is our own we can sweep and adorn and cherish.

The young tenant in the chair allowed these thoughts to file, soft-shod, through his mind, while there drifted into the room furnished sounds and furnished scents. He heard in one room a tittering and incontinent slack laughter; in others the monologue of a scold, the rattling of dice, a lullaby, and one crying dully; above him a banjo tinkled with spirit. Doors banged somewhere; the elevated trains roared intermittently; a cat yowled miserably upon a back fence. And he breathed the breath of the house – a dank savor rather than a smell – a cold, musty effluvium as from underground vaults mingled with the reeking exhalations of linoleum and mildewed and rotten woodwork.

Then suddenly, as he rested there, the room was filled with the strong, sweet odor of mignonette. It came as upon a single buffet of wind with such sureness and fragrance and emphasis that it almost seemed a living visitant. And the man cried aloud: 'What, dear?' as if he had been called, and sprang up and faced about. The rich odor clung to him and wrapped him around. He reached out his arms for it, all his senses for the time confused and commingled. How could one be peremptorily called by an odor? Surely it must have been a sound. But, was it not the sound that had touched, that had caressed him?

'She has been in this room,' he cried, and he sprang to wrest from it a token, for he knew he would recognize the smallest thing that had belonged to her or that she had touched. This enveloping scent of mignonette, the odor that she had loved and made her own – whence came it?

The room had been but carelessly set in order. Scattered upon the flimsy dresser scarf were half a dozen hairpins – those discreet, indistinguishable friends of womankind, feminine of gender, infinite mood and uncommunicative of tense. These he ignored, conscious of their triumphant lack of identity. Ransacking the drawers of the dresser he came upon a discarded, tiny, ragged handkerchief. He pressed it to his face. It was racy and insolent with heliotrope; he hurled it to the floor. In another drawer he found odd buttons, a theater programme, a pawnbroker's card, two lost marshmallows, a book on the divination of dreams. In the last was a woman's black satin hair bow, which halted him, poised between ice and fire. But the black satin hair bow also is femininity's demure, impersonal common ornament and tells no tales.

And then he traversed the room like a hound on the scent, skimming the walls, considering the corners of the bulging matting on his hands and knees, rummaging mantel and tables, the curtains and hangings, the drunken cabinet in the corner, for a visible sign, unable to perceive that she was there beside, around, against, within, above him, clinging to him, wooing him, calling him so poignantly through the finer senses that even his grosser ones became cognizant of the call. Once again he answered loudly: 'Yes, dear!' and turned, wild-eyed, to gaze on vacancy, for he could not yet discern form and color and love and out-stretched arms in the odor of mignonette. Oh, God! whence that odor, and since when have odors had a voice to call? Thus he groped.

He burrowed in crevices and corners, and found corks and ciga-rettes. These he passed in passive contempt. But once he found in a fold of the matting a half-smoked cigar, and this he ground beneath his heel with a green and trenchant oath. He sifted the room from end to end. He found dreary and ignoble small records of many a peripatetic tenant; but of her whom he sought, and who may have lodged there, and whose spirit seemed to hover there, he found no trace.

And then he thought of the housekeeper.

He ran from the haunted room downstairs and to a door that showed a crack of light. She came out to his knock. He smoth-ered his excitement as well as he could.

'Will you tell me, madam,' he besought her, 'who occupied the room I have before I came?'

'Yes, sir. I can tell you again. 'Twas Sprowls and Mooney, as I said. Miss B'retta Sprowls it was in the theaters, but Missis Mooney she was. My house is well known for respectability. The marriage certificate hung, framed, on a nail over —'

'What kind of a lady was Miss Sprowls – in looks, I mean?'

'Why, black-haired, sir, short, and stout, with a comical face. They left a week ago Tuesday.'

'And before they occupied it?'

'Why, there was a single gentleman connected with the dray-ing business. He left owing me a week. Before him was Missis Crowder and her two children, that stayed four months; and back of them was old Mr Doyle, whose sons paid for him. He kept the room six months. That goes back a year, sir, and further I do not remember.'

He thanked her and crept back to his room. The room was dead. The essence that had vivified it was gone. The perfume of mignonette had departed. In its place was the old, stale odor of moldy house furniture, of atmosphere in storage.

The ebbing of his hope drained his faith. He sat staring at the yellow, singing gaslight. Soon he walked to the bed and began to tear the sheets into strips. With the blade of his knife he drove them tightly into every crevice around windows and door. When all was snug and taut he turned out the light, turned the gas full on again and laid himself gratefully upon the bed.

It was Mrs McCool's night to go with the can for beer. So she fetched it and sat with Mrs Purdy in one of those subterranean retreats where housekeepers foregather and the worm dieth seldom.

'I rented out my third-floor-back this evening,' said Mrs Purdy, across a fine circle of foam. 'A young man took it. He went up to bed two hours ago.'

'Now, did ye, Mrs Purdy, ma'am?' said Mrs McCool, with intense admiration. 'You do be a wonder for rentin' rooms of that kind. And did ye tell him, then?' she concluded in a husky whisper laden with mystery.

'Rooms,' said Mrs Purdy, in her furriest tones, 'are furnished for to rent. I did not tell him, Mrs McCool.'

' 'Tis right ye are, ma'am; 'tis by renting rooms we kape alive. Ye have the rale sense for business, ma'am. There be many people will rayjict the rentin' of a room if they be tould a suicide has been after dyin' in the bed of it.'

'As you say, we has our living to be making,' remarked Mrs Purdy.

'Yis, ma'am; 'tis true. 'Tis just one wake ago this day I helped ye lay out the third-floor-back. A pretty slip of a colleen she was to be killin' herself wid the gas – a swate little face she had, Mrs Purdy, ma'am.'

'She'd a-been called handsome, as you say,' said Mrs Purdy, assenting but critical, 'but for that mole she had a-growin' by her left eyebrow. Do fill up your glass again, Mrs McCool.'

# The Trimmed Lamp

Of course there are two sides to the question. Let us look at the other. We often hear 'shop-girls' spoken of. No such persons exist. There are girls who work in shops. They make their living that way. But why turn their occupation into an adjective? Let us be fair. We do not refer to the girls who live on Fifth Avenue as 'marriage-girls.'

Lou and Nancy were chums. They came to the big city to find work because there was not enough to eat at their homes to go around. Nancy was nineteen; Lou was twenty. Both were pretty, active country girls who had no ambition to go on the stage.

The little cherub that sits up aloft guided them to a cheap and respectable boarding-house. Both found positions and became wage-earners. They remained chums. It is at the end of six months that I would beg you to step forward and be introduced to them. Meddlesome Reader: My Lady Friends, Miss Nancy and Miss Lou. While you are shaking hands please take notice – cautiously – of their attire. Yes, cautiously; for they are as quick to resent a stare as a lady in a box at the horse show is.

Lou is a piece-work ironer in a hand laundry. She is clothed in a badly fitting purple dress, and her hat plume is four inches too long; but her ermine muff and scarf cost $25, and its fellow beasts will be ticketed in the windows at $7.98 before the season is over. Her cheeks are pink, and her light blue eyes bright. Contentment radiates from her.

Nancy you would call a shop-girl – because you have the habit. There is no type; but a perverse generation is always seeking a type; so this is what the type should be. She has the high-ratted pompadour and the exaggerated straight-front. Her skirt is shoddy,

42

but has the correct flare. No furs protect her against the bitter spring air, but she wears her short broadcloth jacket as jauntily as though it were Persian lamb. On her face and in her eyes, remorseless type-seeker, is the typical shop-girl expression. It is a look of silent but contemptuous revolt against cheated womanhood; of sad prophecy of the vengeance to come. When she laughs her loudest the look is still there. The same look can be seen in the eyes of Russian peasants; and those of us left will see it some day on Gabriel's face when he comes to blow us up. It is a look that should wither and abash man; but he has been known to smirk at it and offer flowers – with a string tied to them.

Now lift your hat and come away, while you receive Lou's cheery 'See you again,' and the sardonic, sweet smile of Nancy that seems, somehow, to miss you and go fluttering like a white moth up over the housetops to the stars.

The two waited on the corner for Dan. Dan was Lou's steady company. Faithful? Well, he was on hand when Mary would have had to hire a dozen subpoena servers to find her lamb.

'Ain't you cold, Nancy?' said Lou. 'Say, what a chump you are for working in that old store for $8 a week! I made $18.50 last week. Of course ironing ain't as swell work as selling lace behind a counter, but it pays. None of us ironers make less than $10. And I don't know that it's any less respectful work, either.'

'You can have it,' said Nancy, with uplifted nose. 'I'll take my eight a week and hall bedroom. I like to be among nice things and swell people. And look what a chance I've got! Why, one of our glove girls married a Pittsburgh – a steel maker, or blacksmith or something – the other day worth a million dollars. I'll catch a swell myself sometime. I ain't bragging on my looks or anything; but I'll take my chances where there's big prizes offered. What show would a girl have in a laundry?'

'Why, that's where I met Dan,' said Lou, triumphantly. 'He came in for his Sunday shirt and collars and saw me at the first board, ironing. We all try to get to work at the first board. Ella

43

Maginnis was sick that day, and I had her place. He said he noticed my arms first, how round and white they was. I had my sleeves rolled up. Some nice fellows come into laundries. You can tell 'em by their bringing their clothes in suit cases, and turning in the door sharp and sudden.'

'How can you wear a waist like that, Lou?' said Nancy, gazing down at the offending article with sweet scorn in her heavy-lidded eyes. 'It shows fierce taste.'

'This waist?' said Lou, with wide-eyed indignation. 'Why, I paid $16 for this waist. It's worth twenty-five. A woman left it to be laundered, and never called for it. The boss sold it to me. It's got yards and yards of hand embroidery on it. Better talk about that ugly, plain thing you've got on.'

'This ugly, plain thing,' said Nancy, calmly, 'was copied from one that Mrs Van Alstyne Fisher was wearing. The girls say her bill in the store last year was $12,000. I made mine, myself. It cost me $1.50. Ten feet away you couldn't tell it from hers.'

'Oh, well,' said Lou, good-naturedly, 'if you want to starve and put on airs, go ahead. But I'll take my job and good wages; and after hours give me something as fancy and attractive to wear as I am able to buy.'

But just then Dan came – a serious young man with a ready-made necktie, who had escaped the city's brand of frivolity – an electrician earning $30 per week who looked upon Lou with the sad eyes of Romeo, and thought her embroidered waist a web in which any fly should delight to be caught.

'My friend, Mr Owens – shake hands with Miss Danforth,' said Lou.

'I'm mighty glad to know you, Miss Danforth,' said Dan, with outstretched hand. 'I've heard Lou speak of you so often.'

'Thanks,' said Nancy, touching his fingers with the tips of her cool ones, 'I've heard her mention you – a few times.'

Lou giggled.

'Did you get that handshake from Mrs Van Alstyne Fisher, Nance?' she asked.

'If I did, you can feel safe in copying it,' said Nancy.

'Oh, I couldn't use it at all. It's too stylish for me. It's intended to set off diamond rings, that high shake is. Wait till I get a few and then I'll try it.'

'Learn it first,' said Nancy, wisely, 'and you'll be more likely to get the rings.'

'Now, to settle this argument,' said Dan, with his ready, cheerful smile, 'let me make a proposition. As I can't take both of you up to Tiffany's and do the right thing, what do you say to a little vaudeville? I've got the tickets. How about looking at stage diamonds since we can't shake hands with the real sparklers?'

The faithful squire took his place close to the curb; Lou next, a little peacocky in her bright and pretty clothes; Nancy on the inside, slender, and soberly clothed as the sparrow, but with the true Van Alstyne Fisher walk – thus they set out for their evening's moderate diversion.

I do not suppose that many look upon a great department store as an educational institution. But the one in which Nancy worked was something like that to her. She was surrounded by beautiful things that breathed taste and refinement. If you live in an atmosphere of luxury, luxury is yours whether your money pays for it, or another's.

The people she served were mostly women whose dress, manners, and position in the social world were quoted as criterions. From them Nancy began to take toll – the best from each according to her view.

From one she would copy and practice a gesture, from another an eloquent lifting of an eyebrow, from others, a manner of walking, of carrying a purse, of smiling, of greeting a friend, of addressing 'inferiors in station.' From her best beloved model, Mrs Van Alstyne Fisher, she made requisition for the excellent thing, a soft, low voice as clear as silver and as perfect in articulation as the notes of a thrush. Suffused in the aura of this high social refinement and good breeding, it was impossible for her to escape a deeper effect of it. As good habits are said to be better than good principles, so, perhaps, good manners are better than good habits. The teachings of your parents may not keep alive your New England conscience; but if you sit on a straight-back chair and repeat the words 'prisms and pilgrims' forty times the devil will flee from you. And when Nancy spoke in the Van Alstyne Fisher tones she felt the thrill of *noblesse oblige* to her very bones.

There was another source of learning in the great departmental school. Whenever you see three or four shop-girls gather in a bunch and jingle their wire bracelets as an accompaniment to apparently frivolous conversation, do not think that they are there for the purpose of criticizing the way Ethel does her back hair. The meeting may lack the dignity of the deliberative bodies of man; but it has all the importance of the occasion on which Eve and her first daughter first put their heads together to make Adam understand his proper place in the household. It is Woman's Conference for Common Defense and Exchange of Strategical Theories of Attack and Repulse upon and against the World, which is a Stage, and Man, its Audience who Persists in Throwing Bouquets Thereupon. Woman, the most helpless of the young of any animal – with the fawn's grace but without its fleetness; with the bird's beauty but without its power of flight; with the honey-bee's burden of sweetness but without its – Oh, let's drop that metaphor – some of us may have been stung.

During this council of war they pass weapons one to another, and exchange stratagems that each has devised and formulated out of the tactics of life.

'I says to 'im,' says Sadie, 'ain't you the fresh thing! Who do you suppose I am, to be addressing such a remark to me? And what do you think he says back to me?'

The heads, brown, black, flaxen, red, and yellow bob together;

the answer is given; and the parry to the thrust is decided upon, to be used by each thereafter in passages-at-arms with the common enemy, man.

Thus Nancy learned the art of defense; and to women successful defense means victory.

The curriculum of a department store is a wide one. Perhaps no other college could have fitted her as well for her life's ambition – the drawing of a matrimonial prize.

Her station in the store was a favored one. The music room was near enough for her to hear and become familiar with the works of the best composers – at least to acquire the familiarity that passed for appreciation in the social world in which she was vaguely trying to set a tentative and aspiring foot. She absorbed the educating influence of art wares, of costly and dainty fabrics, of adornments that are almost culture to women.

The other girls soon became aware of Nancy's ambition. 'Here comes your millionaire, Nancy,' they would call to her whenever any man who looked the rôle approached her counter. It got to be a habit of men, who were hanging about while their women folk were shopping, to stroll over to the handkerchief counter and dawdle over the cambric squares. Nancy's imitation high-bred air and genuine dainty beauty was what attracted. Many men thus came to display their graces before her. Some of them may have been millionaires; others were certainly no more than their sedulous apes. Nancy learned to discriminate. There was a window at the end of the handkerchief counter; and she could see the rows of vehicles waiting for the shoppers in the street below. She looked and perceived that automobiles differ as well as do their owners.

Once a fascinating gentleman bought four dozen handkerchiefs, and wooed her across the counter with a King Cophetua air. When he had gone one of the girls said:

'What's wrong, Nance, that you didn't warm up to that fellow? He looks the swell article, all right, to me.'

'Him?' said Nancy, with her coolest, sweetest, most impersonal, Van Alstyne Fisher smile; 'not for me. I saw him drive up outside. A 12 H. P. machine and an Irish chauffeur! And you saw what kind of handkerchiefs he bought – silk! And he's got dactylis on him. Give me the real thing or nothing, if you please.'

Two of the most 'refined' women in the store – a forelady and a cashier – had a few 'swell gentlemen friends' with whom they now and then dined. Once they included Nancy in an invitation. The dinner took place in a spectacular café whose tables are engaged for New Year's Eve a year in advance. There were two 'gentlemen friends' – one without any hair on his head – high living ungrew it; and we can prove it – the other a young man whose worth and sophistication he impressed upon you in two convincing ways – he swore that all the wine was corked; and he wore diamond cuff buttons. This young man perceived irresistible excellencies in Nancy. His taste ran to shop-girls; and here was one that added the voice and manners of his high social world to the franker charms of her own caste. So, on the following day, he appeared in the store and made her a serious proposal of marriage over a box of hemstitched, grass-bleached Irish linens. Nancy declined. A brown pompadour ten feet away had been using her eyes and ears. When the rejected suitor had gone she heaped carboys of upbraidings and horror upon Nancy's head.

'What a terrible little fool you are! That fellow's a millionaire – he's nephew of old Van Skittles himself. And he was talking on the level, too. Have you gone crazy, Nance?'

'Have I?' said Nancy. 'I didn't take him, did I? He isn't a millionaire so hard that you could notice it, anyhow. His family only allows him $20,000 a year to spend. The bald-headed fellow was guying him about it the other night at supper.'

The brown pompadour came nearer and narrowed her eyes.

'Say, what do you want?' she inquired, in a voice hoarse for lack of chewing-gum. 'Ain't that enough for you? Do you want to be a Mormon, and marry Rockefeller and Gladstone Dowie and the

King of Spain and the whole bunch? Ain't $20,000 a year good enough for you?'

Nancy flushed a little under the level gaze of the black, shallow eyes.

'It wasn't altogether the money, Carrie,' she explained. 'His friend caught him in a rank lie the other night at dinner. It was about some girl he said he hadn't been to the theater with. Well, I can't stand a liar. Put everything together – I don't like him; and that settles it. When I sell out it's not going to be on any bargain day. I've got to have something that sits up in a chair like a man, anyhow. Yes, I'm looking out for a catch; but it's got to be able to do something more than make a noise like a toy bank.'

'The physiopathic ward for you!' said the brown pompadour, walking away.

These high ideas – if not ideals – Nancy continued to cultivate on $8 per week. She bivouacked on the trail of the great unknown 'catch' eating her dry bread and tightening her belt day by day. On her face was the faint, soldierly, sweet, grim smile of the preordained man-hunter. The store was her forest; and many times she raised her rifle at game that seemed broad-antlered and big; but always some deep unerring instinct – perhaps of the huntress, perhaps of the woman – made her hold her fire and take up the trail again.

Lou flourished in the laundry. Out of her $18.50 per week she paid $6 for her room and board. The rest went mainly for clothes. Her opportunities for bettering her taste and manners were few compared with Nancy's. In the steaming laundry there was nothing but work, work and her thoughts of the evening pleasures to come. Many costly and showy fabrics passed under her iron; and it may be that her growing fondness for dress was thus transmitted to her through the conducting metal.

When the day's work was over Dan awaited her outside, her faithful shadow in whatever light she stood.

Sometimes he cast an honest and troubled glance at Lou's

49

clothes that increased in conspicuity rather than in style; but this was no disloyalty; he deprecated the attention they called to her in the streets.

And Lou was no less faithful to her chum. There was a law that Nancy should go with them on whatsoever outings they might take. Dan bore the extra burden heartily and in good cheer. It might be said that Lou furnished the color, Nancy the tone, and Dan the weight of the distraction-seeking trio. The escort, in his neat but obviously ready-made suit, his ready-made tie and unfailing, genial, ready-made wit never startled or clashed. He was of that good kind that you are likely to forget while they are present, but remember distinctly after they are gone.

To Nancy's superior taste the flavor of these ready-made pleasures was sometimes a little bitter: but she was young; and youth is a gourmand, when it cannot be a gourmet.

'Dan is always wanting me to marry him right away,' Lou told her once. 'But why should I? I'm independent. I can do as I please with the money I earn; and he never would agree for me to keep on working afterward. And say, Nance, what do you want to stick to that old store for, and half starve and half dress yourself? I could get you a place in the laundry right now if you'd come. It seems to me that you could afford to be a little less stuck-up if you could make a good deal more money.'

'I don't think I'm stuck-up, Lou,' said Nancy, 'but I'd rather live on half rations and stay where I am. I suppose I've got the habit. It's the chance that I want. I don't expect to be always behind a counter. I'm learning something new every day. I'm right up against refined and rich people all the time – even if I do only wait on them; and I'm not missing any pointers that I see passing around.'

'Caught your millionaire yet?' asked Lou with her teasing laugh.

'I haven't selected one yet,' answered Nancy. 'I've been looking them over.'

'Goodness! The idea of picking over 'em! Don't you ever let

one get by you, Nance – even if he's a few dollars shy. But of course you're joking – millionaires don't think about working girls like us.'

'It might be better for them if they did,' said Nancy, with cool wisdom. 'Some of us could teach them how to take care of their money.'

'If one was to speak to me,' laughed Lou, 'I know I'd have a duck-fit.'

'That's because you don't know any. The only difference between swells and other people is you have to watch 'em closer. Don't you think that red silk lining is just a little bit too bright for that coat, Lou?'

Lou looked at the plain, dull olive jacket of her friend.

'Well, no, I don't – but it may seem so beside that faded-looking thing you've got on.'

'This jacket,' said Nancy, complacently, 'has exactly the cut and fit of one that Mrs Van Alstyne Fisher was wearing the other day. The material cost me $3.98. I suppose hers cost about $100 more.'

'Oh, well,' said Lou, lightly, 'it don't strike me as millionaire bait. Shouldn't wonder if I catch one before you do, anyway.'

Truly it would have taken a philosopher to decide upon the values of the theories held by the two friends. Lou, lacking that certain pride and fastidiousness that keeps stores and desks filled with girls working for the barest living, thumped away gaily with her iron in the noisy and stifling laundry. Her wages supported her even beyond the point of comfort; so that her dress profited until sometimes she cast a sidelong glance of impatience at the neat but inelegant apparel of Dan – Dan the constant, the immutable, the undeviating.

As for Nancy, her case was one of tens of thousands. Silk and jewels and laces and ornaments and the perfume and music of the fine world of good-breeding and taste – these were made for woman; they are her equitable portion. Let her keep near them if they are a part of life to her, and if she will. She is no traitor to herself, as Esau was; for she keeps her birthright and the pottage she earns is often very scant.

In this atmosphere Nancy belonged; and she throve in it and ate her frugal meals and schemed over her cheap dresses with a determined and contented mind. She already knew woman; and she was studying man, the animal, both as to his habits and eligibility. Some day she would bring down the game that she wanted; but she promised herself it would be what seemed to her the biggest and the best, and nothing smaller.

Thus she kept her lamp trimmed and burning to receive the bridegroom when he should come.

But another lesson she learned, perhaps unconsciously. Her standard of values began to shift and change. Sometimes the dollar-mark grew blurred in her mind's eye, and shaped itself into letters that spelled such words as 'truth' and 'honor' and now and then just 'kindness.' Let us make a likeness of one who hunts the moose or elk in some mighty wood. He sees a little dell, mossy and embowered, where a rill trickles, babbling to him of rest and comfort. At these times the spear of Nimrod himself grows blunt.

So, Nancy wondered sometimes if Persian lamb was always quoted at its market value by the hearts that it covered.

One Thursday evening Nancy left the store and turned across Sixth Avenue westward to the laundry. She was expected to go with Lou and Dan to a musical comedy.

Dan was just coming out of the laundry when she arrived. There was a queer, strained look on his face.

'I thought I would drop around to see if they had heard from her,' he said.

'Heard from who?' asked Nancy. 'Isn't Lou there?'

'I thought you knew,' said Dan. 'She hasn't been here or at the house where she lived since Monday. She moved all her things from there. She told one of the girls in the laundry she might be going to Europe.'

'Hasn't anybody seen her anywhere?' asked Nancy.

Dan looked at her with his jaws set grimly, and a steely gleam in his steady gray eyes.

'They told me in the laundry,' he said, harshly, 'that they saw her pass yesterday – in an automobile. With one of the millionaires, I suppose, that you and Lou were forever busying your brains about.'

For the first time Nancy quailed before a man. She laid her hand that trembled slightly on Dan's sleeve.

'You've no right to say such a thing to me, Dan – as if I had anything to do with it!'

'I didn't mean it that way,' said Dan, softening. He fumbled in his vest pocket.

'I've got the tickets for the show to-night,' he said, with a gallant show of lightness. 'If you —'

Nancy admired pluck whenever she saw it.

'I'll go with you, Dan,' she said.

Three months went by before Nancy saw Lou again.

At twilight one evening the shop-girl was hurrying home along the border of a little quiet park. She heard her name called, and wheeled about in time to catch Lou rushing into her arms.

After the first embrace they drew their heads back as serpents do, ready to attack or to charm, with a thousand questions trembling on their swift tongues. And then Nancy noticed that prosperity had descended upon Lou, manifesting itself in costly furs, flashing gems, and creations of the tailor's art.

'You little fool!' cried Lou, loudly and affectionately. 'I see you are still working in that store, and as shabby as ever. And how about that big catch you were going to make – nothing doing yet, I suppose?'

And then Lou looked, and saw that something better than prosperity had descended upon Nancy – something that shone brighter than gems in her eyes and redder than a rose in her cheeks, and that danced like electricity anxious to be loosed from the tip of her tongue.

'Yes, I'm still in the store,' said Nancy, 'but I'm going to leave it next week. I've made my catch – the biggest catch in the world. You won't mind now, Lou, will you? – I'm going to be married to Dan – to Dan! – he's my Dan now – why, Lou!'

Around the corner of the park strolled one of those new-crop, smooth-faced young policemen that are making the force more endurable – at least to the eye. He saw a woman with an expensive fur coat and diamond-ringed hands crouching down against the iron fence of the park sobbing turbulently, while a slender, plainly dressed working girl leaned close, trying to console her. But the Gibsonian cop, being of the new order, passed on, pretending not to notice, for he was wise enough to know that these matters are beyond help so far as the power he represents is concerned, though he rap the pavement with his nightstick till the sound goes up to the furthermost stars.

# The Pendulum

'Eighty-first street – let 'em out, please,' yelled the shepherd in blue.

A flock of citizen sheep scrambled out and another flock scrambled aboard. Ding-ding! The cattle cars of the Manhattan Elevated rattled away, and John Perkins drifted down the stairway of the station with the released flock.

John walked slowly toward his flat. Slowly, because in the lexicon of his daily life there was no such word as 'perhaps.' There are no surprises awaiting a man who has been married two years and lives in a flat. As he walked John Perkins prophesied to himself with gloomy and downtrodden cynicism the foregone conclusions of the monotonous day.

Katy would meet him at the door with a kiss flavored with cold cream and butter-scotch. He would remove his coat, sit upon a macadamized lounge and read, in the evening paper, of Russians and Japs slaughtered by the deadly linotype. For dinner there would be pot roast, a salad flavored with a dressing warranted not to crack or injure the leather, stewed rhubarb and the bottle of strawberry marmalade blushing at the certificate of chemical purity on its label. After dinner Katy would show him the new patch in her crazy quilt that the iceman had cut for her off the end of his four-in-hand. At half-past seven they would spread newspapers over the furniture to catch the pieces of plastering that fell when the fat man in the flat overhead began to take his physical culture exercises. Exactly at eight Hickey & Mooney, of the vaudeville team (unbooked) in the flat across the hall, would yield to the gentle influence of delirium tremens and begin to overturn chairs under the delusion that Hammerstein was pursuing them with a five-hundred-dollar-a-week contract. Then the gent at the window across the air-shaft would get out his flute; the nightly gas leak would steal forth to frolic in the highways; the dumb-waiter would slip off its trolley; the janitor would drive Mrs Zanowitski's five children once more across the Yalu; the lady with the champagne shoes and the Skye terrier would trip downstairs and paste her Thursday name over her bell and letter-box – and the evening routine of the Frogmore flats would be under way.

John Perkins knew these things would happen. And he knew that at a quarter past eight he would summon his nerve and reach for his hat, and that his wife would deliver this speech in a querulous tone:

'Now, where are you going, I'd like to know, John Perkins?'

'Thought I'd drop up to McCloskey's,' he would answer, 'and play a game or two of pool with the fellows.'

Of late such had been John Perkins's habit. At ten or eleven he would return. Sometimes Katy would be asleep; sometimes waiting up, ready to melt in the crucible of her ire a little more gold plating from the wrought steel chains of matrimony. For these things Cupid will have to answer when he stands at the bar of justice with his victims from the Frogmore flats.

To-night John Perkins encountered a tremendous upheaval of the commonplace when he reached his door. No Katy was there with her affectionate, confectionate kiss. The three rooms seemed in portentous disorder. All about lay her things in confusion. Shoes in the middle of the floor, curling tongs, hair bows, kimonos, powder box, jumbled together on dresser and chairs – this was not Katy's way. With a sinking heart John saw the comb with a curling cloud of her brown hair among its teeth. Some unusual hurry and perturbation must have possessed her for she always carefully placed these combings in the little blue vase on the mantel to be some day formed into the coveted feminine 'rat.'

Hanging conspicuously to the gas jet by a string was a folded paper. John seized it. It was a note from his wife running thus:

Dear John:

I just had a telegram saying mother is very sick. I am going to take the 4:30 train. Brother Sam is going to meet me at the depot there. There is cold mutton in the icebox. I hope it isn't her quinzy again. Pay the milkman 50 cents. She had it bad last spring. Don't forget to write to the company about the gas meter, and your good socks are in the top drawer. I will write to-morrow.

Hastily,
Katy.

Never during their two years of matrimony had he and Katy been separated for a night. John read the note over and over in a dumbfounded way. Here was a break in a routine that had never varied, and it left him dazed.

There on the back of a chair hung, pathetically empty and formless, the red wrapper with black dots that she always wore while getting the meals. Her week-day clothes had been tossed here and there in her haste. A little paper bag of her favorite butter-scotch lay with its string yet unwound. A daily paper sprawled on the floor, gaping rectangularly where a railroad time-table had been clipped from it. Everything in the room spoke of a loss, of an essence gone, of its soul and life departed. John Perkins stood among the dead remains with a queer feeling of desolation in his heart.

He began to set the rooms tidy as well as he could. When he touched her clothes a thrill of something like terror went through him. He had never thought what existence would be without Katy. She had become so thoroughly annealed into his life that she was like the air he breathed – necessary but scarcely noticed.

Now, without warning, she was gone, vanished, as completely absent as if she had never existed. Of course it would be only for a few days, or at most a week or two, but it seemed to him as if the very hand of death had pointed a finger at his secure and uneventful home.

John dragged the cold mutton from the icebox, made coffee, and sat down to a lonely meal face to face with the strawberry marmalade's shameless certificate of purity. Bright among withdrawn blessings now appeared to him the ghosts of pot roasts and the salad with tan polish dressing. His home was dismantled. A quinzied mother-in-law had knocked his lares and penates sky-high. After his solitary meal John sat at a front window.

He did not care to smoke. Outside the city roared to him to come join in its dance of folly and pleasure. The night was his. He might go forth unquestioned and thrum the strings of jollity as free as any gay bachelor there. He might carouse and wander and have his fling until dawn if he liked; and there would be no wrathful Katy waiting for him, bearing the chalice that held the dregs of his joy. He might play pool at McCloskey's with his roistering friends until Aurora dimmed the electric bulbs if he chose. The hymeneal strings that had curbed him always when the Frogmore flats had palled upon him were loosened. Katy was gone.

John Perkins was not accustomed to analyzing his emotions. But as he sat in his Katy-bereft 10 × 12 parlor he hit unerringly upon the keynote of his discomfort. He knew now that Katy was necessary to his happiness. His feeling for her, lulled into unconsciousness by the dull round of domesticity, had been sharply stirred by the loss of her presence. Has it not been dinned into us by proverb and sermon and fable that we never prize the music till the sweet-voiced bird has flown – or in other no less florid and true utterances?

'I'm a double-dyed dub,' mused John Perkins, 'the way I've been treating Katy. Off every night playing pool and bumming with the boys instead of staying home with her. The poor girl here all alone with nothing to amuse her, and me acting that way! John Perkins, you're the worst kind of a shine. I'm going to make it up for the little girl. I'll take her out and let her see some amusement. And I'll cut out the McCloskey gang right from this minute.'

Yes, there was the city roaring outside for John Perkins to come dance in the train of Momus. And at McCloskey's the boys were knocking the balls idly into the pockets against the hour for the nightly game. But no primrose way nor clicking cue could woo the remorseful soul of Perkins the bereft. The thing that was his, lightly held and half scorned, had been taken away from him, and he wanted it. Backward to a certain man named Adam, whom the cherubim bounced from the orchard, could Perkins, the remorseful, trace his descent.

Near the right hand of John Perkins stood a chair. On the back of it stood Katy's blue shirtwaist. It still retained something of her contour. Midway of the sleeves were fine, individual wrinkles made by the movements of her arms in working for his comfort and pleasure. A delicate but impelling odor of bluebells came from it. John took it and looked long and soberly at the unresponsive grenadine. Katy had never been unresponsive. Tears: – yes, tears – came into John Perkins's eyes. When she came back things would be different. He would make up for all his neglect. What was life without her?

The door opened. Katy walked in carrying a little hand satchel. John stared at her stupidly.

'My! I'm glad to get back,' said Katy. 'Ma wasn't sick to amount to anything. Sam was at the depot, and said she just had a little spell, and got all right soon after they telegraphed. So I took the next train back. I'm just dying for a cup of coffee.'

Nobody heard the click and rattle of the cogwheels as the third-floor-front of the Frogmore flats buzzed its machinery back into the Order of Things. A band slipped, a spring was touched, the gear was adjusted and the wheels revolved in their old orbit.

John Perkins looked at the clock. It was 8:15. He reached for his hat and walked to the door.

'Now, where are you going, I'd like to know, John Perkins?' asked Katy, in a querulous tone.

'Thought I'd drop up to McCloskey's,' said John, 'and play a game or two of pool with the fellows.'

# *Brickdust Row*

Blinker was displeased. A man of less culture and poise and wealth would have sworn. But Blinker always remembered that he was a gentleman – a thing that no gentleman should do. So he merely looked bored and sardonic while he rode in a hansom to the center of disturbance, which was the Broadway office of Lawyer Oldport, who was agent for the Blinker estate.

'I don't see,' said Blinker, 'why I should be always signing confounded papers. I am packed, and was to have left for the North Woods this morning. Now I must wait until to-morrow morning. I hate night trains. My best razors are, of course, at the bottom of some unidentifiable trunk. It is a plot to drive me to bay rum and a monologing, thumb-handed barber. Give me a pen that doesn't scratch. I hate pens that scratch.'

'Sit down,' said double-chinned, gray Lawyer Oldport. 'The worst has not been told you. Oh, the hardships of the rich! The papers are not yet ready to sign. They will be laid before you to-morrow at eleven. You will miss another day. Twice shall the barber tweak the helpless nose of a Blinker. Be thankful that your sorrows do not embrace a haircut.'

'If,' said Blinker, rising, 'the act did not involve more signing of papers I would take my business out of your hands at once. Give me a cigar, please.'

'If,' said Lawyer Oldport, 'I had cared to see an old friend's son gulped down at one mouthful by sharks I would have ordered you to take it away long ago. Now, let's quit fooling, Alexander. Besides the grinding task of signing your name some thirty times to-morrow, I must impose upon you the consideration of a matter of business – of business, and I may say humanity or right. I spoke to you about this five years ago, but you would not listen – you were in a hurry for a coaching trip, I think. The subject has come up again. The property –'

'Oh, property!' interrupted Blinker. 'Dear Mr Oldport, I think you mentioned to-morrow. Let's have it all at one dose to-morrow – signatures and property and snappy rubber bands and that smelly sealing-wax and all. Have luncheon with me? Well, I'll try to remember to drop in at eleven to-morrow. Morning.'

The Blinker wealth was in lands, tenements, and heredita-ments, as the legal phrase goes. Lawyer Oldport had once taken Alexander in his little pulmonary gasoline runabout to see the many buildings and rows of buildings that he owned in the city. For Alexander was sole heir. They had amused Blinker very much. The houses looked so incapable of producing the big sums of money that Lawyer Oldport kept piling up in banks for him to spend.

In the evening Blinker went to one of his clubs, intending to dine. Nobody was there except some old fogies playing whist who spoke to him with grave politeness and glared at him with savage contempt. Everybody was out of town. But here he was kept in like a schoolboy to write his name over and over on pieces of paper. His wounds were deep.

Blinker turned his back on the fogies, and said to the club stew-ard who had come forward with some nonsense about cold fresh salmon roe:

'Symons, I'm going to Coney Island.' He said it as one might say: 'All's off, I'm going to jump into the river.'

The joke pleased Symons. He laughed within a sixteenth of a note of the audibility permitted by the laws governing employees.

'Certainly, sir,' he tittered. 'Of course, sir, I think I can see you at Coney, Mr Blinker.'

Blinker got a paper and looked up the movements of Sunday steamboats. Then he found a cab at the first corner and drove to a North River pier. He stood in line, as democratic as you or I, and bought a ticket, and was trampled upon and shoved forward until, at last, he found himself on the upper deck of the boat staring brazenly at a girl who sat alone upon a camp stool. But Blinker did not intend to be brazen; the girl was so wonderfully good looking that he forgot for one minute that he was the prince incog, and behaved just as he did in society.

She was looking at him, too, and not severely. A puff of wind threatened Blinker's straw hat. He caught it warily and settled it again. The movement gave the effect of a bow. The girl nodded and smiled, and in another instant he was seated at her side. She was dressed all in white, she was paler than Blinker imagined milkmaids and girls of humble stations to be, but she was as tidy as a cherry blossom, and her steady, supremely frank gray eyes looked out from the intrepid depths of an unshadowed and untroubled soul.

'How dare you raise your hat to me?' she asked, with a smile-redeemed severity.

'I didn't,' Blinker said, but he quickly covered the mistake by extending it to 'I didn't know how to keep from it after I saw you.'

'I do not allow gentlemen to sit by me to whom I have not been introduced,' she said with a sudden haughtiness that deceived him. He rose reluctantly, but her clear, teasing laugh brought him down to his chair again.

'I guess you weren't going far,' she declared, with beauty's magnificent self-confidence.

'Are you going to Coney Island?' asked Blinker.

'Me?' She turned upon him wide-open eyes full of bantering surprise. 'Why, what a question! Can't you see that I'm riding a bicycle in the park?' Her drollery took the form of impertinence.

'And I'm laying bricks on a tall factory chimney,' said Blinker. 'Mayn't we see Coney together? I'm all alone and I've never been there before.'

'It depends,' said the girl, 'on how nicely you behave. I'll consider your application until we get there.'

Blinker took pains to provide against the rejection of his application. He strove to please. To adopt the metaphor of his nonsensical phrase, he laid brick upon brick on the tall chimney of his devoirs until, at length, the structure was stable and complete. The manners of the best society come around finally to simplicity; and as the girl's way was that naturally, they were on a mutual plane of communication from the beginning.

He learned that she was twenty, and her name was Florence; that she trimmed hats in a millinery shop; that she lived in a furnished room with her best chum Ella, who was cashier in a shoe store; and that a glass of milk from the bottle on the window-sill and an egg that boils itself while you twist up your hair makes a breakfast good enough for anyone. Florence laughed when she heard 'Blinker.'

'Well,' she said. 'It certainly shows that you have imagination. It gives the "Smiths" a chance for a little rest, anyhow.'

They landed at Coney, and were dashed on the crest of a great human wave of mad pleasure-seekers into the walks and avenues of Fairyland gone into vaudeville.

With a curious eye, a critical mind, and a fairly withheld judgment Blinker considered the temples, pagodas and kiosks of popularized delights. Hoi polloi trampled, hustled, and crowded him. Basket parties bumped him; sticky children tumbled, howling, under his feet, candying his clothes. Insolent youths strolling among the booths with hard-won canes under one arm and easily won girls on the other, blew defiant smoke from cheap cigars into his face. The publicity gentlemen with megaphones, each before his own stupendous attraction, roared like Niagara in his ears. Music of all kinds that could be tortured from brass, reed, hide, or string, fought in the air to gain space for its vibrations against its competitors. But what held Blinker in awful fascination was the mob, the multitude, the proletariat shrieking, struggling, hurrying, panting, hurling itself in incontinent frenzy, with unabashed abandon, into the ridiculous sham palaces of trumpery and tinsel pleasures. The vulgarity of it, its brutal overriding of all the tenets of repression and taste that were held by his caste, repelled him strongly.

In the midst of his disgust he turned and looked down at Florence by his side. She was ready with her quick smile and upturned, happy eyes, as bright and clear as the water in trout pools. The eyes were saying that they had the right to be shining and happy, for was their owner not with her (for the present) Man, her gentleman Friend and holder of the keys to the enchanted city of fun.

Blinker did not read her look accurately, but by some miracle he suddenly saw Coney aright.

He no longer saw a mass of vulgarians seeking gross joys. He now looked clearly upon a hundred thousand true idealists. Their offenses were wiped out. Counterfeit and false though the garish joys of these spangled temples were, he perceived that deep under the gilt surface they offered saving and apposite balm and satisfaction to the restless human heart. Here, at least, was the husk of Romance, the empty but shining casque of Chivalry, the breath-catching though safe-guarded dip and flight of Adventure, the magic carpet that transports you to the realms of fairyland, though its journey be through but a few poor yards of space. He no longer saw a rabble, but his brothers seeking the ideal. There was no magic of poesy here or of art; but the glamor of their imagination turned yellow calico into cloth of gold and the megaphone into the silver trumpets of joy's heralds.

Almost humbled, Blinker rolled up the shirt sleeves of his mind and joined the idealists.

'You are the lady doctor,' he said to Florence. 'How shall we go about doing this jolly conglomeration of fairy tales, incorporated?'

'We will begin there,' said the Princess, pointing to a fun pagoda on the edge of the sea, 'and we will take them all in, one by one.'

They caught the eight o'clock returning boat and sat, filled with pleasant fatigue, against the rail in the bow, listening to the Italians' fiddle and harp. Blinker had thrown off all care. The North Woods seemed to him an uninhabitable wilderness. What a fuss he had made over signing his name – pooh! he could sign it a hundred times. And her name was as pretty as she was – 'Florence,' he said it to himself a great many times.

As the boat was nearing its pier in the North River a two-funneled, drab, foreign-looking sea-going steamer was dropping down toward the bay. The boat turned its nose in towards its slip. The steamer veered as if to seek mid-stream, and then yawed, seemed to increase its speed and struck the Coney boat on the side near the stern, cutting into it with a terrifying shock and crash.

While the six hundred passengers on the boat were mostly tumbling about the decks in a shrieking panic the captain was shouting at the steamer that it should not back off and leave the rent exposed for the water to enter. But the steamer tore its way out like a savage sawfish and cleaved its heartless way, full speed ahead.

The boat began to sink at its stern, but moved slowly toward the slip. The passengers were a frantic mob, unpleasant to behold.

Blinker held Florence tightly until the boat had righted itself. She made no sound or sign of fear. He stood on a camp stool, ripped off the slats above his head and pulled down a number of the life preservers. He began to buckle one around Florence. The rotten canvas split and the fraudulent granulated cork came pouring out in a stream. Florence caught a handful of it and laughed gleefully.

'It looks like breakfast food,' she said. 'Take it off. They're no good.'

She unbuckled it and threw it on the deck. She made Blinker sit down and sat by his side and put her hand in his. 'What'll you bet we don't reach the pier all right?' she said, and began to hum a song.

And now the captain moved among the passengers and compelled order. The boat would undoubtedly make her slip, he said, and ordered the women and children to the bow, where they would land first. The boat, very low in the water at the stern, tried gallantly to make his promise good.

'Florence,' said Blinker, as she held him close by an arm and hand, 'I love you.'

'That's what they all say,' she replied, lightly.

'I am not one of "they all,"' he persisted. 'I never knew any one I could love before. I could pass my life with you and be happy every day. I am rich. I can make things all right for you.'

'That's what they all say,' said the girl again, weaving the words into her little, reckless song.

'Don't say that again,' said Blinker in a tone that made her look at him in frank surprise.

'Why shouldn't I say it?' she asked, calmly. 'They all do.'

'Who are "they"?' he asked, jealous for the first time in his existence.

'Why, the fellows I know.'

'Do you know so many?'

'Oh, well, I'm not a wall flower,' she answered with modest complacency.

'Where do you see these – these men? At your home?'

'Of course not. I meet them just as I did you. Sometimes on the boat, sometimes in the park, sometimes on the street. I'm a pretty good judge of a man. I can tell in a minute if a fellow is one who is likely to get fresh.'

'What do you mean by "fresh"?'

'Who try to kiss you – me, I mean.'

'Do any of them try that?' asked Blinker, clenching his teeth.

'Sure. All men do. You know that.'

'Do you allow them?'

'Some. Not many. They won't take you out anywhere unless you do.'

She turned her head and looked searchingly at Blinker. Her eyes were as innocent as a child's. There was a puzzled look in them, as though she did not understand him.

'What's wrong about my meeting fellows?' she asked, wonderingly.

'Everything,' he answered, almost savagely. 'Why don't you entertain your company in the house where you live? Is it necessary to pick up Tom, Dick, and Harry on the street?'

She kept her absolutely ingenuous eyes upon his.

'If you could see the place where I live you wouldn't ask that. I live in Brickdust Row. They call it that because there's red dust from the bricks crumbling over everything. I've lived there for more than four years. There's no place to receive company. You can't have anybody come to your room. What else is there to do? A girl has got to meet the men, hasn't she?'

'Yes,' he said hoarsely. 'A girl has got to meet a – has got to meet the men.'

'The first time one spoke to me on the street,' she continued, 'I ran home and cried all night. But you get used to it. I meet a good many nice fellows at church. I go on rainy days and stand in the vestibule until one comes up with an umbrella. I wish there was a parlor, so I could ask you to call, Mr Blinker – are you really sure it isn't "Smith," now?'

The boat landed safely. Blinker had a confused impression of walking with the girl through quiet crosstown streets until she stopped at a corner and held out her hand.

'I live just one more block over,' she said. 'Thank you for a very pleasant afternoon.'

Blinker muttered something and plunged northward till he found a cab. A big, gray church loomed slowly at his right. Blinker shook his fist at it through the window.

'I gave you a thousand dollars last week,' he cried under his breath, 'and she meets them in your very doors. There is something wrong; there is something wrong.'

At eleven the next day Blinker signed his name thirty times with a new pen provided by Lawyer Oldport.

'Now let me get to the woods,' he said, surlily.

'You are not looking well,' said Lawyer Oldport. 'The trip will do you good. But listen, if you will, to that little matter of business of which I spoke to you yesterday, and also five years ago. There are some buildings, fifteen in number, of which there are new five-year leases to be signed. Your father contemplated a change in the lease provisions, but never made it. He intended that the parlors of these houses should not be sublet, but that the tenants should be allowed to use them for reception rooms. These houses are in the shopping districts, and are mainly tenanted by young working girls. As it is they are forced to seek companionship outside. This row of red brick –'

Blinker interrupted him with a loud, discordant laugh.

'Brickdust Row for an even hundred,' he cried. 'And I own it. Have I guessed right?'

'The tenants have some such name for it,' said Lawyer Oldport.

Blinker arose and jammed his hat down to his eyes.

'Do what you please with it,' he said, harshly. 'Remodel it, burn it, raze it to the ground. But, man, it's too late, I tell you. It's too late. It's too late. It's too late. It's too late.'

# The Making of a New Yorker

Besides many things, Raggles was a poet. He was called a tramp; but that was only an elliptical way of saying that he was a philosopher, an artist, a traveler, a naturalist, and a discoverer. But most of all he was a poet. In all his life he never wrote a line of verse; he lived his poetry. His Odyssey would have been a Limerick, had it been written. But, to linger with the primary proposition, Raggles was a poet.

Raggles's specialty, had he been driven to ink and paper, would have been sonnets to the cities. He studied cities as women study their reflections in mirrors; as children study the glue and sawdust of a dislocated doll; as the men who write about wild animals study the cages in the zoo. A city to Raggles was not merely a pile of bricks and mortar, peopled by a certain number of inhabitants; it was a thing with soul characteristic and distinct; an individual conglomeration of life, with its own peculiar essence, flavor, and feeling. Two thousand miles to the north and south, east and west, Raggles wandered in poetic fervor, taking the cities to his breast. He footed it on dusty roads, or sped magnificently in freight cars, counting time as of no account. And when he had found the heart of a city and listened to its secret confession, he strayed on, restless, to another. Fickle Raggles! – but perhaps he had not met the civic corporation that could engage and hold his critical fancy.

Through the ancient poets we have learned that the cities are feminine. So they were to poet Raggles; and his mind carried a concrete and clear conception of the figure that symbolized and typified each one that he had wooed.

Chicago seemed to swoop down upon him with a breezy

suggestion of Mrs Partington, plumes and patchouli, and to disturb his rest with a soaring and beautiful song of future promise. But Raggles would awake to a sense of shivering cold and a haunting impression of ideals lost in a depressing aura of potato salad and fish.

Thus Chicago affected him. Perhaps there is a vagueness and inaccuracy in the description; but that is Raggles's fault. He should have recorded his sensations in magazine poems.

Pittsburgh impressed him as the play of 'Othello' performed in the Russian language in a railroad station by Dockstader's minstrels. A royal and generous lady this Pittsburgh, though – homely, hearty, with flushed face, washing the dishes in a silk dress and white kid slippers, and bidding Raggles sit before the roaring fireplace and drink champagne with his pigs' feet and fried potatoes.

New Orleans had simply gazed down upon him from a balcony. He could see her pensive, starry eyes and catch the flutter of her fan, and that was all. Only once he came face to face with her. It was at dawn, when she was flushing the red bricks of the banquette with a pail of water. She laughed and hummed a chansonette and filled Raggles's shoes with ice-cold water. Allons!

Boston construed herself to the poetic Raggles in an erratic and singular way. It seemed to him that he had drunk cold tea and that the city was a white, cold cloth that had been bound tightly around his brow to spur him to some unknown but tremendous mental effort. And, after all, he came to shovel snow for a livelihood; and the cloth, becoming wet, tightened its knots and could not be removed.

Indefinite and unintelligible ideas, you will say; but your disapprobation should be tempered with gratitude, for these are poets' fancies – and suppose you had come upon them in verse!

One day Raggles came and laid siege to the heart of the great city of Manhattan. She was the greatest of all; and he wanted to learn her note in the scale; to taste and appraise and classify and solve and label her and arrange her with the other cities that had given him up the secret of their individuality. And here we cease to be Raggles's translator and become his chronicler.

Raggles landed from a ferry-boat one morning and walked into the core of the town with the blasé air of a cosmopolite. He was dressed with care to play the rôle of an 'unidentified man.' No country, race, class, clique, union, party clan, or bowling association could have claimed him. His clothing, which had been donated to him piece-meal by citizens of different height, but same number of inches around the heart, was not yet as uncomfortable to his figure as those specimens of raiment, self-measured, that are railroaded to you by trans-continental tailors with a suit case, suspenders, silk handkerchief and pearl studs as a bonus. Without money – as a poet should be – but with the ardor of an astronomer discovering a new star in the chorus of the Milky Way, or a man who has seen ink suddenly flow from his fountain pen, Raggles wandered into the great city.

Late in the afternoon he drew out of the roar and commotion with a look of dumb terror on his countenance. He was defeated, puzzled, discomfited, frightened. Other cities had been to him as long primer to read; as country maidens quickly to fathom; as send-price-of-subscription-with-answer rebuses to solve; as oyster cocktails to swallow; but here was one as cold, glittering, serene, impossible as a four-carat diamond in a window to a lover outside fingering damply in his pocket his ribbon-counter salary.

The greetings of the other cities he had known – their homespun kindliness, their human gamut of rough charity, friendly curses, garrulous curiosity, and easily estimated credulity or indifference. This city of Manhattan gave him no clue; it was walled against him. Like a river of adamant it flowed past him in the streets. Never an eye was turned upon him; no voice spoke to him. His heart yearned for the clap of Pittsburgh's sooty hand on his shoulder; for Chicago's menacing but social yawp in his ear; for the pale and eleemosynary stare through the Bostonian eyeglass – even for the precipitate but unmalicious boot-toe of Louisville or St Louis.

On Broadway Raggles, successful suitor of many cities, stood, bashful, like any country swain. For the first time he experienced the poignant humiliation of being ignored. And when he tried to reduce this brilliant, swiftly changing, ice-cold city to a formula he failed utterly. Poet though he was, it offered him no color similes, no points of comparison, no flaw in its polished facets, no handle by which he could hold it up and view its shape and structure, as he familiarly and often contemptuously had done with other towns. The houses were interminable ramparts loopholed for defense; the people were bright but bloodless specters passing in sinister and selfish array.

The thing that weighed heaviest on Raggles's soul and clogged his poet's fancy was the spirit of absolute egotism that seemed to saturate the people as toys are saturated with paint. Each one that he considered appeared a monster of abominable and insolent conceit. Humanity was gone from them; they were toddling idols of stone and varnish, worshiping themselves and greedy for though oblivious of worship from their fellow graven images. Frozen, cruel, implacable, impervious, cut to an identical pattern, they hurried on their ways like statues brought by some miracle to motion, while soul and feeling lay unaroused in the reluctant marble.

Gradually Raggles became conscious of certain types. One was an elderly gentleman with a snow-white, short beard, pink, unwrinkled face, and stony, sharp blue eyes, attired in the fashion of a gilded youth, who seemed to personify the city's wealth, ripeness and frigid unconcern. Another type was a woman, tall, beautiful, clear as a steel engraving, goddess-like, calm, clothed like the princesses of old, with eyes as coldly blue as the reflection of sunlight on a glacier. And another was a by-product of this town of marionettes – a broad, swaggering, grim, threateningly sedate fellow, with a jowl as large as a harvested wheat field, the complexion of a baptized infant, and the knuckles of a prize-fighter. This type leaned against cigar signs and viewed the world with frappéd contumely.

A poet is a sensitive creature, and Raggles soon shriveled in the bleak embrace of the undecipherable. The chill, sphinx-like, ironical, illegible, unnatural, ruthless expression of the city left him downcast and bewildered. Had it no heart? Better the woodpile, the scolding of vinegar-faced housewives at back doors, the kindly spleen of bartenders behind provincial free-lunch counters, the amiable truculence of rural constables, the kicks, arrests, and happy-go-lucky chances of the other vulgar, loud, crude cities than this freezing heartlessness.

Raggles summoned his courage and sought alms from the populance. Unheeding, regardless, they passed on without the wink of an eyelash to testify that they were conscious of his existence. And then he said to himself that this fair but pitiless city of Manhattan was without a soul; that its inhabitants were mannikins moved by wires and springs, and that he was alone in a great wilderness.

Raggles started to cross the street. There was a blast, a roar, a hissing and a crash as something struck him and hurled him over and over six yards from where he had been. As he was coming down like the stick of a rocket, the earth and all the cities thereof turned to a fractured dream.

Raggles opened his eyes. First an odor made itself known to him – an odor of the earliest spring flowers of Paradise. And then a hand soft as a falling petal touched his brow. Bending over him was the woman clothed like the princess of old, with blue eyes, now soft and humid with human sympathy. Under his head on the pavement were silks and furs. With Raggles's hat in his hand and with his face pinker than ever from a vehement outburst of oratory against reckless driving, stood the elderly gentleman who personified the city's wealth and ripeness. From a near-by café hurried the by-product with the vast jowl and baby complexion, bearing a glass full of crimson fluid that suggested delightful possibilities.

'Drink dis, sport,' said the by-product, holding the glass to Raggles's lips.

Hundreds of people huddled around in a moment, their faces wearing the deepest concern. Two flattering and gorgeous policemen got into the circle and pressed back the overplus of Samaritans. An old lady in a black shawl spoke loudly of camphor; a newsboy slipped one of his papers beneath Raggles's elbow, where it lay on the muddy pavement. A brisk young man with a notebook was asking for names.

A bell clanged importantly, and the ambulance cleaned a lane through the crowd. A cool surgeon slipped into the midst of affairs.

'How do you feel, old man?' asked the surgeon, stooping easily to his task. The princess of silks and satins wiped a red drop or two from Raggles's brow with a fragrant cobweb.

'Me?' said Raggles, with a seraphic smile. 'I feel fine.'

He had found the heart of his new city.

In three days they let him leave his cot for the convalescent ward in the hospital. He had been in there an hour when the attendants heard sounds of conflict. Upon investigation they found that Raggles had assaulted and damaged a brother convalescent – a glowering transient whom a freight train collision had sent in to be patched up.

'What's all this about?' inquired the head nurse.

'He was runnin' down me town,' said Raggles.

'What town?' asked the nurse.

'Noo York,' said Raggles.

# The Last Leaf

In a little district west of Washington Square the streets have run crazy and broken themselves into small strips called 'places.' These 'places' make strange angles and curves. One street crosses itself a time or two. An artist once discovered a valuable possibility in this street. Suppose a collector with a bill for paints, paper and canvas should, in traversing this route, suddenly meet himself coming back, without a cent having been paid on account!

So, to quaint old Greenwich Village the art people soon came prowling, hunting for north windows and eighteenth-century gables and Dutch attics and low rents. Then they imported some pewter mugs and a chafing dish or two from Sixth Avenue, and became a 'colony.'

At the top of a squatty, three-story brick Sue and Johnsy had their studio. 'Johnsy' was familiar for Joanna. One was from Maine; the other from California. They had met at the *table d'hôte* of an Eighth Street 'Delmonico's,' and found their tastes in art, chicory salad and bishop sleeves so congenial that the joint studio resulted.

That was in May. In November a cold, unseen stranger, whom the doctors called Pneumonia, stalked about the colony, touching one here and there with his icy fingers. Over on the east side this ravager strode boldly, smiting his victims by scores, but his feet trod slowly through the maze of the narrow and moss-grown 'places.'

Mr Pneumonia was not what you would call a chivalric old gentleman. A mite of a little woman with blood thinned by California zephyrs was hardly fair game for the red-fisted, short-breathed old duffer. But Johnsy he smote; and she lay, scarcely moving, on her painted iron bedstead, looking through the small Dutch window-panes at the blank side of the next brick house.

One morning the busy doctor invited Sue into the hallway with a shaggy, gray eyebrow.

'She has one chance in – let us say, ten,' he said as he shook down the mercury in his clinical thermometer. 'And that chance is for her to want to live. This way people have of lining-up on the side of the undertaker makes the entire pharmacopeia look silly. Your little lady has made up her mind that she's not going to get well. Has she anything on her mind?'

'She – she wanted to paint the Bay of Naples some day,' said Sue.

'Paint? – bosh! Has she anything on her mind worth thinking about twice – a man for instance?'

'A man?' said Sue, with a Jew's-harp twang in her voice. 'Is a man worth – but, no, doctor; there is nothing of the kind.'

'Well, it is the weakness, then,' said the doctor. 'I will do all that science, so far as it may filter through my efforts, can accomplish. But whenever my patient begins to count the carriages in her funeral procession I subtract 50 per cent from the curative power of medicines. If you will get her to ask one question about the new winter styles in cloak sleeves, I will promise you a one-in-five chance for her, instead of one in ten.'

After the doctor had gone Sue went into the workroom and cried a Japanese napkin to a pulp. Then she swaggered into Johnsy's room with her drawing board, whistling ragtime.

Johnsy lay, scarcely making a ripple under the bedclothes, with her face toward the window. Sue stopped whistling, thinking she was asleep.

She arranged her board and began a pen-and-ink drawing to illustrate a magazine story. Young artists must pave their way to Art by drawing pictures for magazine stories that young authors write to pave their way to Literature.

As Sue was sketching a pair of elegant horseshow riding trousers and a monocle on the figure of the hero, an Idaho cowboy, she heard a low sound, several times repeated. She went quickly to the bedside.

Johnsy's eyes were open wide. She was looking out the window and counting – counting backward.

'Twelve,' she said, and a little later 'eleven'; and then 'ten,' and 'nine'; and then 'eight' and 'seven,' almost together.

Sue looked solicitously out of the window. What was there to count? There was only a bare, dreary yard to be seen, and the blank side of the brick house twenty feet away. An old, old ivy vine, gnarled and decayed at the roots, climbed half way up the brick wall. The cold breath of autumn had stricken its leaves from the vine until its skeleton branches clung, almost bare, to the crumbling bricks.

'What is it, dear?' asked Sue.

'Six,' said Johnsy, in almost a whisper. 'They're falling faster now. Three days ago there were almost a hundred. It made my head ache to count them. But now it's easy. There goes another one. There are only five left now.'

'Five what, dear? Tell your Sudie.'

'Leaves. On the ivy vine. When the last one falls I must go, too. I've known that for three days. Didn't the doctor tell you?'

'Oh, I never heard of such nonsense,' complained Sue, with magnificent scorn. 'What have old ivy leaves to do with your getting well? And you used to love that vine so, you naughty girl. Don't be a goosey. Why, the doctor told me this morning that your chances for getting well real soon were – let's see exactly what he said – he said the chances were ten to one! Why, that's almost as good a chance as we have in New York when we ride on the street cars or walk past a new building. Try to take some broth now, and let Sudie go back to her drawing, so she can sell the editor man with it, and buy port wine for her sick child, and pork chops for her greedy self.'

'You needn't get any more wine,' said Johnsy, keeping her eyes fixed out the window. 'There goes another. No, I don't want any broth. That leaves just four. I want to see the last one fall before it gets dark. Then I'll go, too.'

'Johnsy, dear,' said Sue, bending over her, 'will you promise me to keep your eyes closed, and not look out the window until I am done working? I must hand those drawings in by to-morrow. I need the light, or I would draw the shade down.'

'Couldn't you draw in the other room?' asked Johnsy, coldly.

'I'd rather be here by you,' said Sue. 'Besides, I don't want you to keep looking at those silly ivy leaves.'

'Tell me as soon as you have finished,' said Johnsy, closing her eyes, and lying white and still as a fallen statue, 'because I want to see the last one fall. I'm tired of waiting. I'm tired of thinking. I want to turn loose my hold on everything, and go sailing down, down, just like one of those poor, tired leaves.'

'Try to sleep,' said Sue. 'I must call Behrman up to be my model for the old hermit miner. I'll not be gone a minute. Don't try to move 'til I come back.'

Old Behrman was a painter who lived on the ground floor beneath them. He was past sixty and had a Michelangelo's Moses beard curling down from the head of a satyr along the body of an imp. Behrman was a failure in art. Forty years he had wielded the brush without getting near enough to touch the hem of his Mistress's robe. He had been always about to paint a master-piece, but had never yet begun it. For several years he had painted nothing except now and then a daub in the line of commerce or advertising. He earned a little by serving as a model to those young artists in the colony who could not pay the price of a pro-fessional. He drank gin to excess, and still talked of his coming masterpiece. For the rest he was a fierce little old man, who scoffed terribly at softness in anyone, and who regarded himself as espe-cial mastiff-in-waiting to protect the two young artists in the studio above.

Sue found Behrman smelling strongly of juniper berries in his dimly lighted den below. In one corner was a blank canvas on an easel that had been waiting there for twenty-five years to receive the first line of the masterpiece. She told him of Johnsy's fancy, and how she feared she would, indeed, light and fragile as a leaf herself, float away, when her slight hold upon the world grew weaker.

Old Behrman, with his red eyes plainly streaming, shouted his contempt and derision for such idiotic imaginings.

'Vass!' he cried. 'Is dere people in de world mit der foolishness to die because leafs dey drop off from a confounded vine? I haf not heard of such a thing. No, I will not bose as a model for your fool hermit-dunderhead. Vy do you allow dot silly pusiness to come in der brain of her? Ach, dot poor leetle Miss Yohnsy.'

'She is very ill and weak,' said Sue, 'and the fever has left her mind morbid and full of strange fancies. Very well, Mr Behrman, if you do not care to pose for me, you needn't. But I think you are a horrid old – old flibbertigibbet.'

'You are just like a woman!' yelled Behrman. 'Who said I will not bose? Go on. I come mit you. For half an hour I haf peen trying to say dot I am ready to bose. Gott! dis is not any blace in which one so good as Miss Yohnsy shall lie sick. Some day I vill baint a masterpiece, and ve shall all go away. Gott! yes.'

Johnsy was sleeping when they went upstairs. Sue pulled the shade down to the window-sill, and motioned Behrman into the other room. In there they peered out the window fearfully at the ivy vine. Then they looked at each other for a moment without speaking. A persistent, cold rain was falling, mingled with snow. Behrman, in his old blue shirt, took his seat as the hermit miner on an upturned kettle for a rock.

When Sue awoke from an hour's sleep the next morning she found Johnsy with dull, wide-open eyes staring at the drawn green shade.

'Pull it up; I want to see,' she ordered, in a whisper.

Wearily Sue obeyed.

But, lo! after the beating rain and fierce gusts of wind that had endured through the livelong night, there yet stood out against the brick wall one ivy leaf. It was the last on the vine. Still dark green near its stem, but with its serrated edges tinted with the yellow of dissolution and decay, it hung bravely from a branch some twenty feet above the ground.

'It is the last one,' said Johnsy. 'I thought it would surely fall during the night. I heard the wind. It will fall to-day, and I shall die at the same time.'

'Dear, dear!' said Sue, leaning her worn face down to the pillow, 'think of me, if you won't think of yourself. What would I do?'

But Johnsy did not answer. The lonesomest thing in all the world is a soul when it is making ready to go on its mysterious, far journey. The fancy seemed to possess her more strongly as one by one the ties that bound her to friendship and to earth were loosed.

The day wore away, and even through the twilight they could see the lone ivy leaf clinging to its stem against the wall. And then, with the coming of the night the north wind was again loosed, while the rain still beat against the windows and pattered down from the low Dutch eaves.

When it was light enough Johnsy, the merciless, commanded that the shade be raised.

The ivy leaf was still there.

Johnsy lay for a long time looking at it. And then she called to Sue, who was stirring her chicken broth over the gas stove.

'I've been a bad girl, Sudie,' said Johnsy. 'Something has made that last leaf stay there to show me how wicked I was. It is a sin to want to die. You may bring me a little broth now, and some milk with a little port in it, and – no; bring me a hand-mirror first, and then pack some pillows about me, and I will sit up and watch you cook.'

An hour later she said:

'Sudie, some day I hope to paint the Bay of Naples.'

The doctor came in the afternoon, and Sue had an excuse to go into the hallway as he left.

'Even chances,' said the doctor, taking Sue's thin, shaking hand in his. 'With good nursing you'll win. And now I must see another case I have downstairs. Behrman, his name is – some kind of an artist, I believe. Pneumonia, too. He is an old, weak man, and the attack is acute. There is no hope for him; but he goes to the hospital to-day to be made more comfortable.'

The next day the doctor said to Sue: 'She's out of danger. You've won. Nutrition and care now – that's all.'

And that afternoon Sue came to the bed where Johnsy lay, contentedly knitting a very blue and very useless woolen shoulder scarf, and put one arm around her, pillows and all.

'I have something to tell you, white mouse,' she said. 'Mr Behrman died of pneumonia to-day in the hospital. He was ill only two days. The janitor found him on the morning of the first day in his room downstairs helpless with pain. His shoes and clothing were wet through and icy cold. They couldn't imagine where he had been on such a dreadful night. And then they found a lantern, still lighted, and a ladder that had been dragged from its place, and some scattered brushes, and a palette with green and yellow colors mixed on it, and – look out the window, dear, at the last ivy leaf on the wall. Didn't you wonder why it never fluttered or moved when the wind blew? Ah, darling, it's Behrman's masterpiece – he painted it there the night that the last leaf fell.'

# The Count and the Wedding Guest

One evening when Andy Donovan went to dinner at his Second Avenue boarding-house, Mrs Scott introduced him to a new boarder, a young lady, Miss Conway. Miss Conway was small and unobtrusive. She wore a plain, snuffy-brown dress, and bestowed her interest, which seemed languid, upon her plate. She lifted her indifferent eyelids and shot one perspicuous, judicial glance at Mr Donovan, politely murmured his name, and returned to her mutton. Mr Donovan bowed with the grace and beaming smile that were rapidly winning for him social, business and political advancement, and erased the snuffy-brown one from the tablets of his consideration.

Two weeks later Andy was sitting on the front steps enjoying his cigar. There was a soft rustle behind and above him and Andy turned his head – and had his head turned.

Just coming out of the door was Miss Conway. She wore a night-black dress of *crêpe de – crêpe de – oh*, this thin black goods. Her hat was black, and from it drooped and fluttered an ebony veil, flimsy as a spider's web. She stood on the top step and drew on black silk gloves. Not a speck of white or a spot of color about her dress anywhere. Her rich golden hair was drawn, with scarcely a ripple, into a shining, smooth knot low on her neck. Her face was plain rather than pretty, but it was now illuminated and made almost beautiful by her large gray eyes that gazed above the houses across the street into the sky with an expression of the most appealing sadness and melancholy.

Gather the idea, girls – all black, you know, with the preference for *crêpe de – oh, crêpe de Chine* – that's it. All black, and that sad, far-away look, and the hair shining under the black veil (you have to be a blonde, of course), and try to look as if, although your young life had been blighted just as it was about to give a hop-skip-and-a-jump over the threshold of life, a walk in the park might do you good, and be sure to happen out the door at the right moment, and – oh, it'll fetch 'em every time. But it's fierce, now, how cynical I am, ain't it? – to talk about mourning costumes this way.'

Mr Donovan suddenly reinscribed Miss Conway upon the tablets of his consideration. He threw away the remaining inch and a quarter of his cigar, that would have been good for eight minutes yet, and quickly shifted his center of gravity to his low-cut patent leathers.

'It's a fine, clear evening, Miss Conway,' he said; and if the Weather Bureau could have heard the confident emphasis of his tones it would have hoisted the square white signal, and nailed it to the mast.

'To them that has the heart to enjoy it, it is, Mr Donovan,' said Miss Conway, with a sigh.

Mr Donovan, in his heart, cursed fair weather. Heartless weather! It should hail and blow and snow to be consonant with the mood of Miss Conway.

'I hope none of your relatives – I hope you haven't sustained a loss?' ventured Mr Donovan.

'Death has claimed,' said Miss Conway, hesitating – 'not a relative, but one who – but I will not intrude my grief upon you, Mr Donovan.'

'Intrude?' protested Mr Donovan. 'Why, say, Miss Conway, I'd be delighted, that is, I'd be sorry – I mean I'm sure nobody could sympathize with you truer than I would.'

Miss Conway smiled a little smile. And oh, it was sadder than her expression in repose.

' "Laugh, and the world laughs with you; weep, and they give you the laugh," ' she quoted. 'I have learned that, Mr Donovan. I have no friends or acquaintances in this city. But you have been kind to me. I appreciate it highly.'

He had passed her the pepper twice at the table.

'It's tough to be alone in New York – that's a cinch,' said Mr Donovan. 'But, say – whenever this little old town does loosen up and get friendly it goes the limit. Say you took a little stroll in the park, Miss Conway – don't you think it might chase away some of your mullygrubs? And if you'd allow me –'

'Thanks, Mr Donovan. I'd be pleased to accept of your escort if you think the company of one whose heart is filled with gloom could be anyways agreeable to you.'

Through the open gates of the iron-railed, old, downtown park, where the elect once took the air, they strolled, and found a quiet bench.

There is this difference between the grief of youth and that of old age; youth's burden is lightened by as much of it as another shares; old age may give and give, but the sorrow remains the same.

'He was my fiancé,' confided Miss Conway, at the end of an hour. 'We were going to be married next spring. I don't want you to think that I am stringing you, Mr Donovan, but he was a real Count. He had an estate and a castle in Italy. Count Fernando Mazzini was his name. I never saw the beat of him for elegance. Papa objected, of course, and once we eloped, but Papa overtook us, and took us back. I thought sure Papa and Fernando would fight a duel. Papa has a livery business – in P'kipsee, you know.

'Finally, Papa came 'round, all right, and said we might be married next spring. Fernando showed him proofs of his title and wealth, and then went over to Italy to get the castle fixed up for us. Papa's very proud and, when Fernando wanted to give me several thousand dollars for my trousseau he called him down something awful. He wouldn't even let me take a ring or any presents from him. And when Fernando sailed I came to the city and got a position as cashier in a candy store.

'Three days ago I got a letter from Italy, forwarded from P'kipsee, saying that Fernando had been killed in a gondola accident.

'That is why I am in mourning. My heart, Mr Donovan, will remain forever in his grave. I guess I am poor company, Mr Donovan, but I cannot take any interest in no one. I should not care to keep you from gaiety and your friends who can smile and entertain you. Perhaps you would prefer to walk back to the house?'

Now, girls, if you want to observe a young man hustle out after a pick and shovel, just tell him that your heart is in some other fellow's grave. Young men are grave-robbers by nature. Ask any widow. Something must be done to restore that missing organ to weeping angels in *crêpe de Chine*. Dead men certainly get the worst of it from all sides.

'I'm awful sorry,' said Mr Donovan, gently. 'Now we won't walk back to the house just yet. And don't say you haven't no friends in this city, Miss Conway. I'm awful sorry, and I want you to believe I'm your friend, and that I'm awful sorry.'

'I've got his picture here in my locket,' said Miss Conway, after wiping her eyes with her handkerchief. 'I never showed it to anybody; but I will to you, Mr Donovan, because I believe you to be a true friend.'

Mr Donovan gazed long and with much interest at the photograph in the locket that Miss Conway opened for him. The face of Count Mazzini was one to command interest. It was a smooth, intelligent, bright, almost a handsome face – the face of a strong, cheerful man who might well be a leader among his fellows.

'I have a larger one, framed, in my room,' said Miss Conway. 'When we return I will show you that. They are all I have to remind me of Fernando. But he ever will be present in my heart, that's a sure thing.'

A subtle task confronted Mr Donovan – that of supplanting the unfortunate Count in the heart of Miss Conway. This his admiration for her determined him to do. But the magnitude of the undertaking did not seem to weigh upon his spirits. The sympathetic but cheerful friend was the rôle he essayed; and he played it so successfully that the next half-hour found them conversing pensively across two plates of ice-cream, though yet there was no diminution of the sadness in Miss Conway's large gray eyes.

Before they parted in the hall that evening she ran upstairs and brought down the framed photograph wrapped lovingly in a white silk scarf. Mr Donovan surveyed it with inscrutable eyes.

'He gave me this the night he left for Italy,' said Miss Conway. 'I had the one for the locket made from this.'

'A fine-looking man,' said Mr Donovan, heartily. 'How would it suit you, Miss Conway, to give me the pleasure of your company to Coney next Sunday afternoon?'

A month later they announced their engagement to Mrs Scott and the other boarders. Miss Conway continued to wear black.

A week after the announcement the two sat on the same bench in the downtown park, while the fluttering leaves of the trees made a dim kinetoscopic picture of them in the moonlight. But Donovan had worn a look of abstracted gloom all day. He was so silent to-night that love's lips could not keep back any longer the question that love's heart propounded.

'What's the matter, Andy, you are so solemn and grouchy to-night?'

'Nothing, Maggie.'

'I know better. Can't I tell? You never acted this way before. What is it?'

'It's nothing much, Maggie.'

'Yes it is; and I want to know. I'll bet it's some other girl you are thinking about. All right. Why don't you go get her if you want her? Take your arm away, if you please.'

'I'll tell you then,' said Andy, wisely, 'but I guess you won't understand it exactly. You've heard of Mike Sullivan, haven't you? "Big Mike" Sullivan, everybody calls him.'

'No, I haven't,' said Maggie. 'And I don't want to, if he makes you act like this. Who is he?'

'He's the biggest man in New York,' said Andy, almost reverently. 'He can about do anything he wants to with Tammany or any other old thing in the political line. He's a mile high and as broad as East River. You say anything against Big Mike, and you'll have a million men on your collarbone in about two seconds. Why, he made a visit over to the old country a while back, and the kings took to their holes like rabbits.

'Well, Big Mike's a friend of mine. I ain't more than deuce-high in the district as far as influence goes, but Mike's as good a friend to a little man, or a poor man, as he is to a big one. I met him to-day on the Bowery, and what do you think he does? Comes up and shakes hands. "Andy," says he. "I've been keeping cases on you. You've been putting in some good licks over on your side of the street, and I'm proud of you. What'll you take to drink?" He takes a cigar and I take a highball. I told him I was going to get married in two weeks. "Andy," says he, "send me an invitation, so I'll keep in mind of it, and I'll come to the wedding." That's what Big Mike says to me; and he always does what he says.

'You don't understand it, Maggie, but I'd have one of my hands cut off to have Big Mike Sullivan at our wedding. It would be the proudest day of my life. When he goes to a man's wedding, there's a guy being married that's made for life. Now, that's why I'm maybe looking sore to-night.'

'Why don't you invite him, then, if he's so much to the mustard?' said Maggie, lightly.

'There's a reason why I can't,' said Andy, sadly. 'There's a reason why he mustn't be there. Don't ask me what it is, for I can't tell you.'

'Oh, I don't care,' said Maggie. 'It's something about politics, of course. But it's no reason why you can't smile at me.'

'Maggie,' said Andy, presently, 'do you think as much of me as you did of your – as you did of the Count Mazzini?'

He waited a long time, but Maggie did not reply. And then, suddenly she leaned against his shoulder and began to cry – to cry and shake with sobs, holding his arm tightly, and wetting the *crêpe de Chine* with tears.

'There, there, there!' soothed Andy, putting aside his own trouble. 'And what is it, now?'

'Andy,' sobbed Maggie, 'I've lied to you, and you'll never marry me, or love me any more. But I feel that I've got to tell. Andy, there never was so much as the little finger of a count. I never had a beau in my life. But all the other girls had; and they talked about 'em; and that seemed to make the fellows like 'em more. And, Andy, I look swell in black – you know I do. So I went out to a photograph store and bought that picture, and had a little one made for my locket, and made up all that story about the Count and about his being killed, so I could wear black. And nobody can love a liar, and you'll shake me, Andy, and I'll die for shame. Oh, there never was anybody I liked but you – and that's all.'

But instead of being pushed away, she found Andy's arm holding her closer. She looked up and saw his face cleared and smiling.

'Could you – could you forgive me, Andy?'

'Sure,' said Andy. 'It's all right about that. Back to the cemetery for the Count. You've straightened everything out, Maggie. I was in hopes you would before the wedding-day. Bully girl!'

'Andy,' said Maggie, with a somewhat shy smile, after she had been thoroughly assured of forgiveness, 'did you believe all that story about the Count?'

'Well, not to any large extent,' said Andy, reaching for his cigar case; 'because it's Big Mike Sullivan's picture you've got in that locket of yours.'

# A Lickpenny Lover

There were 3,000 girls in the Biggest Store. Masie was one of them. She was eighteen and a saleslady in the gents' gloves. Here she became versed in two varieties of human beings – the kind of gents who buy their gloves in department stores and the kind of women who buy gloves for unfortunate gents. Besides this wide knowledge of the human species, Masie had acquired other information. She had listened to the promulgated wisdom of the 2,999 other girls and had stored it in a brain that was as secretive and wary as that of a Maltese cat. Perhaps nature, foreseeing that she would lack wise counsellors, had mingled the saving ingredient of shrewdness along with her beauty, as she has endowed the silver fox of the priceless fur above the other animals with cunning.

For Masie was beautiful. She was a deep-tinted blonde, with the calm poise of a lady who cooks butter cakes in a window. She stood behind her counter in the Biggest Store; and as you closed your hand over the tape-line for your glove measure you thought of Hebe; and as you looked again you wondered how she had come by Minerva's eyes.

When the floorwalker was not looking, Masie chewed tutti frutti; when he was looking she gazed up as if at the clouds and smiled wistfully.

That is the shopgirl smile, and I enjoin you to shun it unless you are well fortified with callosity of the heart, caramels, and a congeniality for the capers of Cupid. This smile belonged to Masie's recreation hours and not to the store; but the floorwalker must have his own. He is the Shylock of the stores. When he comes nosing around the bridge of his nose is a toll-bridge. It is goo-goo eyes or 'git' when he looks toward a pretty girl. Of course not all floorwalkers are thus. Only a few days ago the papers printed news of one over eighty years of age.

One day Irving Carter, painter, millionaire, traveler, poet automobilist, happened to enter the Biggest Store. It is due to him to add that his visit was not voluntary. Filial duty took him by the collar and dragged him inside, while his mother philandered among the bronze and terracotta statuettes.

Carter strolled across to the glove counter in order to shoot a few minutes on the wing. His need for gloves was genuine; he had forgotten to bring a pair with him. But his action hardly calls for apology, because he had never heard of glove-counter flirtations.

As he neared the vicinity of his fate he hesitated, suddenly conscious of this unknown phase of Cupid's less worthy profession.

Three or four cheap fellows, sonorously garbed, were leaning over the counters, wrestling with the mediatorial hand-coverings, while giggling girls played vivacious seconds to their lead upon the strident string of coquetry. Carter would have retreated, but he had gone too far. Masie confronted him behind her counter with a questioning look in eyes as coldly, beautifully, warmly blue as the glint of summer sunshine on an iceberg drifting in Southern seas.

And then Irving Carter, painter, millionaire, etc., felt a warm flush rise to his aristocratically pale face. But not from diffidence. The blush was intellectual in origin. He knew in a moment that he stood in the ranks of the ready-made youths who wooed the giggling girls at other counters. Himself leaned against the oaken trysting place of a cockney Cupid with a desire in his heart for the favor of a glove salesgirl. He was no more than Bill and Jack and Mickey. And then he felt a sudden tolerance for them, and an elating, courageous contempt for the conventions upon which he had fed, and an unhesitating determination to have this perfect creature for his own.

When the gloves were paid for and wrapped Carter lingered

for a moment. The dimples at the corners of Masie's damask mouth deepened. All gentlemen who bought gloves lingered in just that way. She curved an arm, showing like Psyche's through her shirt-waist sleeve, and rested an elbow upon the show-case edge.

Carter had never before encountered a situation of which he had not been perfect master. But now he stood far more awkward than Bill or Jack or Mickey. He had no chance of meeting this beautiful girl socially. His mind struggled to recall the nature and habits of shopgirls as he had read or heard of them. Somehow he had received the idea that they sometimes did not insist too strictly upon the regular channels of introduction. His heart beat loudly at the thought of proposing an unconventional meeting with this lovely and virginal being. But the tumult in his heart gave him courage.

After a few friendly and well-received remarks on general subjects, he laid his card by her hand on the counter.

'Will you please pardon me,' he said, 'if I seem too bold; but I earnestly hope you will allow me the pleasure of seeing you again. There is my name; I assure you that it is with the greatest respect that I ask the favor of becoming one of your fr — acquaintances. May I not hope for the privilege?'

Masie knew men – especially men who buy gloves. Without hesitation she looked him frankly and smilingly in the eyes, and said:

'Sure. I guess you're all right. I don't usually go out with strange gentlemen, though. It ain't quite ladylike. When should you want to see me again?'

'As soon as I may,' said Carter. 'If you would allow me to call at your home, I —'

Masie laughed musically. 'Oh, gee, no!' she said, emphatically. 'If you could see our flat once! There's five of us in three rooms. I'd just like to see ma's face if I was to bring a gentleman friend there!'

'Anywhere, then,' said the enamored Carter, 'that will be convenient to you.'

'Say,' suggested Masie, with a bright-idea look in her peach-blow face; 'I guess Thursday night will about suit me. Suppose you come to the corner of Eighth Avenue and Forty-eighth Street at 7:30. I live right near the corner. But I've got to be back home by eleven. Ma never lets me stay out after eleven.'

Carter promised gratefully to keep the tryst, and then hastened to his mother, who was looking about for him to ratify her purchase of a bronze Diana.

A salesgirl, with small eyes and an obtuse nose, strolled near Masie, with a friendly leer.

'Did you make a hit with his nobs, Masie?' she asked, familiarly.

'The gentleman asked permission to call,' answered Masie, with a grand air, as she slipped Carter's card into the bosom of her waist.

'Permission to call!' echoed small eyes, with a snigger. 'Did he say anything about dinner in the Waldorf and a spin in his auto afterward?'

'Oh, cheese it!' said Masie, wearily. 'You've been used to swell things, I don't think. You've had a swelled head ever since that horse-cart driver took you out to a chop suey joint. No, he never mentioned the Waldorf; but there's a Fifth Avenue address on his card, and if he buys the supper you can bet your life there won't be no pigtail on the waiter what takes the order.'

As Carter glided away from the Biggest Store with his mother in his electric runabout, he bit his lip with a dull pain at his heart. He knew that love had come to him for the first time in all the twenty-nine years of his life. And that the object of it should make so readily an appointment with him at a street corner, though it was a step toward his desires, tortured him with misgivings.

Carter did not know the shopgirl. He did not know that her home is often either a scarcely habitable tiny room or a domicile filled to overflowing with kith and kin. The street corner is her parlor; the park is her drawing room; the avenue is her garden walk; yet for the most part she is as inviolate mistress of herself in them as is my lady inside her tapestried chamber.

One evening at dusk, two weeks after their first meeting, Carter and Masie strolled arm-in-arm into a little, dimly-lit park. They found a bench, tree-shadowed and secluded, and sat there.

For the first time his arm stole gently around her. Her golden-bronze head slid restfully against his shoulder.

'Gee!' sighed Masie, thankfully. 'Why didn't you ever think of that before?'

'Masie,' said Carter, earnestly, 'you surely know that I love you. I ask you sincerely to marry me. You know me well enough by this time to have no doubts of me. I want you, and I must have you. I care nothing for the difference in our stations.'

'What is the difference?' asked Masie, curiously.

'Well, there isn't any,' said Carter, quickly, 'except in the minds of foolish people. It is in my power to give you a life of luxury. My social position is beyond dispute, and my means are ample.'

'They all say that,' remarked Masie. 'It's the kid they all give you. I suppose you really work in a delicatessen or follow the races. I ain't as green as I look.'

'I can furnish you all the proofs you want,' said Carter, gently. 'And I want you, Masie. I loved you the first day I saw you.'

'They all do,' said Masie, with an amused laugh, 'to hear 'em talk. If I could meet a man that got stuck on me the third time he'd seen me I think I'd get mashed on him.'

'Please don't say such things,' pleaded Carter. 'Listen to me, dear. Ever since I first looked into your eyes you have been the only woman in the world for me.'

'Oh, ain't you the kidder!' smiled Masie. 'How many other girls did you ever tell that?'

But Carter persisted. And at length he reached the flimsy, fluttering little soul of the shopgirl that existed somewhere deep down in her lovely bosom. His words penetrated the heart whose very lightness was its safest armor. She looked up at him with eyes that saw. And a warm glow visited her cool cheeks. Tremblingly, awfully, her moth wings closed, and she seemed about to settle upon the flower of love. Some faint glimmer of life and its possibilities on the other side of her glove counter dawned upon her. Carter felt the change and crowded the opportunity.

'Marry me, Masie,' he whispered, softly, 'and we will go away from this ugly city to beautiful ones. We will forget work and business, and life will be one long holiday. I know where I should take you – I have been there often. Just think of a shore where summer is eternal, where the waves are always rippling on the lovely beach and the people are happy and free as children. We will sail to those shores and remain there as long as you please. In one of those faraway cities there are grand and lovely palaces and towers full of beautiful pictures and statues. The streets of the city are water, and one travels about in —'

'I know,' said Masie, sitting up suddenly. 'Gondolas.'

'Yes,' smiled Carter.

'I thought so,' said Masie.

'And then,' continued Carter, 'we will travel on and see whatever we wish in the world. After the European cities we will visit India and the ancient cities there, and ride on elephants and see the wonderful temples of the Hindoos and the Brahmins and the Japanese gardens and the camel trains and chariot races in Persia, and all the queer sights of foreign countries. Don't you think you would like it, Masie?'

Masie rose to her feet.

'I think we had better be going home,' she said, coolly. 'It's getting late.'

Carter humored her. He had come to know her varying, thistledown moods, and that it was useless to combat them. But he felt a certain happy triumph. He had held for a moment, though but by a silken thread, the soul of his wild Psyche, and hope was stronger within him. Once she had folded her wings and her cool hand had closed about his own.

At the Biggest Store the next day Masie's chum, Lulu, waylaid her in an angle of the counter.

'How are you and your swell friend making it?' she asked.

'Oh, him?' said Masie, patting her side curls. 'He ain't in it any more. Say, Lu, what do you think that fellow wanted me to do?'

'Go on the stage?' guessed Lulu, breathlessly.

'Nit; he's too cheap a guy for that. He wanted me to marry him and go down to Coney Island for a wedding tour!'

# Dougherty's Eye-Opener

Big Jim Dougherty was a sport. He belonged to that race of men. In Manhattan it is a distinct race. They are the Caribs of the North – strong, artful, self-sufficient, clannish, honorable within the law of their race, holding in lenient contempt neighboring tribes who bow to the measure of Society's tape-line. I refer, of course, to the titled nobility of sportdom. There is a class which bears as a qualifying adjective the substantive belonging to a wind instrument made of a cheap and base metal. But the tin mines of Cornwall never produced the material for manufacturing descriptive nomenclature for 'Big Jim' Dougherty.

The habitat of the sport is the lobby or the outside corner of certain hotels and combination restaurants and cafés. They are mostly men of different sizes, running from small to large; but they are unanimous in the possession of a recently shaven, blue-black cheek and chin and dark overcoats (in season) with black velvet collars.

Of the domestic life of the sport little is known. It has been said that Cupid and Hymen sometimes take a hand in the game and copper the queen of hearts to lose. Daring theorists have averred – not content with simply saying – that a sport often contracts a spouse, and even incurs descendants. Sometimes he sits in the game of politics, and then at chowder picnics there is a revelation of a Mrs Sport and little Sports in glazed hats with tin pails.

But mostly the sport is Oriental. He believes his women-folk should not be too patent. Somewhere behind grilles or flower-ornamented fire escapes they await him. There, no doubt, they tread on rugs from Teheran and are diverted by the bulbul and play upon the dulcimer and feed upon sweetmeats. But away

97

from his home the sport is an integer. He does not, as men of other races in Manhattan do, become the convoy in his unoccupied hours of fluttering laces and high heels that tick off delectably the happy seconds of the evening parade. He herds with his own race at corners, and delivers a commentary in his Carib lingo upon the passing show.

'Big Jim' Dougherty had a wife, but he did not wear a button portrait of her upon his lapel. He had a home in one of those brown-stone, iron-railed streets on the west side that look like a recently excavated bowling alley of Pompeii.

To this home of his Mr Dougherty repaired each night when the hour was so late as to promise no further diversion in the arch domains of sport. By that time the occupant of the monogamistic harem would be in dreamland, the bulbul silenced and the hour propitious for slumber.

'Big Jim' always arose at twelve, meridian, for breakfast, and soon afterward he would return to the rendezvous of his 'crowd.'

He was always vaguely conscious that there was a Mrs Dougherty. He would have received without denial the charge that the quiet, neat, comfortable little woman across the table at home was his wife. In fact, he remembered pretty well that they had been married for nearly four years. She would often tell him about the cute tricks of Spot, the canary, and the light-haired lady that lived in the window of the flat across the street.

'Big Jim' Dougherty even listened to this conversation of hers sometimes. He knew that she would have a nice dinner ready for him every evening at seven when he came for it. She sometimes went to matinées, and she had a talking machine with six dozen records. Once when her Uncle Amos blew in on a wind from upstate she went with him to the Eden Musée. Surely these things were diversions enough for any woman.

One afternoon Mr Dougherty finished his breakfast, put on his hat and got away fairly for the door. When his hand was on the knob he heard his wife's voice.

'Jim,' she said, firmly, 'I wish you would take me out to dinner this evening. It has been three years since you have been outside the door with me.'

'Big Jim' was astounded. She had never asked anything like this before. It had the flavor of a totally new proposition. But he was a game sport.

'All right,' he said. 'You be ready when I come at seven. None of this "wait two minutes till I primp an hour or two" kind of business, now, Dele.'

'I'll be ready,' said his wife, calmly.

At seven she descended the stone steps in the Pompeian bowling alley at the side of 'Big Jim' Dougherty. She wore a dinner gown made of a stuff that the spiders must have woven, and of a color that a twilight sky must have contributed. A light coat with many admirably unnecessary capes and adorably inutile ribbons floated downward from her shoulders. Fine feathers do make fine birds; and the only reproach in the saying is for the man who refuses to give up his earnings for the ostrich-tip industry.

'Big Jim' Dougherty was troubled. There was a being at his side whom he did not know. He thought of the sober-hued plumage that this bird of paradise was accustomed to wear in her cage, and this winged revelation puzzled him. In some way she reminded him of the Delia Cullen that he had married four years before. Shyly and rather awkwardly he stalked at her right hand.

'After dinner I'll take you back home, Dele,' said Mr Dougherty, 'and then I'll drop back up to Seltzer's with the boys. You can have swell chuck to-night if you want it. I made a winning on Anaconda yesterday so you can go as far as you like.'

Mr Dougherty had intended to make the outing with his unwonted wife an inconspicuous one. Uxoriousness was a weakness that the precepts of the Caribs did not countenance. If any of his friends of the track, the billiard cloth or the square circle had wives they had never complained of the fact in public. There were a number of *table d'hôte* places on the cross streets near the broad and shining way; and to one of these he had proposed to escort her, so that the bushel might not be removed from the light of his domesticity.

But while on the way Mr Dougherty altered those intentions. He had been casting stealthy glances at his attractive companion and he was seized with the conviction that she was no selling plater. He resolved to parade with his wife past Seltzer's café, where at this time a number of his tribe would be gathered to view the daily evening processions. Yes; and he would take her to dine at Hoogley's, the swellest slow-lunch warehouse on the line, he said to himself.

The congregation of smooth-faced tribal gentlemen were on watch at Seltzer's. As Mr Dougherty and his reorganized Delia passed they stared, momentarily petrified, and then removed their hats – a performance as unusual to them as was the astonishing innovation presented to their gaze by 'Big Jim.' On the latter gentleman's impassive face there appeared a slight flicker of triumph – a faint flicker, no more to be observed than the expression called there by the draft of little casino to a four-card spade flush.

Hoogley's was animated. Electric lights shone – as, indeed, they were expected to do. And the napery, the glassware, and the flowers also meritoriously performed the spectacular duties required of them. The guests were numerous, well-dressed, and gay.

A waiter – not necessarily obsequious – conducted 'Big Jim' Dougherty and his wife to a table.

'Play that menu straight across for what you like, Dele,' said 'Big Jim.' 'It's you for a trough of the gilded oats to-night. It strikes me that maybe we've been sticking too fast to home fodder.'

'Big Jim's' wife gave her order. He looked at her with respect. She had mentioned truffles; and he had not known that she knew what truffles were. From the wine list she designated an appropriate and desirable brand. He looked at her with some admiration.

She was beaming with the innocent excitement that woman

derives from the exercise of her gregariousness. She was talking to him about a hundred things with animation and delight. And as the meal progressed her cheeks, colorless from a life indoors, took on a delicate flush. 'Big Jim' looked around the room and saw that none of the women there had her charm. And then he thought of the three years she had suffered immurement, uncomplaining, and a flush of shame warmed him, for he carried fair play as an item in his creed.

But when the Honorable Patrick Corrigan, leader in Dougherty's district and a friend of his, saw them and came over to the table, matters got to the three-quarter stretch. The Honorable Patrick was a gallant man, both in deeds and words. As for the Blarney stone, his previous actions toward it must have been pronounced. Heavy damages for breach of promise could surely have been obtained had the Blarney stone seen fit to sue the Honorable Patrick.

'Jimmy, old man!' he called; he clapped Dougherty on the back; he shone like a midday sun upon Delia.

'Honorable Mr Corrigan . . . Mrs Dougherty,' said 'Big Jim.'

The Honorable Patrick became a fountain of entertainment and admiration. The waiter had to fetch a third chair for him; he made another at the table, and the wineglasses were refilled.

'You selfish old rascal!' he exclaimed, shaking an arch finger at 'Big Jim,' 'to have kept Mrs Dougherty a secret from us.'

And then 'Big Jim' Dougherty, who was no talker, sat dumb, and saw the wife who had dined every evening for three years at home, blossom like a fairy flower. Quick, witty, charming, full of light and ready talk, she received the experienced attack of the Honorable Patrick on the field of repartee and surprised, vanquished, delighted him. She unfolded her long-closed petals and around her the room became a garden. They tried to include 'Big Jim' in the conversation, but he was without a vocabulary.

And then a stray bunch of politicians and good fellows who lived for sport came into the room. They saw 'Big Jim' and the leader, and over they came and were made acquainted with Mrs Dougherty. And in a few minutes she was holding a salon. Half a dozen men surrounded her, courtiers all, and six found her capable of charming. 'Big Jim' sat, grim, and kept saying to himself: 'Three years, three years!'

The dinner came to an end. The Honorable Patrick reached for Mrs Dougherty's cloak; but that was a matter of action instead of words, and Dougherty's big hand got it first by two seconds.

While the farewells were being said at the door the Honorable Patrick smote Dougherty mightily between the shoulders.

'Jimmy, me boy,' he declared, in a giant whisper, 'the madam is a jewel of the first water. Ye're a lucky dog.'

'Big Jim' walked homeward with his wife. She seemed quite as pleased with the lights and show windows in the streets as with the admiration of the men in Hoogley's. As they passed Seltzer's they heard the sound of many voices in the café. The boys would be starting the drinks around now and discussing past performances.

At the door of their home Delia paused. The pleasure of the outing radiated softly from her countenance. She could not hope for Jim of evenings, but the glory of this one would lighten her lonely hours for a long time.

'Thank you for taking me out, Jim,' she said, gratefully. 'You'll be going back to Seltzer's now, of course.'

'To — with Seltzer's,' said 'Big Jim,' emphatically. 'And d —Pat Corrigan! Does he think I haven't got any eyes?'

And the door closed behind both of them.

# The Defeat of the City

Robert Walmsley's descent upon the city resulted in a Kilkenny struggle. He came out of the fight victor by a fortune and a reputation. On the other hand, he was swallowed up by the city. The city gave him what he demanded and then branded him with its brand. It remodeled, cut, trimmed, and stamped him to the pattern it approves. It opened its social gates to him and shut him in on a close-cropped, formal lawn with the select herd of ruminants. In dress, habits, manners, provincialism, routine, and narrowness he acquired that charming insolence, that irritating completeness, that sophisticated crassness, that over-balanced poise that makes the Manhattan gentleman so delightfully small in his greatness.

One of the up-state rural counties pointed with pride to the successful young metropolitan lawyer as a product of its soil. Six years earlier this county had removed the wheat straw from between its huckleberry-stained teeth and emitted a derisive and bucolic laugh as old man Walmsley's freckle-faced 'Bob' abandoned the certain three per diem meals of the one-horse farm for the discontinuous quick lunch counters of the three-ringed metropolis. At the end of the six years no murder trial, coaching party, automobile accident or cotillion was complete in which the name of Robert Walmsley did not figure. Tailors waylaid him in the street to get a new wrinkle from the cut of his unwrinkled trousers. Hyphenated fellows in the clubs and members of the oldest subpoenaed families were glad to clap him on the back and allow him three letters of his name.

But the Matterhorn of Robert Walmsley's success was not scaled until he married Alicia Van Der Pool. I cite the Matterhorn, for just so high and cool and white and inaccessible was this daughter of the old burghers. The social Alps that ranged about her – over whose bleak passes a thousand climbers struggled – reached only to her knees. She towered in her own atmosphere, serene, chaste, prideful, wading in no fountains, dining no monkeys, breeding no dogs for bench shows. She was a Van Der Pool. Fountains were made to play for her; monkeys were made for other people's ancestors; dogs, she understood, were created to be companions of blind persons and objectionable characters who smoked pipes.

This was the Matterhorn that Robert Walmsley accomplished. If he found, with the good poet with the game foot and artificially curled hair, that he who ascends to mountain tops will find the loftiest peaks most wrapped in clouds and snow, he concealed his chillblains beneath a brave and smiling exterior. He was a lucky man and knew it, even though he were imitating the Spartan boy with an ice-cream freezer beneath his doublet frappéeing the region of his heart.

After a brief wedding tour abroad, the couple returned to create a decided ripple in the calm cistern (so placid and cool and sunless it is) of the best society. They entertained at their red brick mausoleum of ancient greatness in an old square that is a cemetery of crumbled glory. And Robert Walmsley was proud of his wife; although while one of his hands shook his guests', the other held tightly to his alpenstock and thermometer.

One day Alicia found a letter written to Robert by his mother. It was an unerudite letter, full of crops and motherly love and farm notes. It chronicled the health of the pig and the recent red calf, and asked concerning Robert's in return. It was a letter direct from the soil, straight from home, full of biographies of bees, tales of turnips, paeans of new-laid eggs, neglected parents and the slump in dried apples.

'Why have I not been shown your mother's letters?' asked Alicia. There was always something in her voice that made you think of lorgnettes, of accounts at Tiffany's, of sledges smoothly gliding on the trail from Dawson to Forty Mile, of the tinkling of pendent prisms on your grandmothers' chandeliers, of snow lying on a convent roof; of a police sergeant refusing bail. 'Your mother,' continued Alicia, 'invites us to make a visit to the farm. I have never seen a farm. We will go there for a week or two, Robert.'

'We will,' said Robert, with the grand air of an associate Supreme Justice concurring in an opinion. 'I did not lay the invitation before you because I thought you would not care to go. I am much pleased at your decision.'

'I will write to her myself,' answered Alicia, with a faint foreshadowing of enthusiasm. 'Félice shall pack my trunks at once. Seven, I think, will be enough. I do not suppose that your mother entertains a great deal. Does she give many house parties?'

Robert arose, and as attorney for rural places filed a demurrer against six of the seven trunks. He endeavored to define, picture, elucidate, set forth and describe a farm. His own words sounded strange in his ears. He had not realized how thoroughly urbsidized he had become.

A week passed and found them landed at the little country station five hours out from the city. A grinning, stentorian, sarcastic youth driving a mule to a spring wagon hailed Robert savagely.

'Hello, Mr Walmsley. Found your way back at last, have you? Sorry I couldn't bring in the automobile for you, but dad's bulltonguing the ten-acre clover patch with it to-day. Guess you'll excuse my not wearing a dress suit over to meet you – it ain't six o'clock yet, you know.'

'I'm glad to see you, Tom,' said Robert, grasping his brother's hand. 'Yes, I've found my way at last. You've a right to say "at last." It's been over two years since the last time. But it will be oftener after this, my boy.'

Alicia, cool in the summer heat as an Arctic wraith, white as a Norse snow maiden in her flimsy muslin and fluttering lace parasol, came round the corner of the station; and Tom was stripped of his assurance. He became chiefly eyesight clothed in blue jeans, and on the homeward drive to the mule alone did he confide in language the inwardness of his thoughts.

They drove homeward. The low sun dropped a spendthrift flood of gold upon the fortunate fields of wheat. The cities were far away. The road lay curling around wood and dale and hill like a ribbon lost from the robe of careless summer. The wind followed like a whinnying colt in the track of Phoebus's steeds.

By and by the farmhouse peeped gray out of its faithful grove; they saw the long lane with its convoy of walnut trees running from the road to the house; they smelled the wild rose and the breath of cool, damp willows in the creek's bed. And then in unison all the voices of the soil began a chant addressed to the soul of Robert Walmsley. Out of the tilted aisles of the dim wood they came hollowly; they chirped and buzzed from the parched grass; they trilled from the ripples of the creek ford; they floated up in clear Pan's pipe notes from the dimming meadows; the whippoorwills joined in as they pursued midges in the upper air; slow-going cow-bells struck out a homely accompaniment – and this was what each one said: 'You've found your way back at last, have you?'

The old voices of the soil spoke of him. Leaf and bud and blossom conversed with him in the old vocabulary of his careless youth – the inanimate things, the familiar stones and rails, the gates and furrows and roofs and turns of road had an eloquence, too, and a power in the transformation. The country had smiled and he had felt the breath of it, and his heart was drawn as if in a moment back to his old love. The city was far away.

This rural atavism, then, seized Robert Walmsley and possessed him. A queer thing he noticed in connection with it was that Alicia, sitting at his side, suddenly seemed to him a stranger. She did not belong to this recurrent phase. Never before had she seemed so remote, so colorless and high – so intangible and unreal. And yet he had never admired her more than when she sat there by him in the rickety spring wagon, chiming no more with his mood and with her environment than the Matterhorn chimes with a peasant's cabbage garden.

That night when the greetings and the supper were over, the entire family, including Buff, the yellow dog, bestrewed itself upon the front porch. Alicia, not haughty but silent, sat in the shadow dressed in an exquisite pale-gray tea gown. Robert's mother discoursed to her happily concerning marmalade and lumbago. Tom sat on the top step; sisters Millie and Pam on the lowest step to catch the lightning bugs. Mother had the willow rocker. Father sat in the big armchair with one of its arms gone. Buff sprawled in the middle of the porch in everybody's way. The twilight pixies and pucks stole forth unseen and plunged other poignant shafts of memory into the heart of Robert. A rural madness entered his soul. The city was far away.

Father sat without his pipe, writhing in his heavy boots, a sacrifice to rigid courtesy. Robert shouted: 'No, you don't!' He fetched the pipe and lit it; he seized the old gentleman's boots and tore them off. The last one slipped suddenly, and Mr Robert Walmsley, of Washington Square, tumbled off the porch backward with Buff on top of him, howling fearfully. Tom laughed sarcastically.

Robert tore off his coat and vest and hurled them into a lilac bush.

'Come out here, you landlubber,' he cried to Tom, 'and I'll put grass seed on your back. I think you called me a "dude" a while ago. Come along and cut your capers.'

Tom understood the invitation and accepted it with delight. Three times they wrestled on the grass, 'side holds,' even as the giants of the mat. And twice was Tom forced to bite grass at the hands of the distinguished lawyer. Disheveled, panting, each still boasting of his own prowess, they stumbled back to the porch. Millie cast a pert reflection upon the qualities of a city brother. In an instant Robert had secured a horrid katydid in his fingers and bore down upon her. Screaming wildly, she fled up the lane pursued by the avenging glass of form. A quarter of a mile and they returned, she full of apology to the victorious 'dude.' The rustic mania possessed him unabatedly.

'I can do up a cowpenful of you slow hayseeds,' he proclaimed, vaingloriously. 'Bring on your bulldogs, your hired men, and your logrollers.'

He turned handsprings on the grass that prodded Tom to envious sarcasm. And then, with a whoop, he clattered to the rear and brought back Uncle Ike, a battered colored retainer of the family, with his banjo, and strewed sand on the porch and danced 'Chicken in the Bread Tray' and did buck-and-wing wonders for half an hour longer. Incredibly wild and boisterous things he did. He sang, he told stories that set all but one shrieking, he played the yokel, the humorous clodhopper; he was mad, mad with the revival of the old life in his blood.

He became so extravagant that once his mother sought gently to reprove him. Then Alicia moved as though she were about to speak, but she did not. Through it all she sat immovable, a slim, white spirit in the dusk that no man might question or read.

By and by she asked permission to ascend to her room, saying that she was tired. On her way she passed Robert. He was standing in the door, the figure of vulgar comedy, with ruffled hair, reddened face and unpardonable confusion of attire – no trace there of the immaculate Robert Walmsley, the courted clubman and ornament of select circles. He was doing a conjuring trick with some household utensils, and the family, now won over to him without exception, was beholding him with worshipful admiration.

As Alicia passed, Robert started suddenly. He had forgotten for the moment that she was present. Without a glance at him she went on upstairs.

After that the fun grew quiet. An hour passed in talk, and then Robert went up himself.

She was standing by the window when he entered their room. She was still clothed as when they were on the porch. Outside and crowding against the window was a giant apple tree, full blossomed.

Robert sighed and went near the window. He was ready to meet his fate. A confessed vulgarian, he foresaw the verdict of justice in the shape of that still, whiteclad form. He knew the rigid lines that a Van Der Pool would draw. He was a peasant gambling indecorously in the valley, and the pure, cold, white, unthawed summit of the Matterhorn could not but frown on him. He had been unmasked by his own actions. All the polish, the poise, the form that the city had given him had fallen from him like an ill-fitting mantle at the first breath of a country breeze. Dully he awaited the approaching condemnation.

'Robert,' said the calm, cool voice of his judge, 'I thought I married a gentleman.'

Yes, it was coming. And yet, in the face of it, Robert Walmsley was eagerly regarding a certain branch of the apple tree upon which he used to climb out of that very window. He believed he could do it now. He wondered how many blossoms there were on the tree – ten millions? But here was someone speaking again:

'I thought I married a gentleman,' the voice went on, 'but —'

Why had she come and was standing so close by his side?

'But I find that I have married' – was this Alicia talking? – 'something better – a man – Bob, dear, kiss me, won't you?'

The city was far away.

# Squaring the Circle

At the hazard of wearying youth, this tale of vehement emotions must be prefaced by a discourse on geometry.

Nature moves in circles; Art in straight lines. The natural is rounded; the artificial is made up of angles. A man lost in the snow wanders, in spite of himself, in perfect circles; the city man's feet, denaturalized by rectangular streets and floors, carry him ever away from himself.

The round eyes of childhood typify innocence; the narrow lines of the flirt's optic proves the invasion of art. The horizontal mouth is the mark of determined cunning; who has not read Nature's most spontaneous lyric in lips rounded for the candid kiss?

Beauty is Nature in perfection; circularity is its chief attribute. Behold the full moon, the enchanting gold ball, the domes of splendid temples, the huckleberry pie, the wedding ring, the circus ring, the ring for the waiter, and the 'round' of drinks.

On the other hand, straight lines show that Nature has been deflected. Imagine Venus's girdle transformed into a 'straight front!'

When we begin to move in straight lines and turn sharp corners our natures begin to change. The consequence is that Nature, being more adaptive than Art, tries to conform to its sterner regulations. The result is often a rather curious product – for instance: A prize chrysanthemum, wood alcohol whiskey, a Republican Missouri, cauliflower *au gratin*, and a New Yorker.

Nature is lost quickest in a big city. The cause is geometrical, not moral. The straight lines of its streets and architecture, the rectangularity of its laws and social customs, the undeviating pavements, the hard, severe, depressing, uncompromising rules of all its ways – even of its recreation and sports – coldly exhibit a sneering defiance of the curved line of Nature.

Wherefore, it may be said that the big city has demonstrated the problem of squaring the circle. And it may be added that this mathematical introduction precedes an account of the fate of a Kentucky feud that was imported to the city that has a habit of making its importations conform to its angles.

The feud began in the Cumberland Mountains between the Folwell and the Harkness families. The first victim of the home-spun vendetta was a 'possum dog belonging to Bill Harkness. The Harkness family evened up this dire loss by laying out the chief of the Folwell clan. The Folwells were prompt at repartee. They oiled up their squirrel rifles and made it feasible for Bill Harkness to follow his dog to a land where the 'possums come down when treed without the stroke of an ax.

The feud flourished for forty years. Harkness were shot at the plough, through their lamp-lit cabin windows, coming from camp-meetings, asleep, in duello, sober and otherwise, singly and in family groups, prepared and unprepared. Folwells had the branches of their family tree lopped off in similar ways, as the traditions of their country prescribed and authorized.

By and by the pruning left but a single member of each family. And then Cal Harkness, probably reasoning that further pursu-ance of the controversy would give a too decided personal flavor to the feud, suddenly disappeared from the relieved Cumber-lands, balking the avenging hand of Sam, the ultimate opposing Folwell.

A year afterward Sam Folwell learned that his hereditary, unsuppressed enemy was living in New York City. Sam turned over the big iron washpot in the yard, scraped off some of the soot, which he mixed with lard, and shined his boots with the compound. He put on his store clothes of butternut dyed black, a white shirt and collar, and packed a carpet-sack with Spartan *lingerie*. He took his squirrel rifle from its hooks, but put it back again with a sigh. However ethical and plausible the habit might be in the Cumberlands, perhaps New York would not swallow his pose of hunting squirrels among the skyscrapers along Broadway. An ancient but reliable Colt's revolver that he resurrected from a bureau drawer seemed to proclaim itself the pink of weapons for metropolitan adventure and vengeance. This and a hunting-knife in a leather sheath, Sam packed in the carpet-sack. As he started, muleback, for the lowland railroad station the last Folwell turned in his saddle and looked grimly at the little cluster of white-pine slabs in the clump of cedars that marked the Folwell burying-ground.

Sam Folwell arrived in New York in the night. Still moving and living in the free circles of nature, he did not perceive the formidable, pitiless, restless, fierce angles of the great city waiting in the dark to close about the rotundity of his heart and brain and mold him to the form of its millions of reshaped victims. A cabby picked him out of the whirl, as Sam himself had often picked a nut from a bed of wind-tossed autumn leaves, and whisked him away to a hotel commensurate to his boots and carpet-sack.

On the next morning the last of the Folwells made his sortie into the city that sheltered the last Harkness. The Colt was thrust beneath his coat and secured by a narrow leather belt; the hunting-knife hung between his shoulder-blades, with the haft an inch below his coat collar. He knew this much – that Cal Harkness drove an express wagon somewhere in that town, and that he, Sam Folwell, had come to kill him. And as he stepped upon the sidewalk the red came into his eye and the feud-hate into his heart.

The clamor of the central avenues drew him thitherward. He had half expected to see Cal coming down the street in his shirt-sleeves with a jug and a whip in his hand, just as he would have seen him in Frankfort or Laurel City. But an hour went by and Cal did not appear. Perhaps he was waiting in ambush, to shoot him from a door or a window. Sam kept a sharp eye on doors and windows for a while.

About noon the city tired of playing with its mouse and suddenly squeezed him with its straight lines.

Sam Folwell stood where two great, rectangular arteries of the city cross. He looked four ways, and saw the world hurled from its orbit and reduced by spirit level and tape to an edged and cornered plane. All life moved on tracks, in grooves, according to system, within boundaries, by rote. The root of life was the cube root; the measure of existence was square measure. People streamed by in straight rows; the horrible din and crash stupefied him.

Sam leaned against the sharp corner of a stone building. Those faces passed him by thousands, and not one of them was turned toward him. A sudden foolish fear that he had died and was a spirit, and that they could not see him, seized him. And then the city smote him with loneliness.

A fat man dropped out of the stream and stood a few feet distant, waiting for his car. Sam crept to his side and shouted above the tumult into his ear:

'The Rankinses' hogs weighed more'n ourn a whole passel, but the mast in thar neighborhood was a fine chance better than what it was down —'

The fat man moved away unostentatiously, and bought roasted chestnuts to cover his alarm.

Sam felt the need of a drop of mountain dew. Across the street men passed in and out through swinging doors. Brief glimpses could be had of a glistening bar and its bedeckings. The feudist crossed and essayed to enter. Again had Art eliminated the familiar circle. Sam's hand found no door-knob – it slid, in vain, over a rectangular brass plate and polished oak with nothing even so large as a pin's head upon which his fingers might close.

Abashed, reddened, heartbroken, he walked away from the bootless door and sat upon a step. A locust club tickled him in the ribs.

'Take a walk for yourself,' said the policeman. 'You've been loafing around here long enough.'

At the next corner a shrill whistle sounded in Sam's ear. He wheeled around and saw a black-browed villain scowling at him over peanuts heaped on a steaming machine. He started across the street. An immense engine, running without mules, with the voice of a bull and the smell of a smoky lamp, whizzed past, grazing his knee. A cab-driver bumped him with a hub and explained to him that kind words were invented to be used on other occasions. A motorman clanged his bell wildly and, for once in his life, corroborated a cab-driver. A large lady in a changeable silk waist dug an elbow into his back, and a newsy pensively pelted him with banana rinds, murmuring, 'I hates to do it – but if anybody seen me let it pass!'

Cal Harkness, his day's work over and his express wagon stabled, turned the sharp edge of the building that, by the cheek of architects, is modeled upon a safety razor. Out of the mass of hurrying people his eye picked up, three yards away, the surviving bloody and implacable foe of his kith and kin.

He stopped short and wavered for a moment, being unarmed and sharply surprised. But the keen mountaineer's eye of Sam Folwell had picked him out.

There was a sudden spring, a ripple in the stream of passers-by and the sound of Sam's voice crying:

'Howdy, Cal! I'm durned glad to see ye.'

And in the angles of Broadway, Fifth Avenue, and Twenty-third Street the Cumberland feudists shook hands.

# Transients in Arcadia

There is a hotel on Broadway that has escaped discovery by the summer-resort promoters. It is deep and wide and cool. Its rooms are finished in dark oak of a low temperature. Home-made breezes and deep-green shrubbery give it the delights without the inconveniences of the Adirondacks. One can mount its broad staircases or glide dreamily upward in its aerial elevators, attended by guides in brass buttons, with a serene joy that Alpine climbers have never attained. There is a chef in its kitchen who will prepare for you brook trout better than the White Mountains ever served, sea food that would turn Old Point Comfort – 'by Gad, sah!' – green with envy, and Maine venison that would melt the official heart of the game warden.

A few have found out this oasis in the July desert of Manhattan. During that month you will see the hotel's reduced array of guests scattered luxuriously about in the cool twilight of its lofty dining-room, gazing at one another across the snowy waste of unoccupied tables, silently congratulatory.

Superfluous, watchful, pneumatically moving waiters hover near, supplying every want before it is expressed. The temperature is perpetual April. The ceiling is painted in water colors to counterfeit a summer sky across which delicate clouds drift and do not vanish as those of nature do to our regret.

The pleasing, distant roar of Broadway is transformed in the imagination of the happy guests to the noise of a waterfall filling the woods with its restful sound. At every strange footstep the guests turn an anxious ear, fearful lest their retreat be discovered and invaded by the restless pleasure-seekers who are forever hounding Nature to her deepest lairs.

Thus in the depopulated caravansary the little band of connoisseurs jealously hide themselves during the heated season, enjoying to the uttermost delights of mountain and seashore that art and skill have gathered and served to them.

In this July came to the hotel one whose card that she sent to the clerk for her name to be registered read 'Mme. Héloise D'Arcy Beaumont.'

Madame Beaumont was a guest such as the Hotel Lotus loved. She possessed the fine air of the elite, tempered and sweetened by a cordial graciousness that made the hotel employees her slaves. Bell-boys fought for the honor of answering her ring; the clerks, but for the question of ownership, would have deeded to her the hotel and its contents; the other guests regarded her as the final touch of feminine exclusiveness and beauty that rendered the entourage perfect.

This super-excellent guest rarely left the hotel. Her habits were consonant with the customs of the discriminating patrons of the Hotel Lotus. To enjoy that delectable hostelry one must forgo the city as though it were leagues away. By night a brief excursion to the nearby roofs is in order; but during the torrid day one remains in the umbrageous fastnesses of the Lotus as a trout hangs poised in the pellucid sanctuaries of his favorite pool.

Though alone in the Hotel Lotus, Madame Beaumont preserved the state of a queen whose loneliness was of position only. She breakfasted at ten, a cool, sweet, leisurely, delicate being who glowed softly in the dimness like a jasmine flower in the dusk.

But at dinner was Madame's glory at its height. She wore a gown as beautiful and immaterial as the mist from an unseen cataract in a mountain gorge. The nomenclature of this gown is beyond the guess of the scribe. Always pale-red roses reposed against its lace-garnished front. It was a gown that the headwaiter viewed with respect and met at the door. You thought of Paris when you saw it, and maybe of mysterious countesses, and

certainly of Versailles and rapiers and Mrs Fiske and rouge-et-
noir. There was an untraceable rumor in the Hotel Lotus that
Madame was a cosmopolite, and that she was pulling with her
slender white hands certain strings between the nations in the
favor of Russia. Being a citizeness of the world's smoothest roads
it was small wonder that she was quick to recognize in the refined
purlieus of the Hotel Lotus the most desirable spot in America
for a restful sojourn during the heat of midsummer.

On the third day of Madame Beaumont's residence in the
hotel a young man entered and registered himself as a guest. His
clothing – to speak of his points in approved order – was quietly
in the mode; his features good and regular; his expression that of
a poised and sophisticated man of the world. He informed the
clerk that he would remain three or four days, inquired concerning the sailing of European steamships, and sank into the blissful
inanition of the nonpareil hotel with the contented air of a traveler in his favorite inn.

The young man – not to question the veracity of the register –
was Harold Farrington. He drifted into the exclusive and calm
current of life in the Lotus so tactfully and silently that not a ripple alarmed his fellow seekers-after-rest. He ate in the Lotus and
of its patronym, and was lulled into blissful peace with the other
fortunate mariners. In one day he acquired his table and his
waiter and the fear lest the panting chasers after repose that kept
Broadway warm should pounce upon and destroy this contigu-
ous but covert haven.

After dinner on the next day after the arrival of Harold Farrington Madame Beaumont dropped her handkerchief in passing
out. Mr Farrington recovered and returned it without the effu-
siveness of a seeker after acquaintance.

Perhaps there was a mystic freemasonry between the discriminating guests of the Lotus. Perhaps they were drawn one to
another by the fact of their common good fortune in discovering
the acme of summer resorts in a Broadway hotel. Words delicate

in courtesy and tentative in departure from formality passed between the two. And, as if in the expedient atmosphere of a real summer resort, an acquaintance grew, flowered and fructified on the spot as does the mystic plant of the conjuror. For a few moments they stood on a balcony upon which the corridor ended, and tossed the feathery ball of conversation.

'One tires of the old resorts,' said Madame Beaumont, with a faint but sweet smile. 'What is the use to fly to the mountains or the seashore to escape noise and dust when the very people that make both follow us there?'

'Even on the ocean,' remarked Farrington sadly, 'the Philistines be upon you. The most exclusive steamers are getting to be scarcely more than ferry boats. Heaven help us when the summer resorter discovers that the Lotus is further away from Broadway than Thousand Islands or Mackinac.'

'I hope our secret will be safe for a week, anyhow,' said Madame, with a sigh and a smile. 'I do not know where I would go if they should descend upon the dear Lotus. I know of but one place so delightful in summer, and that is the castle of Count Polinski, in the Ural Mountains.'

'I hear that Baden-Baden and Cannes are almost deserted this season,' said Farrington. 'Year by year the old resorts fall into disrepute. Perhaps many others, like ourselves, are seeking out the quiet nooks that are overlooked by the majority.'

'I promise myself three days more of this delicious rest,' said Madame Beaumont. 'On Monday the *Cedric* sails.'

Harold Farrington's eyes proclaimed his regret. 'I too must leave on Monday,' he said, 'but I do not go abroad.'

Madame Beaumont shrugged one round shoulder in a foreign gesture.

'One cannot hide here forever, charming though it may be. The château has been in preparation for me longer than a month. Those house parties that one must give – what a nuisance! But I shall never forget my week in the Hotel Lotus.'

'Nor shall I,' said Farrington in a low voice, 'and I shall never *forgive* the *Cedric*.'

On Sunday evening, three days afterward, the two sat at a little table on the same balcony. A discreet waiter brought ices and small glasses of claret cup.

Madame Beaumont wore the same beautiful evening gown that she had worn each day at dinner. She seemed thoughtful. Near her hand on the table lay a small chatelaine purse. After she had eaten her ice she opened the purse and took out a one-dollar bill.

'Mr Farrington,' she said, with the smile that had won the Hotel Lotus, 'I want to tell you something. I'm going to leave before breakfast in the morning, because I've got to go back to my work. I'm behind the hosiery counter at Casey's Mammoth Store, and my vacation's up at eight o'clock to-morrow. That paper dollar is the last cent I'll see till I draw my eight dollars salary next Saturday night. You're a real gentleman, and you've been good to me, and I wanted to tell you before I went.

'I've been saving up out of my wages for a year just for this vacation. I wanted to spend one week like a lady if I never do another one. I wanted to get up when I please instead of having to crawl out at seven every morning; and I wanted to live on the best and be waited on and ring bells for things just like rich folks do. Now I've done it, and I've had the happiest time I ever expect to have in my life. I'm going back to my work and my little hall bedroom satisfied for another year. I wanted to tell you about it, Mr Farrington, because I – I thought you kind of liked me, and I – I liked you. But, oh, I couldn't help deceiving you up till now, for it was all just like a fairy tale to me. So I talked about Europe and the things I've read about in other countries, and made you think I was a great lady.

'This dress I've got on – it's the only one I have that's fit to wear – I bought from O'Dowd & Levinsky on the installment plan.

'Seventy-five dollars is the price, and it was made to measure. I paid $10 down, and they're to collect $1 a week till it's paid for.

That'll be about all I have to say, Mr Farrington, except that my name is Mamie Siviter instead of Madame Beaumont, and I thank you for your attentions. This dollar will pay the instalment due on the dress to-morrow. I guess I'll go up to my room now.'

Harold Farrington listened to the recital of the Lotus's loveliest guest with an impassive countenance. When she had concluded he drew a small book like a checkbook from his coat pocket. He wrote upon a blank form in this with a stub of pencil, tore out the leaf, tossed it over to his companion and took up the paper dollar.

'I've got to go to work, too, in the morning,' he said, 'and I might as well begin now. There's a receipt for the dollar install- ment. I've been a collector for O'Dowd & Levinsky for three years. Funny, ain't it, that you and me both had the same idea about spending our vacation? I've always wanted to put up at a swell hotel, and I saved up out of my twenty per, and did it. Say, Mame, how about a trip to Coney Saturday night on the boat – what?'

The face of the pseudo Madame Héloise D'Arcy Beaumont beamed.

'Oh, you bet I'll go, Mr Farrington. The store closes at twelve on Saturdays. I guess Coney'll be all right even if we did spend a week with the swells.'

Below the balcony the sweltering city growled and buzzed in the July night. Inside the Hotel Lotus the tempered, cool shadows reigned, and the solicitous waiter single-footed near the low win- dows, ready at a nod to serve Madame and her escort.

At the door of the elevator Farrington took his leave, and Mad- ame Beaumont made her last ascent. But before they reached the noiseless cage he said: 'Just forget that "Harold Farrington," will you? – McManus is the name – James McManus. Some call me Jimmy.'

'Good-night, Jimmy,' said Madame.

# The Memento

Miss Lynnette D'Armande turned her back on Broadway. This was but tit for tat, because Broadway had often done the same thing to Miss D'Armande. Still, the 'tats' seemed to have it, for the ex-leading lady of the 'Reaping the Whirlwind' company had everything to ask of Broadway, while there was no vice-versa.

So Miss Lynnette D'Armande turned the back of her chair to her window that overlooked Broadway, and sat down to stitch in time the lisle-thread heel of a black silk stocking. The tumult and glitter of the roaring Broadway beneath her window had no charm for her; what she greatly desired was the stifling air of a dressing-room on that fairyland street and the roar of an audience gathered in that capricious quarter. In the meantime, those stockings must not be neglected. Silk does wear out so, but – after all, isn't it just the only goods there is?

The Hotal Thalia looks on Broadway as Marathon looks on the sea. It stands like a gloomy cliff above the whirlpool where the tides of two great thoroughfares clash. Here the player-bands gather at the end of their wanderings to loosen the buskin and dust the sock. Thick in the streets around it are booking-offices, theaters, agents, schools, and the lobster-places to which those thorny paths lead.

Wandering through the eccentric halls of the dim and fusty Thalia, you seem to have found yourself in some great ark or caravan about to sail, or fly, or roll away on wheels. About the house lingers a sense of unrest, of expectation, of transientness, even of anxiety and apprehension. The halls are a labyrinth. Without a guide, you wander like a lost soul in a Sam Lloyd puzzle.

Turning any corner, a dressing-sack or a *cul-de-sac* may bring you up short. You meet alarming tragedians talking in bath-robes in search of rumored bathrooms. From hundreds of rooms come the buzz of talk, scraps of new and old songs, and the ready laughter of the convened players.

Summer has come; their companies have disbanded, and they take their rest in their favorite caravansary, while they besiege the managers for engagements for the coming season.

At this hour of the afternoon the day's work of tramping the rounds of the agents' offices is over. Past you, as you ramble distractedly through the mossy halls, flit audible visions of houris, with veiled, starry eyes, flying tag-ends of things and a swish of silk, bequeathing to the dull hallways an odor of gaiety and a memory of *frangipanni*. Serious young comedians, with versatile Adam's apples, gather in doorways and talk of Booth. Far-reaching from somewhere comes the smell of ham and red cabbage, and the crash of dishes on the American plan.

The indeterminate hum of life in the Thalia is enlivened by the discreet popping – at reasonable and salubrious intervals – of beer-bottle corks. Thus punctuated, life in the genial hostel scans easily – the comma being the favorite mark, semicolons frowned upon, and periods barred.

Miss D'Armande's room was a small one. There was room for her rocker between the dresser and the wash-stand if it were placed longitudinally. On the dresser were its usual accoutrements, plus the ex-leading lady's collected souvenirs of road engagements and photographs of her dearest and best professional friends.

At one of these photographs she looked twice or thrice as she darned, and smiled friendlily.

'I'd like to know where Lee is just this minute,' she said, half-aloud.

If you had been privileged to view the photograph thus flattered, you would have thought at the first glance that you saw the picture of a many-petaled white flower, blown through the air by a storm. But the floral kingdom was not responsible for that swirl of petalous whiteness.

You saw the filmy, brief skirt of Miss Rosalie Ray as she made a complete heels-over-head turn in her wisteria-entwined swing, far out from the stage, high above the heads of the audience. You saw the camera's inadequate representation of the graceful, strong kick, with which she, at this exciting moment, sent flying, high and far, the yellow silk garter that each evening spun from her agile limb and descended upon the delighted audience below.

You saw, too, amid the black-clothed, mainly masculine patrons of select vaudeville a hundred hands raised with the hope of staying the flight of the brilliant aerial token.

Forty weeks of the best circuits this act had brought Miss Rosalie Ray, for each of two years. She did other things during her twelve minutes – a song and dance, imitations of two or three actors who are but imitations of themselves, and a balancing feat with a step-ladder and feather-duster; but when the blossom-decked swing was let down from the flies, and Miss Rosalie sprang smiling into the seat, with the golden circlet conspicuous in the place whence it was soon to slide and become a soaring and coveted guerdon – then it was that the audience rose in its seat as a single man – or presumably so – and indorsed the specialty that made Miss Ray's name a favorite in the booking-offices.

At the end of two years Miss Ray suddenly announced to her dear friend, Miss D'Armande, that she was going to spend the summer at an antediluvian village on the north shore of Long Island, and that the stage would see her no more.

Seventeen minutes after Miss Lynnette D'Armande had expressed her wish to know the whereabouts of her old chum, there were sharp raps at her door.

Doubt not that it was Rosalie Ray. At the shrill command to enter she did so, with something of a tired flutter, and dropped a heavy hand-bag on the floor. Upon my word, it was Rosalie, in a loose, travel-stained automobileless coat, closely tied brown veil with yard-long flying ends, gray walking suit, and tan oxfords with lavender over-gaiters.

When she threw off her veil and hat, you saw a pretty enough face, now flushed and disturbed by some unusual emotion, and restless, large eyes with discontent marring their brightness. A heavy pile of dull auburn hair, hastily put up, was escaping in crinkly, waving strands and curling, small locks from the confining combs and pins.

The meeting of the two was not marked by the effusion vocal, gymnatical, osculatory and catechetical that distinguishes the greetings of their unprofessional sisters in society. There was a brief clinch, two simultaneous labial dabs, and they stood on the same footing as the old days. Very much like the short salutations of soldiers or of travelers in foreign wilds are the welcomes between the strollers at the corners of their criss-cross roads.

'I've got the hall-room two flights up above yours,' said Rosalie, 'but I came straight to see you before going up. I didn't know you were here till they told me.'

'I've been in since the last of April,' said Lynnette. 'And I'm going on the road with a "Fatal Inheritance" Company. We open next week in Elizabeth. I thought you'd quit the stage, Lee. Tell me about yourself.'

Rosalie settled herself with a skillful wriggle on the top of Miss D'Armande's wardrobe trunk, and leaned her head against the papered wall. From long habit, thus can peripatetic leading ladies and their sisters make themselves as comfortable as though the deepest armchairs embraced them.

'I'm going to tell you, Lynn,' she said, with a strangely sardonic and yet carelessly resigned look on her youthful face. 'And then to-morrow I'll strike the old Broadway trail again, and wear some more paint off the chairs in the agents' offices. If anybody had told me any time in the last three months up to four o'clock this afternoon that I'd ever listen to that "Leave-your-name-and-address" rot of the booking bunch again, I'd have given 'em the real Mrs Fiske laugh. Loan me a handkerchief, Lynn. Gee! but those Long Island trains are fierce. I've got enough soft-coal cinders on my face to go on and play *Topsy* without using the cork. And, speaking of corks – got anything to drink, Lynn?'

Miss D'Armande opened a door of the washstand and took out a bottle.

'There's nearly a pint of Manhattan. There's a cluster of carnations in the drinking glass, but —'

'Oh, pass the bottle. Save the glass for company. Thanks! That hits the spot. The same to you. My first drink in three months!

'Yes, Lynn, I quit the stage at the end of last season. I quit it because I was sick of the life. And especially because my heart and soul were sick of men – of the kind of men we stage people have to be up against. You know what the game is to us – it's a fight against 'em all the way down the line from the manager who wants us to try his new motor-car to the bill-posters who want to call us by our front names.

'And the men we have to meet after the show are the worst of all. The stage-door kind, and the manager's friends who take us to supper and show their diamonds and talk about seeing "Dan" and "Dave" and "Charlie" for us. They're beasts, and I hate 'em.

'I tell you, Lynn, it's the girls like us on the stage that ought to be pitied. It's girls from good homes that are honestly ambitious and work hard to rise in the profession, but never do get there. You hear a lot of sympathy sloshed around on chorus girls and their fifteen dollars a week. Piffle! There ain't a sorrow in the chorus that a lobster cannot heal.

'If there's any tears to shed, let 'em fall for the actress that gets a salary of from thirty to forty-five dollars a week for taking a leading part in a bum show. She knows she'll never do any better but she hangs on for years, hoping for the "chance" that never comes.

'And the fool plays we have to work in! Having another girl roll you around the stage by the hind legs in a "Wheelbarrow

Chorus" in a musical comedy is dignified drama compared with the idiotic things I've had to do in the thirty-centers.

'But what I hated most was the men – the men leering and blathering at you across tables, trying to buy you with Würzburger or Extra Dry, according to their estimate of your price. And the men in the audiences, clapping, yelling, snarling, crowding, writhing, gloating – like a lot of wild beasts, with their eyes fixed on you, ready to eat you up if you come in reach of their claws. Oh how I hate 'em!

'Well, I'm not telling you much about myself, am I, Lynn?

'I had two hundred dollars saved up, and I cut the stage the first of the summer. I went over on Long Island and found the sweetest little village that ever was, called Soundport, right on the water. I was going to spend the summer there, and study up on elocution, and try to get a class in the fall. There was an old widow lady with a cottage near the beach who sometimes rented a room or two just for company, and she took me in. She had another boarder, too – the Reverend Arthur Lyle.

'Yes, he was the head-liner. You're on, Lynn. I'll tell you all of it in a minute. It's only a one-act play.

'The first time he walked on, Lynn, I felt myself going; the first lines he spoke, he had me. He was different from the men in audiences. He was tall and slim, and you never heard him come in the room, but you *felt* him. He had a face like a picture of a knight – like one of that Round Table bunch – and a voice like a 'cello solo. And his manners!

'Lynn, if you'd take John Drew in his best drawing-room scene and compare the two, you'd have John arrested for disturbing the peace.

'I'll spare you the particulars; but in less than a month Arthur and I were engaged. He preached at a little one-night stand of a Methodist church. There was to be a parsonage the size of a lunch-wagon, and hens and honeysuckles when we were married. Arthur used to preach to me a good deal about Heaven, but he never could get my mind quite off those honeysuckles and hens.

'No; I didn't tell him I'd been on the stage. I hated the business and all that went with it; I'd cut it out forever, and I didn't see any use of stirring things up. I was a good girl, and I didn't have anything to confess, except being an elocutionist, and that was about all the strain my conscience would stand.

'Oh, I tell you, Lynn, I was happy. I sang in the choir and attended the sewing and society, and recited that "Annie Laurie" thing with the whistling stunt in it, "in a manner bordering upon the professional," as the weekly village paper reported it. And Arthur and I went rowing, and walking in the woods and clamming, and that poky little village seemed to me the best place in the world. I'd have been happy to live there always, too, if —

'But one morning old Mrs Gurley, the widow lady, got gossipy while I was helping her string beans on the back porch, and began to gush information, as folks who rent out their rooms usually do. Mr Lyle was her idea of a saint on her earth – as he was mine, too. She went over all his virtues and graces, and wound up by telling me that Arthur had an extremely romantic love-affair, not long before, that had ended unhappily. She didn't seem to be on to the details, but she knew that he had been hit pretty hard. He was paler and thinner, she said, and he had some kind of a remembrance or keepsake of the lady in a little rosewood box that he kept locked in his desk drawer in his study.

' "Several times," says she, "I've seen him gloomerin' over that box of evenings, and he always locks it up right away if anybody comes into the room."

'Well, you can imagine how long it was before I got Arthur by the wrist and led him down stage and hissed in his ear.

'That same afternoon we were lazying around in a boat among the waterlilies at the edge of the bay.

' "Arthur," says I, "you never told me you'd had another

love-affair. But Mrs Gurley did," I went on, to let him know I knew. I hate to hear a man lie.

' "Before you came," says he, looking me frankly in the eye, "there was a previous affection – a strong one. Since you know of it, I will be perfectly candid with you."

' "I am waiting," says I.

' "My dear Ida," says Arthur – of course I went by my real name, while I was in Soundport – "this former affection was a spiritual one, in fact. Although the lady aroused my deepest sentiments, and was, as I thought, my ideal woman, I never met her, and never spoke to her. It was an ideal love. My love for you, while no less ideal, is different. You wouldn't let that come between us."

' "Was she pretty?" I asked.

' "She was very beautiful," said Arthur.

' "Did you see her often?" I asked.

' "Something like a dozen times," says he.

' "Always from a distance?" says I.

' "Always from quite a distance," says he.

' "And you loved her?" I asked.

' "She seemed my ideal of beauty and grace – and soul," says Arthur.

' "And this keepsake that you keep under lock and key, and moon over at times, is that a remembrance from her?"

' "A memento," says Arthur, "that I have treasured."

' "Did she send it to you?"

' "It came from her," says he.

' "In a roundabout way?" I asked.

' "Somewhat roundabout," says he, "and yet rather direct."

' "Why didn't you ever meet her?" I asked. "Were your positions in life so different?"

' "She was far above me," says Arthur. "Now, Ida," he goes on, "this is all of the past. You're not going to be jealous, are you?"

' "Jealous!" says I. "Why, man, what are you talking about? It makes me think ten times as much of you as I did before I knew about it."

'And it did, Lynn – if you can understand it. That ideal love was a new one on me, but it struck me as being the most beautiful and glorious thing I'd ever heard of. Think of a man loving a woman he'd never even spoken to, and being faithful just to what his mind and heart pictured her! Oh, it sounded great to me. The men I'd always known come at you with either diamonds, knock-out drops, or a raise of salary – and their ideals – well, we'll say no more.

'Yes, it made me think more of Arthur than I did before. I couldn't be jealous of that far-away divinity that he used to worship, for I was going to have him myself. And I began to look upon him as a saint on earth, just as old lady Gurley did.

'About four o'clock this afternoon a man came to the house for Arthur to go and see somebody that was sick among his church bunch. Old lady Gurley was taking her afternoon snore on the couch, so that left me pretty much alone.

'In passing by Arthur's study I looked in, and saw his bunch of keys hanging in the drawer of his desk, where he'd forgotten 'em. Well, I guess we're all to the Mrs Bluebeard now and then, ain't we, Lynn? I made up my mind I'd have a look at that memento he kept so secret. Not that I cared what it was – it was just curiosity.

'While I was opening the drawer I imagined one or two things it might be. I thought it might be a dried rosebud she'd dropped down to him from a balcony, or maybe a picture of her he'd cut out of a magazine, she being so high up in the world.

'I opened the drawer, and there was the rosewood casket about the size of a gent's collar box. I found the little key in the bunch that fitted it, and raised the lid.

'I took one look at that memento, and then I went to my room and packed my trunk. I threw a few things into my grip, gave my hair a flirt or two with a side-comb, put on my hat, and went in and gave the old lady's foot a kick. I'd tried awfully hard to use proper and correct language while I was there for Arthur's sake, and I had the habit down pat, but it left me then.

'"Stop sawing gourds," says I, "and sit up and take notice. The ghost's about to walk. I'm going away from here, and I owe you eight dollars. The expressman will call for my trunk."

'I handed her the money.

'"Dear me, Miss Crosby!" said she. "Is anything wrong? I thought you were pleased here. Dear me, young women are so hard to understand, and so different from what you expect 'em to be."

'"You're damn right," says I. "Some of 'em are. But you can't say that about men. *When you know one man you know 'em all!* That settles the human race question."

'And then I caught the four-thirty-eight, soft-coal unlimited; and here I am.'

'You didn't tell me what was in that box, Lee,' said Miss D'Armande, anxiously.

'One of those yellow silk garters that I used to kick off my leg into the audience during that old vaudeville swing act of mine. Is there any of the cocktail left, Lynn?'

# Roads of Destiny

*I go to seek on many roads*
  *What is to be.*
*True heart and strong, with love to light –*
*Will they not bear me in the fight*
*To order, shun or wield or mould*
  *My Destiny?*

Unpublished Poems of David Mignot

The song was over. The words were David's; the air, one of the countryside. The company about the inn table applauded heartily, for the young poet paid for the wine. Only the notary, M. Papineau, shook his head a little at the lines, for he was a man of books, and he had not drunk with the rest.

David went out into the village street, where the night air drove the wine vapor from his head. And then he remembered that he and Yvonne had quarreled that day, and that he had resolved to leave his home that night to seek fame and honor in the great world outside.

'When my poems are on every man's tongue,' he told himself, in a fine exhilaration, 'she will, perhaps, think of the hard words she spoke this day.'

Except the roysterers in the tavern, the village folk were abed. David crept softly into his room in the shed of his father's cottage and made a bundle of his small store of clothing. With this upon a staff, he set his face outward upon the road that ran from Vernoy.

He passed his father's herd of sheep huddled in their nightly pen – the sheep he herded daily, leaving them to scatter while he wrote verses on scraps of paper. He saw a light yet shining in Yvonne's window, and a weakness shook his purpose of a sudden. Perhaps that light meant that she rued, sleepless, her anger, and that morning might – But, no! His decision was made. Vernoy was no place for him. Not one soul there could share his thoughts. Out along that road lay his fate and his future.

Three leagues across the dim, moonlit champaign ran the road, straight as a plowman's furrow. It was believed in the village that the road ran to Paris, at least; and this name the poet whispered often to himself as he walked. Never so far from Vernoy had David traveled before.

## The Left Branch

*Three leagues, then, the road ran, and turned into a puzzle. It joined with another and a larger road at right angles. David stood, uncertain, for a while, and then took the road to the left.*

Upon this more important highway were, imprinted in the dust, wheel tracks left by the recent passage of some vehicle. Some half an hour later these traces were verified by the sight of a ponderous carriage mired in a little brook at the bottom of a steep hill. The driver and postilions were shouting and tugging at the horses' bridles. On the road at one side stood a huge, black-clothed man and a slender lady wrapped in a long, light cloak.

David saw the lack of skill in the efforts of the servants. He quietly assumed control of the work. He directed the outriders to cease their clamor at the horses and to exercise their strength upon the wheels. The driver alone urged the animals with his familiar voice; David himself heaved a powerful shoulder at the rear of the carriage, and with one harmonious tug the great vehicle rolled up on solid ground. The outriders climbed to their places.

David stood for a moment upon one foot. The huge gentleman

waved a hand. 'You will enter the carriage,' he said, in a voice large, like himself, but smoothed by art and habit. Obedience belonged in the path of such a voice. Brief as was the young poet's hesitation, it was cut shorter still by a renewal of the command. David's foot went to the step. In the darkness he perceived dimly the form of the lady upon the rear seat. He was about to seat himself opposite, when the voice again swayed him to its will. 'You will sit at the lady's side.'

The gentleman swung his great weight to the forward seat. The carriage proceeded up the hill. The lady was shrunk, silent, into her corner. David could not estimate whether she was old or young, but a delicate, mild perfume from her clothes stirred his poet's fancy to the belief that there was loveliness beneath the mystery. Here was an adventure such as he had often imagined. But as yet he held no key to it, for no word was spoken while he sat with his impenetrable companions.

In an hour's time David perceived through the window that the vehicle traversed the street of some town. Then it stopped in front of a closed and darkened house, and a postilion alighted to hammer impatiently upon the door. A latticed window above flew wide and a night-capped head popped out.

'Who are ye that disturb honest folk at this time of night? My house is closed. 'Tis too late for profitable travelers to be abroad. Cease knocking at my door, and be off.'

'Open!' spluttered the postilion, loudly; 'open for Monseigneur, the Marquis de Beaupertuys.'

'Ah!' cried the voice above. 'Ten thousand pardons, my lord. I did not know – the hour is so late – at once shall the door be opened, and the house placed at my lord's disposal.'

Inside was heard the clink of chain and bar, and the door was flung open. Shivering with chill and apprehension, the landlord of the Silver Flagon stood, half clad, candle in hand, upon the threshold.

David followed the marquis out of the carriage. 'Assist the

lady,' he was ordered. The poet obeyed. He felt her small hand tremble as he guided her descent. 'Into the house,' was the next command.

The room was the long dining-hall of the tavern. A great oak table ran down its length. The huge gentleman seated himself in a chair at the nearer end. The lady sank into another against the wall, with an air of great weariness. David stood, considering how best he might now take his leave and continue upon his way.

'My lord,' said the landlord, bowing to the floor, 'h-had I ex-expected this honor, entertainment would have been ready. T-t-there is wine and cold fowl and m-m-maybe —'

'Candles,' said the marquis, spreading the fingers of one plump white hand in a gesture he had.

'Y-yes, my lord.' He fetched half a dozen candles, lighted them, and set them upon the table.

'If monsieur would, perhaps, deign to taste a certain Burgundy – there is a cask —'

'Candles,' said monsieur, spreading his fingers.

'Assuredly – quickly – I fly, my lord.'

A dozen more lighted candles shone in the hall. The great bulk of the marquis overflowed his chair. He was dressed in fine black from head to foot save for the snowy ruffles at his wrist and throat. Even the hilt and scabbard of his sword were black. His expression was one of sneering pride. The ends of an upturned moustache reached nearly to his mocking eyes.

The lady sat motionless, and now David perceived that she was young, and possessed a pathetic and appealing beauty. He was startled from the contemplation of her forlorn loveliness by the booming voice of the marquis.

'What is your name and pursuit?'

'David Mignot. I am a poet.'

The moustache of the marquis curled nearer to his eyes.

'How do you live?'

'I am also a shepherd; I guarded my father's flock,' David answered, with his head high, but a flush upon his cheek.

'Then listen, master shepherd and poet, to the fortune you have blundered upon to-night. This lady is my niece, Mademoiselle Lucie de Varennes. She is of noble descent and is possessed of ten thousand francs a year in her own right. As to her charms, you have but to observe for yourself. If the inventory pleases your shepherd's heart, she becomes your wife at a word. Do not interrupt me. To-night I conveyed her to the château of the Comte de Villemaur, to whom her hand had been promised. Guests were present; the priest was waiting; her marriage to one eligible in rank and fortune was ready to be accomplished. At the altar this demoiselle, so meek and dutiful, turned upon me like a leopardess, charged me with cruelty and crimes, and broke, before the gaping priest, the troth I had plighted for her. I swore there and then, by ten thousand devils, that she should marry the first man we met after leaving the château, be he prince, charcoalburner, or thief. You, shepherd, are the first. Mademoiselle must be wed this night. If not you, then another. You have ten minutes in which to make your decision. Do not vex me with words or questions. Ten minutes, shepherd; and they are speeding.'

The marquis drummed loudly with his white fingers upon the table. He sank into a veiled attitude of waiting. It was as if some great house had shut its doors and windows against approach. David would have spoken, but the huge man's bearing stopped his tongue. Instead, he stood by the lady's chair and bowed.

'Mademoiselle,' he said, and he marveled to find his words flowing easily before so much elegance and beauty. 'You have heard me say I was a shepherd. I have also had the fancy, at times, that I am a poet. If it be the test of a poet to adore and cherish the beautiful, that fancy is now strengthened. Can I serve you in any way, mademoiselle?'

The young woman looked up at him with eyes dry and mournful. His frank, glowing face, made serious by the gravity of the adventure, his strong, straight figure and the liquid sympathy in his blue eyes, perhaps, also, her imminent need of long-denied help and kindness, thawed her to sudden tears.

'Monsieur,' she said, in low tones, 'you look to be true and kind. He is my uncle, the brother of my father, and my only relative. He loved my mother, and he hates me because I am like her. He has made my life one long terror. I am afraid of his very looks, and never before dared to disobey him. But to-night he would have married me to a man three times my age. You will forgive me for bringing this vexation upon you, monsieur. You will, of course, decline this mad act he tries to force upon you. But let me thank you for your generous words, at least. I have had none spoken to me in so long.'

There was now something more than generosity in the poet's eyes. Poet he must have been, for Yvonne was forgotten; this fine, new loveliness held him with its freshness and grace. The subtle perfume from her filled him with strange emotions. His tender look fell warmly upon her. She leaned to it, thirstily.

'Ten minutes,' said David, 'is given me in which to do what I would devote years to achieve. I will not say I pity you, mademoiselle; it would not be true – I love you. I cannot ask love from you yet, but let me rescue you from this cruel man, and, in time, love may come. I think I have a future, I will not always be a shepherd. For the present I will cherish you with all my heart and make your life less sad. Will you trust your fate to me, mademoiselle?'

'Ah, you would sacrifice yourself from pity!'

'From love. The time is almost up, mademoiselle.'

'You will regret it, and despise me.'

'I will live only to make you happy, and myself worthy of you.'

Her fine small hand crept into his from beneath her cloak.

'I will trust you,' she breathed, 'with my life. And – and love – may not be so far off as you think. Tell him. Once away from the power of his eyes I may forget.'

David went and stood before the marquis. The black figure stirred, and the mocking eyes glanced at the great hall clock.

'Two minutes to spare. A shepherd requires eight minutes to decide whether he will accept a bride of beauty and income! Speak up, shepherd, do you consent to become mademoiselle's husband?'

'Mademoiselle,' said David, standing proudly, 'has done me the honor to yield to my request that she become my wife.'

'Well said!' said the marquis. 'You have yet the making of a courtier in you, master shepherd. Mademoiselle could have drawn a worse prize, after all. And now to be done with the affair as quick as the Church and the devil will allow!'

He struck the table soundly with his sword hilt. The landlord came, knee-shaking, bringing more candles in the hope of anticipating the great lord's whims. 'Fetch a priest,' said the marquis, 'a priest; do you understand? In ten minutes have a priest here, or —'

The landlord dropped his candles and flew.

The priest came, heavy-eyed and ruffled. He made David Mignot and Lucie de Varennes man and wife, pocketed a gold piece that the marquis tossed him, and shuffled out again into the night.

'Wine,' ordered the marquis, spreading his ominous fingers at the host.

'Fill glasses,' he said, when it was brought. He stood up at the head of the table in the candlelight, a black mountain of venom and conceit, with something like the memory of an old love turned to poison in his eye, as it fell upon his niece.

'Monsieur Mignot,' he said, raising his wine-glass, 'drink after I say this to you: You have taken to be your wife one who will make your life a foul and wretched thing. The blood in her is an inheritance running black lies and red ruin. She will bring you shame and anxiety. The devil that descended to her is there in her eyes and skin and mouth that stoop even to beguile a peasant.

'There is your promise, monsieur poet, for a happy life. Drink your wine. At last, mademoiselle, I am rid of you.'

The marquis drank. A little grievous cry, as if from a sudden wound, came from the girl's lips. David, with his glass in his hand, stepped forward three paces and faced the marquis. There was little of a shepherd in his bearing.

'Just now,' he said calmly, 'you did me the honor to call me "monsieur." May I hope, therefore, that my marriage to mademoiselle has placed me somewhat nearer to you in – let us say – reflected rank, has given me the right to stand more as an equal to monseigneur in a certain little piece of business I have in my mind?'

'You may hope, shepherd,' sneered the marquis.

'Then,' said David, dashing his glass of wine into the contemptuous eyes that mocked him, 'perhaps you will condescend to fight me.'

The fury of the great lord outbroke in one sudden curse like a blast from a horn. He tore his sword from its black sheath; he called to the hovering landlord: 'A sword there, for this lout!' He turned to the lady, with a laugh that chilled her heart, and said: 'You put much labor upon me, madame. It seems I must find you a husband and make you a widow in the same night.'

'I know not sword-play,' said David. He flushed to make the confession before his lady.

' "I know not sword-play," ' mimicked the marquis. 'Shall we fight like peasants with oaken cudgels? *Hola!* François, my pistols!'

A postilion brought two shining great pistols ornamented with carven silver from the carriage holsters. The marquis tossed one upon the table near David's hand. 'To the other end of the table,' he cried; 'even a shepherd may pull a trigger. Few of them attain the honor to die by the weapon of a De Beaupertuys.'

The shepherd and the marquis faced each other from the ends of the long table. The landlord, in an ague of terror, clutched the air and stammered: 'M-M-Monseigneur, for the love of Christ! not in my house! – do not spill blood – it will ruin my custom —' The look of the marquis, threatening him, paralyzed his tongue.

'Coward,' cried the lord of Beaupertuys, 'cease chattering your teeth long enough to give the word for us, if you can.'

Mine host's knees smote the floor. He was without a vocabulary. Even sounds were beyond him. Still, by gestures he seemed to beseech peace in the name of his house and custom.

'I will give the word,' said the lady, in a clear voice. She went up to David and kissed him sweetly. Her eyes were sparkling bright, and color had come to her cheek. She stood against the wall, and the two men leveled their pistols for her count.

'*Un – deux – trois!*'

The two reports came so nearly together that the candles flickered but once. The marquis stood, smiling, the fingers of his left hand resting, outspread, upon the end of the table. David remained erect, and turned his head very slowly, searching for his wife with his eyes. Then, as a garment falls from where it is hung, he sank, crumpled, upon the floor.

With a little cry of terror and despair, the widowed maid ran and stooped above him. She found his wound, and then looked up with her old look of pale melancholy. 'Through his heart,' she whispered. 'Oh, his heart!'

'Come,' boomed the great voice of the marquis, 'out with you to the carriage! Daybreak shall not find you on my hands. Wed you shall be again, and to a living husband, this night. The next we come upon, my lady, highwayman or peasant. If the road yields no other, then the churl that opens my gates. Out with you to the carriage!'

The marquis, implacable and huge, the lady wrapped again in the mystery of her cloak, the postilion bearing the weapons – all moved out to the waiting carriage. The sound of its ponderous wheels rolling away echoed through the slumbering village. In the hall of the Silver Flagon the distracted landlord wrung his hands above the slain poet's body, while the flames of the four and twenty candles danced and flickered on the table.

## The Right Branch

*Three leagues, then, the road ran, and turned into a puzzle. It joined with another and a larger road at right angles. David stood, uncertain, for a while, and then took the road to the right.*

Whither it led he knew not, but he was resolved to leave Vernoy far behind that night. He traveled a league and then passed a large château which showed testimony of recent entertainment. Lights shone from every window; from the great stone gateway ran a tracery of wheel tracks drawn in the dust by the vehicles of the guests.

Three leagues farther and David was weary. He rested and slept for a while on a bed of pine boughs at the roadside. Then up and on again along the unknown way.

Thus for five days he traveled the great road, sleeping upon Nature's balsamic beds or in peasants' ricks, eating of their black, hospitable bread, drinking from streams or the willing cup of the goatherd.

At length he crossed a great bridge and set his foot within the smiling city that has crushed or crowned more poets than all the rest of the world. His breath came quickly as Paris sang to him in a little undertone her vital chant of greeting – the hum of voice and foot and wheel.

High up under the eaves of an old house in the Rue Conti David paid for lodging, and set himself, in a wooden chair, to his poems. The street, once sheltering citizens of import and consequence, was now given over to those who ever follow in the wake of decline.

The houses were tall and still possessed of a ruined dignity, but many of them were empty save for dust and the spider. By night there was the clash of steel and the cries of brawlers straying restlessly from inn to inn. Where once gentility abode was now but a rancid and rude incontinence. But here David found housing commensurate to his scant purse. Daylight and candlelight found him at pen and paper.

One afternoon he was returning from a foraging trip to the lower world, with bread and curds and a bottle of thin wine. Halfway up his dark stairway he met – or rather came upon, for she rested on the stair – a young woman of a beauty that should balk even the justice of a poet's imagination. A loose, dark cloak, flung open, showed a rich gown beneath. Her eyes changed swiftly with every little shade of thought. Within one moment they would be round and artless like a child's, and long and cozening like a gypsy's. One hand raised her gown, undraping a little shoe, high-heeled, with its ribbons dangling, untied. So heavenly she was, so unfitted to stoop, so qualified to charm and command! Perhaps she had seen David coming, and had waited for his help there.

Ah, would monsieur pardon that she occupied the stairway, but the shoe! – the naughty shoe! Alas! it would not remain tied. Ah! if monsieur *would* be so gracious!

The poet's fingers trembled as he tied the contrary ribbons. Then he would have fled from the danger of her presence, but the eyes grew long and cozening, like a gypsy's, and held him. He leaned against the balustrade, clutching his bottle of sour wine.

'You have been so good,' she said, smiling. 'Does monsieur, perhaps, live in the house?'

'Yes, madame. I – I think so, madame.'

'Perhaps in the third story, then?'

'No, madame; higher up.'

The lady fluttered her fingers with the least possible gesture of impatience.

'Pardon. Certainly I am not discreet in asking. Monsieur will forgive me? It is surely not becoming that I should inquire where he lodges.'

'Madame, do not say so. I live in the —'

'No, no, no; do not tell me. Now I see that I erred. But I cannot lose the interest I feel in this house and all that is in it. Once it was my home. Often I come here but to dream of those happy days again. Will you let that be my excuse?'

'Let me tell you, then, for you need no excuse,' stammered the poet. 'I live in the top floor – the small room where the stairs turn.'

'In the front room?' asked the lady, turning her head sidewise.

'The rear, madame.'

The lady sighed, as if with relief.

'I will detain you no longer, then, monsieur,' she said, employing the round and artless eye. 'Take good care of my house. Alas! only the memories of it are mine now. Adieu, and accept my thanks for your courtesy.'

She was gone, leaving but a smile and a trace of sweet perfume. David climbed the stairs as one in slumber. But he awoke from it, and the smile and the perfume lingered with him and never afterward did either seem quite to leave him. This lady of whom he knew nothing drove him to lyrics of eyes, chansons of swiftly conceived love, odes to curling hair, and sonnets to slippers on slender feet.

Poet he must have been, for Yvonne was forgotten; this fine, new loveliness held him with its freshness and grace. The subtle perfume about her filled him with strange emotions.

On a certain night three persons were gathered about a table in a room on the third floor of the same house. Three chairs and the table and a lighted candle upon it was all the furniture. One of the persons was a huge man, dressed in black. His expression was one of sneering pride. The ends of his upturned moustache reached nearly to his mocking eyes. Another was a lady, young and beautiful, with eyes that could be round and artless, like a child's, or long and cozening, like a gypsy's, but were now keen and ambitious, like any other conspirator's. The third was a man of action, a combatant, a bold and impatient executive, breathing fire and steel. He was addressed by the others as Captain Desrolles.

This man struck the table with his fist, and said, with controlled violence:

'To-night. To-night as he goes to midnight mass. I am tired of the plotting that gets nowhere. I am sick of signals and ciphers and secret meetings and such *baragouin*. Let us be honest traitors. If France is to be rid of him, let us kill in the open, and not hunt with snares and traps. To-night, I say. I back my words. My hand will do the deed. To-night, as he goes to mass.'

The lady turned upon him a cordial look. Woman, however wedded to plots, must ever thus bow to rash courage. The big man stroked his upturned moustache.

'Dear captain,' he said, in a great voice, softened by habit, 'this time I agree with you. Nothing is to be gained by waiting. Enough of the palace guards belong to us to make the endeavor a safe one.'

'To-night,' repeated Captain Desrolles, again striking the table. 'You have heard me, marquis; my hand will do the deed.'

'But now,' said the huge man, softly, 'comes a question. Word must be sent to our partisans in the palace, and a signal agreed upon. Our staunchest men must accompany the royal carriage. At this hour what messenger can penetrate so far as the south doorway? Ribout is stationed there; once a message is placed in his hands, all will go well.'

'I will send the message,' said the lady.

'You, countess?' said the marquis, raising his eyebrows. 'Your devotion is great, we know, but —'

'Listen!' exclaimed the lady, rising and resting her hands upon the table; 'in a garret of this house lives a youth from the provinces as guileless and tender as the lambs he tended there. I have met him twice or thrice upon the stairs. I questioned him, fearing that he might dwell too near the room in which we are accustomed to meet. He is mine, if I will. He writes poems in his garret, and I think he dreams of me. He will do what I say. He shall take the message to the palace.'

The marquis rose from his chair and bowed. 'You did not permit me to finish my sentence, countess,' he said. 'I would have said: "Your devotion is great, but your wit and charm are infinitely greater."'

While the conspirators were thus engaged, David was polishing some lines addressed to his *amorette d'escalier*. He heard a timorous knock at his door, and opened it, with a great throb, to behold her there, panting as one in straits, with eyes wide open and artless, like a child's.

'Monsieur,' she breathed, 'I come to you in distress. I believe you to be good and true, and I know of no other help. How I flew through the streets among the swaggering men! Monsieur, my mother is dying. My uncle is a captain of guards in the palace of the king. Someone must fly to bring him. May I hope —'

'Mademoiselle,' interrupted David, his eyes shining with the desire to do her service, 'your hopes shall be my wings. Tell me how I may reach him.'

The lady thrust a sealed paper into his hand.

'Go to the south gate – the south gate, mind – and say to the guards there, "The falcon has left his nest." They will pass you, and you will go to the south entrance to the palace. Repeat the words, and give this letter to the man who will reply, "Let him strike when he will." This is the password, monsieur, entrusted to me by my uncle, for now when the country is disturbed and men plot against the king's life, no one without it can gain entrance to the palace grounds after nightfall. If you will, monsieur, take him this letter so that my mother may see him before she closes her eyes.'

'Give it me,' said David, eagerly. 'But shall I let you return home through the streets alone so late? I —'

'No, no – fly. Each moment is like a precious jewel. Sometime,' said the lady, with eyes long and cozening, like a gypsy's, 'I will try to thank you for your goodness.'

The poet thrust the letter into his breast, and bounded down the stairway. The lady, when he was gone, returned to the room below.

The eloquent eyebrows of the marquis interrogated her.

'He is gone,' she said, 'as fleet and stupid as one of his own sheep, to deliver it.'

The table shook again from the batter of Captain Desrolles's fist.

'Sacred name!' he cried; 'I have left my pistols behind! I can trust no others.'

'Take this,' said the marquis, drawing from beneath his cloak a shining, great weapon, ornamented with carven silver. 'There are none truer. But guard it closely, for it bears my arms and crest, and already I am suspected. Me, I must put many leagues between myself and Paris this night. To-morrow must find me in my château. After you, dear countess.'

The marquis puffed out the candle. The lady, well cloaked, and the two gentlemen softly descended the stairway and flowed into the crowd that roamed along the narrow pavements of the Rue Conti.

David sped. At the south gate of the king's residence a halberd was laid to his breast, but he turned its point with the words: 'The falcon has left his nest.'

'Pass, brother,' said the guard, 'and go quickly.'

On the south steps of the palace they moved to seize him, but again the *mot de passe* charmed the watchers. One among them stepped forward and began: 'Let him strike —' But a flurry among the guards told of a surprise. A man of keen look and soldierly stride suddenly pressed through them and seized the letter which David held in his hand. 'Come with me,' he said, and led him inside the great hall. Then he tore open the letter and read it.

He beckoned to a man uniformed as an officer of musketeers, who was passing. 'Captain Tetreau, you will have the guards at the south entrance and the south gate arrested and confined. Place men known to be loyal in their places.' To David he said: 'Come with me.'

He conducted him through a corridor and an anteroom into a spacious chamber, where a melancholy man, sombrely dressed, sat brooding in a great leather-covered chair. To that man he said:

'Sire, I have told you that the palace is as full of traitors and spies as a sewer is of rats. You have thought, sire, that it was my fancy. This man penetrated to your very door by their connivance. He bore a letter which I have intercepted. I have brought him here that your majesty may no longer think my zeal excessive.'

'I will question him,' said the king, stirring in his chair. He looked at David with heavy eyes dulled by an opaque film. The poet bent his knee.

'From where do you come?' asked the king.

'From the village of Vernoy, in the province of Eure-et-Loir, sire.'

'What do you follow in Paris?'

'I – I would be a poet, sire.'

'What did you in Vernoy?'

'I minded my father's flock of sheep.'

The king stirred again, and the film lifted from his eyes.

'Ah! in the fields?'

'Yes, sire.'

'You lived in the fields; you went out in the cool of the morning and lay among the hedges in the grass. The flock distributed itself upon the hillside; you drank of the living stream; you ate your sweet brown bread in the shade; and you listened, doubtless, to blackbirds piping in the grove. Is not that so, shepherd?'

'It is, sire,' answered David, with a sigh; 'and to the bees at the flowers, and, maybe, to the grape gatherers singing on the hill.'

'Yes, yes,' said the king, impatiently; 'maybe to them; but surely to the blackbirds. They whistled often, in the grove, did they not?'

'Nowhere, sire, so sweetly as in Eure-et-Loir. I have endeavored to express their song in some verses that I have written.'

'Can you repeat those verses?' asked the king, eagerly. 'A long time ago I listened to the blackbirds. It would be something better than a kingdom if one could rightly construe their song. And at night you drove the sheep to the fold and then sat, in peace and tranquillity, to your pleasant bread. Can you repeat those verses, shepherd?'

'They run this way, sire,' said David, with respectful ardor:

> *'Lazy shepherd, see your lambkins*
> *Skip, ecstatic, on the mead;*
> *See the firs dance in the breezes,*
> *Hear Pan blowing at his reed.*
>
> *'Hear us calling from the tree-tops,*
> *See us swoop upon your flock;*
> *Yield us wool to make our nests warm*
> *In the branches of the —'*

'If it please your majesty,' interrupted a harsh voice, 'I will ask a question or two of this rhymester. There is little time to spare. I crave pardon, sire, if my anxiety for your safety offends.'

'The loyalty,' said the king, 'of the Duke d'Aumale is too well proven to give offence.' He sank into his chair, and the film came again over his eyes.

'First,' said the duke, 'I will read you the letter he brought:

"To-night is the anniversary of the dauphin's death. If he goes, as is his custom, to midnight mass to pray for the soul of his son, the falcon will strike, at the corner of the Rue Esplanade. If this be his intention, set a red light in the upper room at the southwest corner of the palace, that the falcon may take heed."

'Peasant,' said the duke, sternly, 'you have heard these words. Who gave you this message to bring?'

'My lord duke,' said David, sincerely, 'I will tell you. A lady gave it me. She said her mother was ill, and that this writing would fetch her uncle to her bedside. I do not know the meaning of the letter, but I will swear that she is beautiful and good.'

'Describe the woman,' commanded the duke, 'and how you came to be her dupe.'

'Describe her!' said David with a tender smile. 'You would command words to perform miracles. Well, she is made of sunshine and deep shade. She is slender, like the alders, and moves with their grace. Her eyes change while you gaze into them; now round, and then half shut as the sun peeps between two clouds. When she comes, heaven is all about her; when she leaves, there is chaos and a scent of hawthorn blossoms. She came to me in the Rue Conti, number twenty-nine.'

'It is the house,' said the duke, turning to the king, 'that we have been watching. Thanks to the poet's tongue, we have a picture of the infamous Countess Quebedaux.'

'Sire and my lord duke,' said David, earnestly, 'I hope my poor words have done no injustice. I have looked into that lady's eyes. I will stake my life that she is an angel, letter or no letter.'

The duke looked at him steadily. 'I will put you to the proof,' he said, slowly. 'Dressed as the king, you shall, yourself, attend mass in his carriage at midnight. Do you accept the test?'

David smiled. 'I have looked into her eyes,' he said. 'I had my proof there. Take yours how you will.'

Half an hour before twelve the Duke d'Aumale, with his own hands, set a red lamp in a southwest window of the palace. At ten minutes to the hour, David, leaning on his arm, dressed as the king, from top to toe, with his head bowed in his cloak, walked slowly from the royal apartments to the waiting carriage. The duke assisted him inside and closed the door. The carriage whirled away along its route to the cathedral.

On the *qui vive* in a house at the corner of the Rue Esplanade was Captain Tetreau with twenty men, ready to pounce upon the conspirators when they should appear.

But it seemed that, for some reason, the plotters had slightly altered their plans. When the royal carriage had reached the Rue Christopher, one square nearer than the Rue Esplanade, forth from it burst Captain Desrolles, with his band of would-be regicides, and assailed the equipage. The guards upon the carriage, though surprised at the premature attack, descended and fought valiantly. The noise of conflict attracted the force of Captain Tetreau, and they came pelting down the street to the rescue. But, in the meantime, the desperate Desrolles had torn open the door of the king's carriage, thrust his weapon against the body of the dark figure inside, and fired.

Now, with loyal reinforcements at hand, the street rang with cries and the rasp of steel, but the frightened horses had dashed away. Upon the cushions lay the dead body of the poor mock king and poet, slain by a ball from the pistol of Monseigneur, the Marquis de Beaupertuys.

## The Main Road

*Three leagues, then, the road ran, and turned into a puzzle. It joined with another and a larger road at right angles. David stood, uncertain, for a while, and then sat himself to rest upon its side.*

Whither those roads led he knew not. Either way there seemed to lie a great world full of chance and peril. And then, sitting there, his eye fell upon a bright star, one that he and Yvonne had named for theirs. That set him thinking of Yvonne, and he wondered if he had not been too hasty. Why should he leave her and his home because a few hot words had come between them? Was love so brittle a thing that jealousy, the very proof of it, could break it? Mornings always brought a cure for the little heartaches of evening. There was yet time for him to return home without any one in the sweetly sleeping village of Vernoy being the wiser. His heart was Yvonne's; there where he had lived always he could write his poems and find his happiness.

David rose, and shook off his unrest and the wild mood that had tempted him. He set his face steadfastly back along the road he had come. By the time he had retraveled the road to Vernoy, his desire to rove was gone. He passed the sheepfold, and the sheep scurried, with a drumming flutter, at his late footsteps, warming his heart by the homely sound. He crept without noise into his little room and lay there, thankful that his feet had escaped the distress of new roads that night.

How well he knew woman's heart! The next evening Yvonne was at the well in the road where the young congregated in order that the *curé* might have business. The corner of her eye was engaged in a search for David, albeit her set mouth seemed unrelenting. He saw the look; braved the mouth, drew from it a recantation and, later, a kiss as they walked homeward together.

Three months afterward they were married. David's father was shrewd and prosperous. He gave them a wedding that was heard of three leagues away. Both the young people were favorites in the village. There was a procession in the streets, a dance on the green; they had the marionettes and a tumbler out from Dreux to delight the guests.

Then a year, and David's father died. The sheep and the cottage descended to him. He already had the seemliest wife in the village. Yvonne's milk pails and her brass kettles were bright – *ouf!* they blinded you in the sun when you passed that way. But you must keep your eyes upon her yard, for her flower beds were so neat and gay they restored to you your sight. And you might hear her sing, aye, as far as the double chestnut tree above Père Gruneau's blacksmith forge.

But a day came when David drew out paper from a longshut drawer, and began to bite the end of a pencil. Spring had come again and touched his heart. Poet he must have been, for now Yvonne was well-nigh forgotten. This fine new loveliness of earth held him with its witchery and grace. The perfume from her woods and meadows stirred him strangely. Daily had he gone forth with his flock, and brought it safe at night. But now he stretched himself under the hedge and pieced words together on his bits of paper. The sheep strayed, and the wolves, perceiving that difficult poems make easy mutton, ventured from the woods and stole his lambs.

David's stock of poems grew larger and his flock smaller. Yvonne's nose and temper waxed sharp and her talk blunt. Her pans and kettles grew dull, but her eyes had caught their flash. She pointed out to the poet that his neglect was reducing the flock and bringing woe upon the household. David hired a boy to guard the sheep, locked himself in the little room in the top of the cottage, and wrote more poems. The boy, being a poet by nature, but not furnished with an outlet in the way of writing, spent his time in slumber. The wolves lost no time in discovering that poetry and sleep are practically the same; so the flock steadily grew smaller. Yvonne's ill temper increased at an equal rate. Sometimes she would stand in the yard and rail at David through his high window. Then you could hear her as far as the double chestnut tree above Père Gruneau's blacksmith forge.

M. Papineau, the kind, wise, meddling old notary, saw this, as he saw everything at which his nose pointed. He went to David, fortified himself with a great pinch of snuff, and said:

'Friend Mignot, I affixed the seal upon the marriage certificate of your father. It would distress me to be obliged to attest a paper signifying the bankruptcy of his son. But that is what you are coming to. I speak as an old friend. Now, listen to what I have to say. You have your heart set, I perceive, upon poetry. At Dreux, I have a friend, one Monsieur Bril – Georges Bril. He lives in a little cleared space in a houseful of books. He is a learned man; he visits Paris each year; he himself has written books. He will tell you when the catacombs were made, how they found out the names of the stars, and why the plover has a long bill. The meaning and the form of poetry is to him as intelligent as the baa of a sheep is to you. I will give you a letter to him, and you shall take him your poems and let him read them. Then you will know if you shall write more, or give your attention to your wife and business.'

'Write the letter,' said David. 'I am sorry you did not speak of this sooner.'

At sunrise the next morning he was on the road to Dreux with the precious roll of poems under his arm. At noon he wiped the dust from his feet at the door of Monsieur Bril. That learned man broke the seal of M. Papineau's letter, and sucked up its contents through his gleaming spectacles as the sun draws water. He took David inside to his study and sat him down upon a little island beat upon by a sea of books.

Monsieur Bril had a conscience. He flinched not even at a mass of manuscript the thickness of a finger length and rolled to an incorrigible curve. He broke the back of the roll against his knee and began to read. He slighted nothing; he bored into the lump as a worm into a nut, seeking for a kernel.

Meanwhile, David sat, marooned, trembling in the spray of so much literature. It roared in his ears. He held no chart or compass for voyaging in that sea. Half the world, he thought, must be writing books.

Monsieur Bril bored to the last page of the poems. Then he took off his spectacles and wiped them with his handkerchief.

'My old friend, Papineau, is well?' he asked.

'In the best of health,' said David.

'How many sheep have you, Monsieur Mignot?'

'Three hundred and nine, when I counted them yesterday. The flock has had ill fortune. To that number it has decreased from eight hundred and fifty.'

'You have a wife and a home, and lived in comfort. The sheep brought you plenty. You went into the fields with them and lived in the keen air and ate the sweet bread of contentment. You had but to be vigilant and recline there upon nature's breast, listening to the whistle of the blackbirds in the grove. Am I right thus far?'

'It was so,' said David.

'I have read all your verses,' continued Monsieur Bril, his eyes wandering about his sea of books as if he conned the horizon for a sail. 'Look yonder, through that window, Monsieur Mignot; tell me what you see in that tree.'

'I see a crow,' said David, looking.

'There is a bird,' said Monsieur Bril, 'that shall assist me where I am disposed to shirk a duty. You know that bird, Monsieur Mignot; he is the philosopher of the air. He is happy through submission to his lot. None so merry or full-crawed as he with his whimsical eye and rollicking step. The fields yield him what he desires. He never grieves that his plumage is not gay, like the oriole's. And you have heard, Monsieur Mignot, the notes that nature has given him? Is the nightingale any happier, do you think?'

David rose to his feet. The crow cawed harshly from his tree.

'I thank you, Monsieur Bril,' he said, slowly. 'There was not, then, one nightingale note among all those croaks?'

'I could not have missed it,' said Monsieur Bril, with a sigh. 'I read every word. Live your poetry, man; do not try to write it any more.'

'I thank you,' said David, again. 'And now I will be going back to my sheep.'

'If you would dine with me,' said the man of books, 'and overlook the smart of it, I will give you reasons at length.'

'No,' said the poet, 'I must be back in the fields cawing at my sheep.'

Back along the road to Vernoy he trudged with his poems under his arm. When he reached his village he turned into the shop of one Zeigler, a Jew out of Armenia, who sold anything that came to his hand.

'Friend,' said David, 'wolves from the forest harass my sheep on the hills. I must purchase firearms to protect them. What have you?'

'A bad day, this, for me, friend Mignot,' said Zeigler, spreading his hands, 'for I perceive that I must sell you a weapon that will not fetch a tenth of its value. Only last week I bought from a peddler a wagon full of goods that he procured at a sale by a *commissionaire* of the crown. The sale was of the château and belongings of a great lord – I know not his title – who has been banished for conspiracy against the king. There are some choice firearms in the lot. This pistol – oh, a weapon fit for a prince! – it shall be only forty francs to you, friend Mignot – if I lost ten by the sale. But perhaps an arquebus —'

'This will do,' said David, throwing the money on the counter. 'Is it charged?'

'I will charge it,' said Zeigler. 'And, for ten francs more, add a store of powder and ball.'

David laid his pistol under his coat and walked to his cottage. Yvonne was not there. Of late she had taken to gadding much among the neighbors. But a fire was glowing in the kitchen stove. David opened the door of it and thrust his poems in upon the coals. As they blazed up they made a singing, harsh sound in the flue.

'The song of the crow!' said the poet.

He went up to his attic room and closed the door. So quiet was the village that a score of people heard the roar of the great pistol. They flocked thither, and up the stairs where the smoke, issuing, drew their notice.

The men laid the body of the poet upon his bed, awkwardly arranging it to conceal the torn plumage of the poor black crow.

The women chattered in a luxury of zealous pity. Some of them ran to tell Yvonne.

M. Papineau, whose nose had brought him there among the first, picked up the weapon and ran his eye over its silver mountings with a mingled air of connoisseurship and grief.

'The arms,' he explained, aside, to the *curé*, 'and crest of Monseigneur, the Marquis de Beaupertuys.'

# A Retrieved Reformation

A guard came to the prison shoe-shop, where Jimmy Valentine was assiduously stitching uppers, and escorted him to the front office. There the warden handed Jimmy his pardon, which had been signed that morning by the governor. Jimmy took it in a tired kind of way. He had served nearly ten months of a four-year sentence. He had expected to stay only about three months, at the longest. When a man with as many friends on the outside as Jimmy Valentine had is received in the 'stir' it is hardly worth while to cut his hair.

'Now, Valentine,' said the warden, 'you'll go out in the morning. Brace up, and make a man of yourself. You're not a bad fellow at heart. Stop cracking safes, and live straight.'

'Me?' said Jimmy, in surprise. 'Why, I never cracked a safe in my life.'

'Oh, no,' laughed the warden. 'Of course not. Let's see, now. How was it you happened to get sent up on that Springfield job? Was it because you wouldn't prove an alibi for fear of compromising somebody in extremely high-toned society? Or was it simply a case of a mean old jury that had it in for you? It's always one or the other with you innocent victims.'

'Me?' said Jimmy, still blankly virtuous. 'Why, warden, I never was in Springfield in my life!'

'Take him back, Cronin,' smiled the warden, 'and fix him up with outgoing clothes. Unlock him at seven in the morning, and let him come to the bull-pen. Better think over my advice, Valentine.'

At a quarter past seven on the next morning Jimmy stood in the warden's outer office. He had on a suit of the villainously fitting, ready-made clothes and a pair of the stiff, squeaky shoes that the state furnishes to its discharged compulsory guests.

The clerk handed him a railroad ticket and the five-dollar bill with which the law expected him to rehabilitate himself into good citizenship and prosperity. The warden gave him a cigar, and shook hands. Valentine, 9762, was chronicled on the books 'Pardoned by Governor,' and Mr James Valentine walked out into the sunshine.

Disregarding the song of the birds, the waving green trees, and the smell of the flowers, Jimmy headed straight for a restaurant. There he tasted the first sweet joys of liberty in the shape of a broiled chicken and a bottle of white wine – followed by a cigar a grade better than the one the warden had given him. From there he proceeded leisurely to the depot. He tossed a quarter into the hat of a blind man sitting by the door, and boarded his train. Three hours set him down in a little town near the state line. He went to the café of one Mike Dolan and shook hands with Mike, who was alone behind the bar.

'Sorry we couldn't make it sooner, Jimmy, me boy,' said Mike. 'But we had that protest from Springfield to buck against, and the governor nearly balked. Feeling all right?'

'Fine,' said Jimmy. 'Got my key?'

He got his key and went upstairs, unlocking the door of a room at the rear. Everything was just as he had left it. There on the floor was still Ben Price's collar-button that had been torn from that eminent detective's shirt-band when they had over-powered Jimmy to arrest him.

Pulling out from the wall a folding-bed, Jimmy slid back a panel in the wall and dragged out a dust-covered suitcase. He opened this and gazed fondly at the finest set of burglar's tools in the East. It was a complete set, made of specially tempered steel, the latest designs in drills, punches, braces and bits, jimmies, clamps, and augers, with two or three novelties invented by Jimmy himself, in which he took pride. Over nine hundred dollars they had cost him to have made at —, a place where they make such things for the profession.

In half an hour Jimmy went downstairs and through the café. He was now dressed in tasteful and well-fitting clothes, and carried his dusted and cleaned suitcase in his hand.

'Got anything on?' asked Mike Dolan, genially.

'Me?' said Jimmy, in a puzzled tone. 'I don't understand. I'm representing the New York Amalgamated Short Snap Biscuit Cracker and Frazzled Wheat Company.'

This statement delighted Mike to such an extent that Jimmy had to take a seltzer-and-milk on the spot. He never touched 'hard' drinks.

A week after the release of Valentine, 9762, there was a neat job of safe-burglary done in Richmond, Indiana, with no clue to the author. A scant eight hundred dollars was all that was secured. Two weeks after that a patented, improved, burglar-proof safe in Logansport was opened like a cheese to the tune of fifteen hundred dollars, currency; securities and silver untouched. That began to interest the rogue-catchers. Then an old-fashioned bank-safe in Jefferson City became active and threw out of its crater an eruption of bank-notes amounting to five thousand dollars. The losses were now high enough to bring the matter up into Ben Price's class of work. By comparing notes, a remarkable similarity in the methods of the burglaries was noticed. Ben Price investigated the scenes of the robberies, and was heard to remark:

'That's Dandy Jim Valentine's autograph. He's resumed business. Look at that combination knob – jerked out as easy as pulling up a radish in wet weather. He's got the only clamps that can do it. And look how clean those tumblers were punched out! Jimmy never has to drill but one hole. Yes, I guess I want Mr Valentine. He'll do his bit next time without any short-time or clemency foolishness.'

Ben Price knew Jimmy's habits. He had learned them while working up the Springfield case. Long jumps, quick get-aways, no confederates, and a taste for good society – these ways had helped Mr Valentine to become noted as a successful dodger of retribution. It was given out that Ben Price had taken up the trail of the elusive cracksman, and other people with burglar-proof safes felt more at ease.

One afternoon Jimmy Valentine and his suitcase climbed out of the mail-hack in Elmore, a little town five miles off the railroad down in the black-jack country of Arkansas. Jimmy, looking like an athletic young senior just home from college, went down the board sidewalk toward the hotel.

A young lady crossed the street, passed him at the corner and entered a door over which was the sign, 'The Elmore Bank.' Jimmy Valentine looked into her eyes, forgot what he was, and became another man. She lowered her eyes and colored slightly. Young men of Jimmy's style and looks were scarce in Elmore.

Jimmy collared a boy that was loafing on the steps of the bank as if he were one of the stock-holders, and began to ask him questions about the town, feeding him dimes at intervals. By and by the young lady came out, looking royally unconscious of the young man with the suitcase, and went her way.

'Isn't that young lady Miss Polly Simpson?' asked Jimmy, with specious guile.

'Naw,' said the boy. 'She's Annabel Adams. Her pa owns this bank. What'd you come to Elmore for? Is that a good watch-chain? I'm going to get a bulldog. Got any more dimes?'

Jimmy went to the Palmer Hotel, registered as Ralph D. Spencer, and engaged a room. He leaned on the desk and declared his platform to the clerk. He said he had come to Elmore to look for a location to go into business. How was the shoe business, now, in the town? He had thought of the shoe business. Was there an opening?

The clerk was impressed by the clothes and manner of Jimmy. He, himself, was something of a pattern of fashion to the thinly gilded youth of Elmore, but he now perceived his shortcomings.

While trying to figure out Jimmy's manner of typing his four-in-hand he cordially gave information.

Yes, there ought to be a good opening in the shoe line. There wasn't an exclusive shoe-store in the place. The dry-goods and general stores handled them. Business in all lines was fairly good. Hoped Mr Spencer would decide to locate in Elmore. He would find it a pleasant town to live in, and the people very sociable.

Mr Spencer thought he would stop over in the town a few days and look over the situation. No, the clerk needn't call the boy. He would carry up his suitcase, himself; it was rather heavy.

Mr Ralph Spencer, the phoenix that arose from Jimmy Valentine's ashes – ashes left by the flame of a sudden and alternative attack of love – remained in Elmore, and prospered. He opened a shoe-store and secured a good run of trade.

Socially he was also a success, and made many friends. And he accomplished the wish of his heart. He met Miss Annabel Adams, and became more and more captivated by her charms.

At the end of a year the situation of Mr Ralph Spencer was this: he had won the respect of the community, his shoe-store was flourishing, and he and Annabel were engaged to be married in two weeks. Mr Adams, the typical, plodding, country banker, approved of Spencer. Annabel's pride in him almost equaled her affection. He was as much at home in the family of Mr Adams and that of Annabel's married sister as if he were already a member.

One day Jimmy sat down in his room and wrote this letter which he mailed to the safe address of one of his old friends in St Louis:

Dear Old Pal:

I want you to be at Sullivan's place, in Little Rock, next Wednesday night at nine o'clock. I want you to wind up some little matters for me. And, also, I want to make you a present of my kit of tools. I know you'll be glad to get them – you couldn't duplicate the lot for a thousand dollars. Say, Billy, I've quit the old business – a year ago. I've got a nice store. I'm making an honest living, and I'm going to marry the finest girl on earth two weeks from now. It's the only life, Billy – the straight one. I wouldn't touch a dollar of another man's money now for a million. After I get married I'm going to sell out and go West, where there won't be so much danger of having old scores brought up against me. I tell you, Billy, she's an angel. She believes in me; and I wouldn't do another crooked thing for the whole world. Be sure to be at Sully's, for I must see you. I'll bring along the tools with me.

Your old friend,
Jimmy

On the Monday night after Jimmy wrote this letter, Ben Price jogged unobtrusively into Elmore in a livery buggy. He lounged about town in his quiet way until he found out what he wanted to know. From the drug-store across the street from Spencer's shoe-store he got a good look at Ralph D. Spencer.

'Going to marry the banker's daughter are you, Jimmy?' said Ben to himself, softly. 'Well, I don't know!'

The next morning Jimmy took breakfast at the Adamses. He was going to Little Rock that day to order his wedding-suit and buy something nice for Annabel. That would be the first time he had left town since he came to Elmore. It had been more than a year now since those last professional 'jobs,' and he thought he could safely venture out.

After breakfast quite a family party went down town together – Mr Adams, Annabel, Jimmy, and Annabel's married sister with her two little girls, aged five and nine. They came by the hotel where Jimmy still boarded, and he ran up to his room and brought along his suitcase. Then they went on to the bank. There stood

Jimmy's horse and buggy and Dolph Gibson, who was going to drive him over to the railroad station.

All went inside the high, carved oak railings into the banking-room – Jimmy included, for Mr Adams' future son-in-law was welcome anywhere. The clerks were pleased to be greeted by the good-looking, agreeable young man who was going to marry Miss Annabel. Jimmy set his suitcase down. Annabel, whose heart was bubbling with happiness and lively youth, put on Jimmy's hat and picked up the suitcase. 'Wouldn't I make a nice drummer?' said Annabel. 'My! Ralph, how heavy it is. Feels like it was full of gold bricks.'

'Lot of nickel-plated shoe-horns in there,' said Jimmy, coolly, 'that I'm going to return. Thought I'd save express charges by taking them up. I'm getting awfully economical.'

The Elmore Bank had just put in a new safe and vault. Mr Adams was very proud of it, and insisted on an inspection by every one. The vault was a small one, but it had a new patented door. It fastened with three solid steel bolts thrown simultaneously with a single handle, and had a time-lock. Mr Adams beamingly explained its workings to Mr Spencer, who showed a courteous but not too intelligent interest. The two children, May and Agatha, were delighted by the shining metal and funny clock and knobs.

While they were thus engaged Ben Price sauntered in and leaned on his elbow, looking casually inside between the railings. He told the teller that he didn't want anything; he was just waiting for a man he knew.

Suddenly there was a scream or two from the women, and a commotion. Unperceived by the elders, May, the nine-year-old girl, in a spirit of play, had shut Agatha in the vault. She had then shot the bolts and turned the knob of the combination as she had seen Mr Adams do.

The old banker sprang to the handle and tugged at it for a moment. 'The door can't be opened,' he groaned. 'The clock hasn't been wound nor the combination set.'

Agatha's mother screamed again, hysterically.

'Hush!' said Mr Adams, raising his trembling hand. 'All be quiet for a moment, Agatha!' he called as loudly as he could: 'Listen to me.' During the following silence they could just hear the faint sound of the child wildly shrieking in the dark vault in a panic of terror.

'My precious darling!' wailed the mother. 'She will die of fright! Open the door! Oh, break it open! Can't you men do something?'

'There isn't a man nearer than Little Rock who can open that door,' said Mr Adams, in a shaky voice. 'My God! Spencer, what shall we do? That child – she can't stand it long in there. There isn't enough air, and, besides, she'll go into convulsions from fright.'

Agatha's mother, frantic now, beat the door of the vault with her hands. Somebody wildly suggested dynamite. Annabel turned to Jimmy, her large eyes full of anguish, but not yet despairing. To a woman nothing seems quite impossible to the powers of the man she worships.

'Can't you do something, Ralph – *try*, won't you?'

He looked at her with a queer, soft smile on his lips and in his keen eyes.

'Annabel,' he said, 'give me that rose you are wearing, will you?'

Hardly believing that she heard him aright, she unpinned the bud from the bosom of her dress, and placed it in his hand. Jimmy stuffed it into his vest-pocket, threw off his coat and pulled up his shirt-sleeves. With that act Ralph D Spencer passed away and Jimmy Valentine took his place.

'Get away from the door, all of you,' he commanded, shortly.

He set his suitcase on the table, and opened it out flat. From that time on he seemed to be unconscious of the presence of anyone else. He laid out the shining, queer implements swiftly and orderly, whistling softly to himself as he always did when at work. In a deep silence and immovable, the others watched him as if under a spell.

In a minute Jimmy's pet drill was biting smoothly into the steel door. In ten minutes – breaking his own burglarious record – he threw back the bolts and opened the door.

Agatha, almost collapsed, but safe, was gathered into her mother's arms.

Jimmy Valentine put on his coat, and walked outside the railings toward the front door. As he went he thought he heard a far-away voice that he once knew call 'Ralph!' But he never hesitated.

At the door a big man stood somewhat in his way.

'Hello, Ben!' said Jimmy, still with his strange smile. 'Got around at last, have you? Well, let's go. I don't know that it makes much difference, now.'

And then Ben Price acted rather strangely.

'Guess you're mistaken, Mr Spencer,' he said. 'Don't believe I recognize you. Your buggy's waiting for you, ain't it?'

And Ben Price turned and strolled down the street.

# The Whirligig of Life

Justice-of-the-peace Benaja Widdup sat in the door of his office smoking his elder-stem pipe. Halfway to the Zenith the Cumberland range rose blue-gray in the afternoon haze. A speckled hen swaggered down the main street of the 'settlement,' cackling foolishly.

Up the road came a sound of creaking axles, and then a slow cloud of dust, and then a bull-cart bearing Ransie Bilbro and his wife. The cart stopped at the Justice's door, and the two climbed down. Ransie was a narrow six feet of sallow brown skin and yellow hair. The imperturbability of the mountains hung upon him like a suit of armor. The woman was calicoed, angled, snuff-brushed, and weary with unknown desires. Through it all gleamed a faint protest of cheated youth unconscious of its loss.

The Justice of the Peace slipped his feet into his shoes, for the sake of dignity, and moved to let them enter.

'We-all,' said the woman, in a voice like the wind blowing through pine boughs, 'wants a divo'ce.' She looked at Ransie to see if he noted any flaw or ambiguity or evasion or partiality or self-partisanship in her statement of their business.

'A divo'ce,' repeated Ransie, with a solemn nod. 'We-all can't git along together nohow. It's lonesome enough fur to live in the mount'ins when a man and a woman keers fur one another. But when she's a-spittin' like a wildcat or a-sullenin' like a hoot-owl in the cabin, a man ain't got no call to live with her.'

'When he's a no-'count varmint,' said the woman, without any special warmth, 'a-traipsin' along of scalawags and moonshiners and a-layin' on his back pizen 'ith co'n whiskey, and a-pesterin' folks with a pack o' hungry, triflin' houn's to feed!'

'When she keeps a-throwin skillet lids,' came Ransie's antiphony 'and slings b'ilin' water on the best coon-dog in the Cumberlands, and sets herself again' cookin' a man's victuals, and keeps him awake o' nights accusin' him of a sight of doin's!'

'When he's al'ays a-fightin' the revenues, and git a hard name in the mount'ins fur a mean man, who' gwine to be able fur to sleep o' nights?'

The Justice of the Peace stirred deliberately to his duties. He placed his one chair and a wooden stool for his petitioners. He opened his book of statutes on the table and scanned the index. Presently he wiped his spectacles and shifted his inkstand.

'The law and the statutes,' said he, 'air silent on the subjeck of divo'ce as fur as the jurisdiction of this co't air concerned. But, accordin' to equity and the Constitution and the golden rule, it's a had barg'in that can't run both ways. If a justice of the peace can marry a couple, it's plain that he is bound to be able to divo'ce 'em. This here office will issue a decree of divo'ce and abide by the decision of the Supreme Co't to hold it good.'

Ransie Bilbro drew a small tobacco-bag from his trousers pocket. Out of this he shook upon the table a five-dollar note. 'Sold a b'arskin and two foxes fur that,' he remarked. 'It's all the money we got.'

'The regular price of a divo'ce in this co't,' said the Justice, 'air five dollars.' He stuffed the bill into the pocket of his homespun vest with a deceptive air of indifference. With much bodily toil and mental travail he wrote the decree upon half a sheet of fools-cap, and then copied it upon the other. Ransie Bilbro and his wife listened to his reading of the document that was to give them freedom:

Know all men by these presents that Ransie Bilbro and his wife, Ariela Bilbro, this day personally appeared before me and promises that hereinafter they will neither love, honor, nor obey each other, neither for better nor worse, being of sound mind and body, and accept summons for divorce according to the peace and dignity of the State. Herein fail not, so help you God. Benaja Widdup, justice of the peace in and for the county of Piedmont, State of Tennessee.

The Justice was about to hand one of the documents to Ransie. The voice of Ariela delayed the transfer. Both men looked at her. Their dull masculinity was confronted by something sudden and unexpected in the woman.

'Judge, don't you give him that air paper yit. 'Tain't all settled, nohow. I got to have my rights first. I got to have my ali-money. 'Tain't no kind of a way to do fur a man to divo'ce his wife 'thout her havin' a cent fur to do with. I'm a-layin' off to be a-goin' up to brother Ed's up on Hogback Mount'in. I'm bound fur to hev a pa'r of shoes and some snuff and things besides. Ef Rance kin affo'd a divo'ce let him pay me ali-money.'

Ransie Bilbro was stricken to dumb perplexity. There had been no previous hint of alimony. Women were always bringing up startling and unlooked-for issues.

Justice Benaja Widdup felt that the point demanded judicial decision. The authorities were also silent on the subject of alimony. But the woman's feet were bare. The trail to Hogback Mountain was steep and flinty.

'Ariela Bilbro,' he asked, in official tones, 'how much did you 'low would be good and sufficient ali-money in the case befo' the co't?'

'I'lowed,' she answered, 'fur the shoes and all, to say five dollars. That ain't much fur ali-money, but I reckon that'll git me up to brother Ed's.'

'The amount,' said the Justice, 'air not unreasonable. Ransie Bilbro, you air ordered by the co't to pay the plaintiff the sum of five dollars befo' the decree of divo'ce air issued.'

'I hain't no mo' money,' breathed Ransie, heavily. 'I done paid you all I had.'

'Otherwise,' said the Justice, looking severely over his spectacles, 'you air in contempt of co't.'

'I reckon if you gimme till to-morrow,' pleaded the husband, 'I mout be able to rake or scrape it up somewhars. I never looked for to be a-payin' no ali-money.'

'The case air adjourned,' said Benaja Widdup, 'till to-morrow, when you-all will present yo'selves and obey the order of the co't. Followin' of which the decrees of divo'ce will be delivered.' He sat down in the door and began to loosen a shoestring.

'We mout as well go down to Uncle Ziah's,' decided Ransie, 'and spend the night.' He climbed into the cart on one side, and Ariela climbed in on the other. Obeying the flat of his rope, the little red bull slowly came around on a tack, and the cart crawled away in the nimbus arising from its wheels.

Justice-of-the-peace Benaja Widdup smoked his elder-stem pipe. Late in the afternoon he got his weekly paper, and read it until the twilight dimmed its lines. Then he lit the tallow candle on his table and read until the moon rose, marking the time for supper. He lived in the double log cabin on the slope near the girdled poplar. Going home to supper he crossed a little branch darkened by a laurel thicket. The dark figure of a man stepped from the laurels and pointed a rifle at his breast. His hat was pulled down low, and something covered most of his face.

'I want yo' money,' said the figure, ' 'thout any talk. I'm gettin' nervous, and my finger's a-wobblin on this here trigger.'

'I've only got f-f-five dollars,' said the Justice, producing it from his vest pocket.

'Roll it up,' came the order, 'and stick it in the end of this here gunbar'l.'

The bill was crisp and new. Even fingers that were clumsy and trembling found little difficulty in making a spill of it and inserting it (this with less ease) into the muzzle of the rifle.

'Now I reckon you kin be goin' along,' said the robber.

The Justice lingered not on his way.

*

The next day came the little red bull, drawing the cart to the office door. Justice Benaja Widdup had his shoes on, for he was expecting the visit. In his presence Ransie Bilbro handed to his wife a five-dollar bill. The official's eye sharply viewed it. It seemed to curl up as though it had been rolled and inserted into the end of a gun-barrel. But the Justice refrained from comment. It is true that other bills might be inclined to curl. He handed each one a decree of divorce. Each stood awkwardly silent, slowly folding the guarantee of freedom. The woman cast a shy glance full of constraint at Ransie.

'I reckon you'll be goin' back up to the cabin,' she said, 'along with the bull-cart. There's bread in the tin box settin' on the shelf. I put the bacon in the bilin'-pot to keep the hounds from gettin' it. Don't forget to wind the clock to-night.'

'You air a-goin' to your brother Ed's?' asked Ransie, with fine unconcern.

'I was 'lowin' to get along up that afore night. I ain't sayin' as they'll pester theyselves any to make me welcome, but I hain't nowhar else fur to go. It's a right smart ways, and I reckon I better be goin'. I'll be a-sayin' good-bye, Ranse – that is, if you keer fur to say so.'

'I don't know as anybody's a hound dog,' said Ransie, in a martyr's voice, 'fur to not want to say good-bye – 'less you air so anxious to git away that you don't want me to say it.'

Ariela was silent. She folded the five-dollar bill and her decree carefully, and placed them in the bosom of her dress. Benaja Widdup watched the money disappear with mournful eyes behind his spectacles.

And then with his next words he achieved rank (as his thoughts ran) with either the great crowd of the world's sympathizers or the little crowd of its great financiers.

'Be kind o' lonesome in the old cabin to-night, Ransie,' he said.

Ransie Bilbro stared out at the Cumberlands, clear blue now in the sunlight. He did not look at Ariela.

'I 'low it might be lonesome,' he said; 'but when folks gits mad and wants a divo'ce, you can't make folks stay.'

'There's others wanted a divo'ce,' said Ariela, speaking to the wooden stool. 'Besides, nobody don't want nobody to stay.'

'Nobody never said they didn't.'

'Nobody never said they did. I reckon I better start on now to brother Ed's.'

'Nobody can't wind that old clock.'

'Want me to go along 'ith you in the cart and wind it fur you, Ranse?'

The mountaineer's countenance was proof against emotion. But he reached out a big hand and enclosed Ariela's thin brown one. Her soul peeped out once through her impassive face, hallowing it.

'Them hounds sha'n't pester you no more,' said Ransie. 'I reckon I been mean and low down. You wind that clock, Ariela.'

'My heart hit's in that cabin, Ranse,' she whispered, 'along 'ith you. I ain't a-goin' to git mad no more. Let's be startin', Ranse, so's we kin git home by sundown.'

Justice-of-the-peace Benaja Widdup interposed as they started for the door, forgetting his presence.

'In the name of the State of Tennessee,' he said, 'I forbid you-all to be a-defyin' of its laws and statutes. This co't is mo' than willin' and full of joy to see the clouds of discord and misunderstandin' rollin' away from two lovin' hearts, but it air the duty of the co't to p'eserve the morals and integrity of the State. The co't reminds you that you air no longer man and wife, but air divo'ced by regular decree, and as such air not entitled to the benefits and 'purtenances of the mattermonal estate.'

Ariela caught Ransie's arm. Did those words mean that she must lose him now when they had just learned the lesson of life?

'But the co't air prepared,' went on the Justice, 'fur to remove the disabilities set up by the decree of divo'ce. The co't air on hand to perform the solemn ceremony of marri'ge, thus fixin' things up and enablin' the parties in the case to resume the honor'ble and elevatin' state of mattermony which they desires. The fee fur performin' said ceremony will be, in this case, to wit, five dollars.'

Ariela caught the gleam of promise in his words. Swiftly her hand went to her bosom. Freely as an alighting dove the bill fluttered to the Justice's table. Her sallow cheek colored as she stood hand in hand with Ransie and listened to the reuniting words.

Ransie helped her into the cart, and climbed in beside her. The little red bull turned once more, and they set out, hand-clasped, for the mountains.

Justice-of-the-peace Benaja Widdup sat in his door and took off his shoes. Once again he fingered the bill tucked down in his vest pocket. Once again he smoked his elder-stem pipe. Once again the speckled hen swaggered down the main street of the 'settlement,' cackling foolishly.

# A Blackjack Bargainer

The most disreputable thing in Yancey Goree's law office was Goree himself, sprawled in his creaky old armchair. The rickety little office, built of red brick, was set flush with the street – the main street of the town of Bethel.

Bethel rested upon the foot-hills of the Blue Ridge. Above it the mountains were piled to the sky. Far below it the turbid Catawba gleamed yellow along its disconsolate valley.

The June day was at its sultriest hour. Bethel dozed in the tepid shade. Trade was not. It was so still that Goree, reclining in his chair, distinctly heard the clicking of the chips in the grand-jury room, where the 'court-house gang' was playing poker. From the open back door of the office a well-worn path meandered across the grassy lot to the court-house. The treading out of that path had cost Goree all he ever had – first inheritance of a few thousand dollars, next the old family home, and, latterly, the last shreds of his self-respect and manhood. The 'gang' had cleaned him out. The broken gambler had turned drunkard and parasite; he had lived to see this day come when the men who had stripped him denied him a seat at the game. His word was no longer to be taken. The daily bout at cards had arranged itself accordingly, and to him was assigned the ignoble part of the onlooker. The sheriff, the county clerk, a sportive deputy, a gay attorney, and a chalk-faced man hailing 'from the valley,' sat at table, and the sheared one was thus tacitly advised to go and grow more wool.

Soon wearying of his ostracism, Goree had departed for his office, muttering to himself as he unsteadily traversed the unlucky pathway. After a drink of corn whiskey from a demijohn under the table he had flung himself into the chair, staring, in a sort of maudlin apathy, out at the mountains immersed in the summer haze. The little white patch he saw away up on the side of Blackjack was Laurel, the village near which he had been born and bred. There, also, was the birthplace of the feud between the Gorees and the Coltranes. Now no direct heir of the Gorees survived except this plucked and singed bird of misfortune. To the Coltranes, also, but one male supporter was left – Colonel Abner Coltrane, a man of substance and standing, a member of the State Legislature, and a contemporary with Goree's father. The feud had been a typical one of the region; it had left a red record of hate, wrong, and slaughter.

But Yancey Goree was not thinking of feuds. His befuddled brain was hopelessly attacking the problem of the future maintenance of himself and his favorite follies. Of late, old friends of the family had seen to it that he had whereof to eat and a place to sleep, but whiskey they would not buy for him, and he must have whiskey. His law business was extinct; no case had been entrusted to him in two years. He had been a borrower and a sponge, and it seemed that if he fell no lower it would be from lack of opportunity. One more chance – he was saying to himself – if he had one more stake at the game, he thought he could win; but he had nothing left to sell, and his credit was more than exhausted.

He could not help smiling, even in his misery, as he thought of the man to whom, six months before, he had sold the old Goree homestead. There had come from 'back yan' ' in the mountains two of the strangest creatures, a man named Pike Garvey and his wife. 'Back yan',' with a wave of the hand toward the hills, was understood among the mountaineers to designate the remotest fastnesses, the unplumbed gorges, the haunts of lawbreakers, the wolf's den, and the boudoir of the bear. In the cabin far up on Blackjack's shoulder, in the wildest part of these retreats, this odd couple had lived for twenty years. They had neither dog nor children to mitigate the heavy silence of the hills. Pike Garvey was little known in the settlements, but all who had dealt with him pronounced him 'crazy as a loon.' He acknowledged no occupation save that of a squirrel hunter, but he 'moonshined' occasionally by way of diversion. Once the 'revenues' had dragged him from his lair, fighting silently and desperately like a terrier, and he had been sent to state's prison for two years. Released, he popped back into his hole like an angry weasel.

Fortune, passing over many anxious wooers, made a freakish flight into Blackjack's bosky pockets to smile upon Pike and his faithful partner.

One day a party of spectacled, knickerbockered, and altogether absurd prospectors invaded the vicinity of the Garveys' cabin. Pike lifted his squirrel rifle off the hook and took a shot at them at long range on the chance of their being revenues. Happily he missed, and the unconscious agents of good luck drew nearer, disclosing their innocence of anything resembling law or justice. Later on, they offered the Garveys an enormous quantity of ready, green, crisp money for their thirty-acre patch of cleared land, mentioning, as an excuse for such a mad action, some irrelevant and inadequate nonsense about a bed of mica underlying the said property.

When the Garveys became possessed of so many dollars that they faltered in computing them, the deficiencies of life on Blackjack began to grow prominent. Pike began to talk of new shoes, a hogshead of tobacco to set in the corner, a new lock to his rifle; and, leading Martella to a certain spot on the mountainside, he pointed out to her how a small cannon – doubtless a thing not beyond the scope of their fortune in price – might be planted so as to command and defend the sole accessible trail to the cabin, to the confusion of revenues and meddling strangers forever.

But Adam reckoned without his Eve. These things represented to him the applied power of wealth, but there slumbered in his dingy cabin an ambition that soared far above his primitive wants. Somewhere in Mrs Garvey's bosom still survived a spot of femininity unstarved by twenty years of Blackjack. For so long a time the sounds in her ears had been the scaly-barks dropping in the woods at noon, and the wolves singing among the rocks at night, and it was enough to have purged her vanities. She had grown fat and sad and yellow and dull. But when the means came, she felt a rekindled desire to assume the perquisites of her sex – to sit at tea tables; to buy inutile things; to whitewash the hideous veracity of life with a little form and ceremony. So she coldly vetoed Pike's proposed system of fortifications, and announced that they would descend upon the world, and gyrate socially.

And thus, at length, it was decided, and the thing done. The village of Laurel was their compromise between Mrs Garvey's preference for one of the large valley towns and Pike's hankering for primeval solitudes. Laurel yielded a halting round of feeble social distractions comportable with Martella's ambitions, and was not entirely without recommendation to Pike, its contiguity to the mountains presenting advantages for sudden retreat in case fashionable society should make it advisable.

Their descent upon Laurel had been coincident with Yancey Goree's feverish desire to convert property into cash, and they bought the old Goree homestead, paying four thousand dollars ready money into the spendthrift's shaking hand.

Thus it happened that while the disreputable last of the Gorees sprawled in his disreputable office, at the end of his row, spurned by the cronies whom he had gorged, strangers dwelt in the halls of his fathers.

A cloud of dust was rolling slowly up the parched street, with something traveling in the midst of it. A little breeze wafted the cloud to one side and a new, brightly painted carryall, drawn by a slothful gray horse, became visible. The vehicle deflected from the middle of the street as it neared Goree's office, and stopped in the gutter directly in front of his door.

On the front seat sat a gaunt, tall man, dressed in black broadcloth, his rigid hands incarcerated in yellow kid gloves. On the back seat was a lady who triumphed over the June heat. Her stout form was armored in a skintight silk dress of the description known as 'changeable,' being a gorgeous combination of shifting hues. She sat erect, waving a much-ornamented fan, with her eyes fixed stonily far down the street. However Martella Garvey's heart might be rejoicing at the pleasures of her new life, Blackjack had done his work with her exterior. He had carved her countenance to the image of emptiness and inanity; had imbued her with the stolidity of his crags and the reserve of his hushed interiors. She always seemed to hear, whatever her surroundings were, the scaly-barks falling and pattering down the mountainside. She could always hear the awful silence of Blackjack sounding through the stillest of nights.

Goree watched this solemn equipage, as it drove to his door, with only faint interest but when the lank driver wrapped the reins about his whip, and awkwardly descended, and stepped into the office, he rose unsteadily to receive him, recognizing Pike Garvey, the new, the transformed, the recently civilized.

The mountaineer took the chair Goree offered him. They who cast doubts upon Garvey's soundness of mind had a strong witness in the man's countenance. His face was too long, a dull saffron in hue, and immobile as a statue's. Pale-blue, unblinking round eyes without lashes added to the singularity of his gruesome visage. Goree was at a loss to account for the visit.

'Everything all right at Laurel, Mr Garvey?' he inquired.

'Everything all right, sir, and mighty pleased is Missis Garvey and me with the property. Missis Garvey likes yo' old place, and she likes the neighborhood. Society is what she 'lows she wants, and she is gettin' of it. The Rogerses, the Hapgoods, the Pratts, and the Torys hev been to see Missis Garvey, and she hev et meals to most of thar houses. The best folks hev axed her to differ'nt kinds of doin's. I cyan't say, Mr Goree, that sech things suits me – fur me, give me them thar.' Garvey's huge, yellow-gloved hand flourished in the direction of the mountains. 'That's whar I b'long 'mongst the wild honey bees and the b'ars. But that ain't what I come fur to say, Mr Goree. That's somethin' you got what me and Missis Garvey wants to buy.'

'Buy!' echoed Goree. 'From me?' Then he laughed harshly. 'I reckon you are mistaken about that. I sold out to you, as you yourself expressed it, "lock, stock, and barrel." There isn't even a ramrod left to sell.'

'You've got it; and we 'uns want it. "Take the money," says Missis Garvey, "and buy it fa'r and squar".' '

Goree shook his head. 'The cupboard's bare,' he said.

'We've riz,' pursued the mountaineer, undeflected from his object, 'a heap. We was poor as opossums, and now we could hev folks to dinner every day. We been reco'nized, Missis Garvey says, by the best society. But there's somethin' we need we ain't got. She says it ought to been put in the 'ventory ov the sale, but it 'tain't thar. "Take the money, then," she says, "and buy it fa'r and squar".' '

'Out with it,' said Goree, his racked nerves growing impatient.

Garvey threw his slouch hat upon the table, and leaned forward, fixing his unblinking eyes upon Goree's.

'There's a old feud,' he said, distinctly and slowly, ' 'tween you 'uns and the Coltranes.'

Goree frowned ominously. To speak of his feud to a feudist is a serious breach of the mountain etiquette. The man from 'back yan' ' knew it as well as the lawyer did.

'Na offense,' he went on, 'but purely in the way of business. Missis Garvey hev studied all about feuds. Most of the quality folks in the mountains hev 'em. The Settles and the Goforths, the Rankins and the Boyds, the Silers and the Galloways, hev all been cyarin' on feuds f'om twenty to a hundred year. The last man to drap was when yo uncle, Jedge Paisley Goree, 'journed co't and shot Len Coltrane f'om the bench. Missis Garvey and me, we come f'om the po' white trash. Nobody wouldn't pick a feud with we'uns, no mo'n with a fam'ly of treetoads. Quality people everywhar, says Missis Garvey, has feuds. We 'uns ain't quality, but we're buyin' into as fur as we can. "Take the money, then," says Missis Garvey, "and buy Mr Goree's feud, fa'r and squar'." '

The squirrel hunter straightened a leg half across the room, drew a roll of bills from his pocket, and threw them on the table.

'Thar's two hundred dollars, Mr Goree, what you would call a fa'r price for a feud that's been 'lowed to run down like yourn hev. Thar's only you left to cyar' on yo' side of it, and you'd make mighty po' killin'. I'll take it off yo' hands, and it'll set me and Missis Garvey up among the quality. Thar's the money.'

The little roll of currency on the table slowly untwisted itself, writhing and jumping as its folds relaxed. In the silence that followed Garvey's last speech the rattling of the poker chips in the court-house could be plainly heard. Goree knew that the sheriff had just won a pot, for the subdued whoop with which he always greeted a victory floated across the square upon the crinkly heat waves. Beads of moisture stood on Goree's brow. Stooping, he drew the wicker-covered demijohn from under the table, and filled a tumbler from it.

'A little corn liquor, Mr Garvey? Of course you are joking about – what you spoke of? Opens quite a new market, doesn't it? Feuds, prime, two-fifty to three. Feuds, slightly damaged – two hundred, I believe you said, Mr Garvey.'

The mountaineer took the glass Goree handed him, and drank the whiskey without a tremor of the lids of his staring eyes. The lawyer applauded the feat by a look of envious admiration. He poured his own drink, and took it like a drunkard, by gulps, and with shudders at the smell and taste.

'Two hundred,' repeated Garvey. 'That's the money.'

A sudden passion flared up in Goree's brain. He struck the table with his fist. One of the bills flipped over and touched his hand. He flinched as if something had stung him.

'Do you come to me,' he shouted, 'seriously with such a ridiculous, insulting, darn-fool proposition?'

'It's fa'r and squar',' said the squirrel hunter, but he reached out his hand as if to take back the money; and then Goree knew that his own flurry of rage had not been from pride or resentment, but from anger at himself, knowing that he would set foot in the deeper depths that were being opened to him. He turned in an instant from an outraged gentleman to an anxious chafferer recommending his goods.

'Don't be in a hurry, Garvey,' he said, his face crimson and his speech thick. 'I accept your p-p-proposition, though it's dirt cheap at two hundred. A t-trade's all right when both p-purchaser and b-buyer are s-satisfied. Shall I w-wrap it up for you, Mr Garvey?'

Garvey rose, and shook out his broadcloth. 'Missis Garvey will be pleased. You air out of it, and it stands Coltrane and Garvey. Just a scrap ov writin', Mr Goree, you bein' a lawyer, to show we traded.'

Goree seized a sheet of paper and a pen. The money was clutched in his moist hand. Everything else suddenly seemed to grow trivial and light.

'Bill of sale, by all means. "Right, title, and interest in and to" . . . "forever warrant and –" No, Garvey, we'll have to leave out that "defend," ' said Goree with a loud laugh. 'You'll have to defend this title yourself.'

The mountaineer received the amazing screed that the lawyer handed him, folded it with immense labor, and placed it carefully in his pocket.

Goree was standing near the window. 'Step here,' he said, raising his finger, 'and I'll show you your recently purchased enemy. There he goes, down the other side of the street.'

The mountaineer crooked his long frame to look through the window in the direction indicated by the other. Colonel Abner Coltrane, an erect, portly gentleman of about fifty wearing the inevitable long, double-breasted frock coat of the Southern lawmaker, and an old high silk hat, was passing on the opposite sidewalk. As Garvey looked, Goree glanced at his face. If there be such a thing as a yellow wolf, here was its counterpart. Garvey snarled as his unhuman eyes followed the moving figure, disclosing long amber-colored fangs.

'Is that him? Why, that's the man who sent me to the pen'tentiary once!'

'He used to be district attorney,' said Goree, carelessly. 'And by the way, he's a first-class shot.'

'I kin hit a squirrel's eye at a hundred yard,' said Garvey. 'So that thar's Coltrane! I made a better trade than I was thinkin'. I'll take keer of this feud, Mr Goree, better'n you ever did!'

He moved toward the door, but lingered there, betraying a slight perplexity.

'Anything else to-day?' inquired Goree with frothy sarcasm. 'Any family traditions, ancestral ghosts, or skeletons in the closet? Prices as low as the lowest.'

'Thar was another thing,' replied the unmoved squirrel hunter 'that Missis Garvey was thinkin' of. ''Tain't so much in my line as t'other, but she wanted partic'lar that I should inquire, and ef you was willin', "pay fur it," she says, "fa'r and squar'." Thar's a buryin' groun', as you know, Mr Goree, in the yard of yo' old place, under the cedars. Them that lies thar is yo' folks what was killed by the Coltranes. The monyments has the names on 'em. Missis Garvey says a fam'ly buryin' groun' is a sho' sign of quality. She says ef we git the feud, that's somethin' else ought to go with it. The names on them monyments is "Goree," but they can be changed to ourn by—'

'Go! Go!' screamed Goree, his face turning purple. He stretched out both hands toward the mountaineer, his fingers hooked and shaking. 'Go, you ghoul! Even a Ch-Chinaman protects the g-graves of his ancestors – go!'

The squirrel hunter slouched out of the door to his carryall. While he was climbing over the wheel Goree was collecting, with feverish celerity, the money that had fallen from his hand to the floor. As the vehicle slowly turned about, the sheep with a coat of newly grown wool was hurrying, in indecent haste, along the path to the courthouse.

At three o'clock in the morning they brought him back to his office shorn and unconscious. The sheriff, the sportive deputy, the county clerk, and the gay attorney carried him, the chalk-faced man 'from the valley' acting as escort.

'On the table,' said one of them and they deposited him there among the litter of his unprofitable books and papers.

'Yance thinks a lot of a pair of deuces when he's liquored up,' sighed the sheriff, reflectively.

'Too much,' said the gay attorney. 'A man has no business to play poker who drinks as much as he does. I wonder how much he dropped to-night.'

'Close to two hundred. What I wonder is whar he got it. Yance ain't had a cent fur over a month, I know.'

'Struck a client, maybe. Well, let's get home before daylight. He'll be all right when he wakes up, except for a sort of beehive about the cranium.'

The gang slipped away through the early morning twilight. The next eye to gaze upon the miserable Goree was the orb of day. He peered through the uncurtained window, first deluging the sleeper in a flood of faint gold, but soon pouring upon the mottled red of his flesh a searching, white, summer heat. Goree stirred, half unconsciously, among the table's débris, and turned his face from the window. His movement dislodged a heavy law book, which crashed upon the floor. Opening his eyes, he saw, bending over him, a man in a black frock coat. Looking higher, he discovered a well-worn silk hat, and beneath it the kindly, smooth face of Colonel Abner Coltrane.

A little uncertain of the outcome, the colonel waited for the other to make some sign of recognition. Not in twenty years had male members of these two families faced each other in peace. Goree's eyelids puckered as he strained his blurred sight toward this visitor, and then he smiled serenely.

'Have you brought Stella and Lucy over to play?' he said, calmly.

'Do you know me, Yancey?' asked Coltrane.

'Of course I do. You brought me a whip with a whistle in the end.'

So he had – twenty-four years ago; when Yancey's father was his best friend.

Goree's eyes wandered about the room. The colonel understood. 'Lie still, and I'll bring you some water,' said he. There was a pump in the yard at the rear, and Goree closed his eyes, listening with rapture to the click of its handle and the bubbling of the falling stream. Coltrane brought a pitcher of the cool water, and held it for him to drink. Presently Goree sat up – a most forlorn object, his summer suit of flax soiled and crumpled, his discreditable head tousled and unsteady. He tried to wave one of his hands toward the colonel.

'Ex-excuse – everything, will you?' he said. 'I must have drunk too much whiskey last night, and gone to bed on the table.' His brows knitted into a puzzled frown.

'Out with the boys a while?' asked Coltrane, kindly.

'No, I went nowhere. I haven't had a dollar to spend in the last two months. Struck the demijohn too often, I reckon, as usual.'

Colonel Coltrane touched him on the shoulder.

'A little while ago, Yancey,' he began, 'you asked me if I had brought Stella and Lucy over to play. You weren't quite awake then, and must have been dreaming you were a boy again. You are awake now, and I want you to listen to me. I have come from Stella and Lucy to their old playmate, and to my old friend's son. They know that I am going to bring you home with me, and you will find them as ready with a welcome as they were in the old days. I want you to come to my house and stay until you are yourself again, and as much longer as you will. We heard of your being down in the world, and in the midst of temptation, and we agreed that you should come over and play at our house once more. Will you come, my boy? Will you drop our old family trouble and come with me?'

'Trouble!' said Goree, opening his eyes wide. 'There was never any trouble between us that I know of. I'm sure we've always been the best of friends. But, good Lord, Colonel, how could I go to your home as I am – a drunken wretch, a miserable, degraded spendthrift and gambler –'

He lurched from the table to his armchair, and began to weep maudlin tears, mingled with genuine drops of remorse and shame. Coltrane talked to him persistently and reasonably, reminding him of the simple mountain pleasures of which he had once been so fond, and insisting upon the genuineness of the invitation.

Finally he landed Goree by telling him he was counting upon his help in the engineering and transportation of a large amount of felled timber from a high mountainside to a waterway. He knew that Goree had once invented a device for this purpose – a series of slides and chutes – upon which he had justly prided himself. In an instant the poor fellow, delighted at the idea of his being of use to anyone, had paper spread upon the table, and was drawing rapid but pitifully shaky lines in demonstration of what he could and would do.

The man was sickened of the husks; his prodigal heart was turning again toward the mountains. His mind was yet strangely clogged, and his thoughts and memories were returning to his brain one by one, like carrier pigeons over a stormy sea. But Coltrane was satisfied with the progress he had made.

Bethel received the surprise of its existence that afternoon when a Coltrane and a Goree rode amicably together through the town. Side by side they rode, out from the dusty streets and gaping townspeople, down across the creek bridge, and up toward the mountain. The prodigal had brushed and washed and combed himself to a more decent figure, but he was unsteady in the saddle, and he seemed to be deep in the contemplation of some vexing problem. Coltrane left him in his mood, relying upon the influence of changed surroundings to restore his equilibrium.

Once Goree was seized with a shaking fit, and almost came to a collapse. He had to dismount and rest at the side of the road. The colonel, foreseeing such a condition, had provided a small flask of whiskey for the journey but when it was offered to him Goree refused it almost with violence, declaring he would never touch it again. By and by he was recovered, and went quietly enough for a mile or two. Then he pulled up his horse suddenly, and said:

'I lost two hundred dollars last night, playing poker. Now, where did I get that money?'

'Take it easy, Yancey. The mountain air will soon clear it up. We'll go fishing, first thing, at the Pinnacle Falls. The trout are jumping there like bullfrogs. We'll take Stella and Lucy along, and have a picnic on Eagle Rock. Have you forgotten how a hickory-cured ham sandwich tastes, Yancey, to a hungry fisherman?'

Evidently the colonel did not believe the story of his lost wealth; so Goree retired again into brooding silence.

By late afternoon they had traveled ten of the twelve miles between Bethel and Laurel. Half a mile this side of Laurel lay the old Goree place; a mile or two beyond the village lived the Col-tranes. The road was now steep and laborious, but the compensations were many. The tilted aisles of the forest were opulent with leaf and bird and bloom. The tonic air put to shame the pharmacopia, the glades were dark with mossy shade and bright with shy rivulets winking from the ferns and laurels. On the lower side they viewed, framed in the near foliage, exquisite sketches of the far valley swooning in its opal haze.

Coltrane was pleased to see that his companion was yielding to the spell of the hills and woods. For now they had but to skirt the base of Painter's Cliff, to cross Elder Branch and mount the hill beyond, and Goree would have to face the squandered home of his fathers. Every rock he passed, every tree, every foot of the road-way, was familiar to him. Though he had forgotten the woods, they thrilled him like the music of 'Home, Sweet Home.'

They rounded the cliff, descended into Elder Branch, and paused there to let the horses drink and splash in the swift water. On the right was a rail fence that cornered there, and followed the road and stream. Inclosed by it was the old apple orchard of the home place; the house was yet concealed by the brow of the steep hill. Inside and along the fence, pokeberries, elders, sassafras, and sumac grew high and dense. At a rustle of their branches, both Goree and Coltrane glanced up, and saw a long, yellow, wolfish face above the fence, staring at them with pale, unblinking eyes. The head quickly disappeared; there was a violent swaying of the bushes, and an ungainly figure ran up through the apple orchard in the direction of the house zigzagging among the trees.

'That's Garvey,' said Coltrane; 'the man you sold out to. There's no doubt but he's considerably cracked. I had to send him up for moonshining once, several years ago, in spite of the fact that I believed him irresponsible. Why, what's the matter, Yancey?'

Goree was wiping his forehead, and his face had lost its color. 'Do I look queer, too?' he asked, trying to smile. 'I'm just remembering a few more things.' Some of the alcohol had evaporated from his brain. 'I recollect now where I got that two hundred dollars.'

'Don't think of it,' said Coltrane, cheerfully. 'Later on we'll figure it all out together.'

They rode out of the branch, and when they reached the foot of the hill Goree stopped again.

'Did you ever suspect I was a very vain kind of fellow, Colonel?' he asked. 'Sort of foolish proud about appearances?'

The colonel's eyes refused to wander to the soiled, sagging suit of flax and the faded slouch hat.

'It seems to me,' he replied, mystified, but humoring him, 'I remember a young buck about twenty, with the tightest coat, the sleekest hair, and the prancingest saddle horse in the Blue Ridge.'

'Right you are,' said Goree, eagerly. 'And it's in me yet, though it don't show. Oh, I'm as vain as a turkey gobbler, and as proud as Lucifer. I'm going to ask you to indulge this weakness of mine in a little matter.'

'Speak out, Yancey. We'll create you Duke of Laurel and Baron of Blue Ridge, if you choose; and you shall have a feather out of Stella's peacock's tail to wear in your hat.'

'I'm in earnest. In a few minutes we'll pass the house up there on the hill where I was born, and where my people have lived for nearly a century. Strangers live there now – and look at me! I am about to show myself to them ragged and poverty-stricken, a wastrel and a beggar. Colonel Coltrane, I'm ashamed to do it. I want you to let me wear your coat and hat until we are out of sight beyond. I know you think it a foolish pride, but I want to make as good a showing as I can when I pass the old place.'

'Now, what does this mean?' said Coltrane to himself, as he compared his companion's sane looks and quiet demeanor with his strange request. But he was already unbuttoning the coat, assenting readily, as if the fancy were in no wise to be considered strange.

The coat and hat fitted Goree well. He buttoned the former about him with a look of satisfaction and dignity. He and Coltrane were nearly the same size – rather tall, portly and erect. Twenty-five years were between them, but in appearance they might have been brothers. Goree looked older than his age; his face was puffy and lined; the colonel had the smooth, fresh complexion of a temperate liver. He put on Goree's disreputable old flax coat and faded slouch hat.

'Now,' said Goree, taking up the reins, 'I'm all right. I want you to ride about ten feet in the rear as we go by, Colonel, so that they can get a good look at me. They'll see I'm no back number yet, by any means. I guess I'll show up pretty well to them once more, anyhow. Let's ride on.'

He set out up the hill at a smart trot, the colonel following, as he had been requested.

Goree sat straight in the saddle, with head erect, but his eyes were turned to the right, sharply scanning every shrub and fence and hiding-place in the old homestead yard. Once he muttered to himself, 'Will the crazy fool try it, or did I dream half of it?'

It was when he came opposite the little family burying ground that he saw what he had been looking for – a puff of white smoke, coming from the thick cedars in one corner. He toppled so slowly to the left that Coltrane had time to urge his horse to that side, and catch him with one arm.

The squirrel hunter had not overpraised his arm. He had sent the bullet where he intended, and where Goree had expected that it would pass through the breast of Colonel Abner Coltrane's black frock coat.

Goree leaned heavily against Coltrane, but he did not fall. The horses kept pace, side by side, and the colonel's arm kept him steady. The little white houses of Laurel shone through the trees, half a mile away. Goree reached out one hand and groped until it rested upon Coltrane's fingers, which held his bridle.

'Good friend,' he said, and that was all.

Thus did Yancey Goree, as he rode past his old home, make, considering all things, the best showing that was in his power.

# One Dollar's Worth

The judge of the United States court of the district lying along the Rio Grande border found the following letter one morning in his mail:

Judge:

When you sent me up for four years you made a talk. Among other hard things, you called me a rattlesnake. Maybe I am one – anyhow, you hear me rattling now. One year after I got to the pen, my daughter died of – well, they said it was poverty and the disgrace together. You've got a daughter, Judge, and I'm going to make you know how it feels to lose one. And I'm going to bite that district attorney that spoke against me. I'm free now, and I guess I've turned to rattlesnake all right. I feel like one. I don't say much, but this is my rattle. Look out what I strike.

Yours respectfully,
Rattlesnake

Judge Derwent threw the letter carelessly aside. It was nothing new to receive such epistles from desperate men whom he had been called up to judge. He felt no alarm. Later on he showed the letter to Littlefield, the young district attorney, for Littlefield's name was included in the threat, and the judge was punctilious in matters between himself and his fellow men.

Littlefield honored the rattle of the writer, as far as it concerned himself, with a smile of contempt; but he frowned a little over the reference to the Judge's daughter, for he and Nancy Derwent were to be married in the fall.

Littlefield went to the clerk of the court and looked over the records with him. They decided that the letter might have been sent by Mexico Sam, a half-breed border desperado who had been imprisoned for manslaughter four years before. Then official duties crowded the matter from his mind, and the rattle of the revengeful serpent was forgotten.

Court was in session in Brownsville. Most of the cases to be tried were charges of smuggling, counterfeiting, post-office robberies, and violations of Federal laws along the border. One case was that of a young Mexican, Rafael Ortiz, who had been rounded up by a clever deputy marshal in the act of passing a counterfeit silver dollar. He had been suspected of many such deviations from rectitude, but this was the first time that anything provable had been fixed upon him. Ortiz languished cozily in jail, smoking brown cigarettes and waiting for trial. Kilpatrick, the deputy, brought the counterfeit dollar and handed it to the district attorney in his office in the court-house. The deputy and a reputable druggist were prepared to swear that Ortiz paid for a bottle of medicine with it. The coin was a poor counterfeit, soft, dull-looking, and made principally of lead. It was the day before the morning on which the docket would reach the case of Ortiz, and the district attorney was preparing himself for the trial.

'Not much need of having in high-priced experts to prove the coin's queer, is there, Kil?' smiled Littlefield, as he thumped the dollar down upon the table, where it fell with no more ring than would have come from a lump of putty.

'I guess the Greaser's as good as behind the bars,' said the deputy, easing up his holsters. 'You've got him dead. If it had been just one time, these Mexicans can't tell good money from bad; but this little yaller rascal belongs to a gang of counterfeiters, I know. This is the first time I've been able to catch him doing the trick. He's got a girl down there in them Mexican jacals on the river bank. I seen her one day when I was watching him. She's as pretty as a red heifer in a flower bed.'

Littlefield shoved the counterfeit dollar into his pocket, and slipped his memoranda of the case into an envelope. Just then a bright, winsome face, as frank and jolly as a boy's, appeared in the doorway, and in walked Nancy Derwent.

'Oh, Bob, didn't court adjourn at twelve to-day until to-morrow?' she asked of Littlefield.

'It did,' said the district attorney, 'and I'm very glad of it. I've got a lot of rulings to look up, and –'

'Now, that's just like you. I wonder you and Father don't turn into law books or rulings or something! I want you to take me out plover-shooting this afternoon. Long Prairie is just alive with them. Don't say no, please! I want to try my new twelve-bore hammer-less. I've sent to the livery stable to engage Fly and Bess for the buckboard; they stand fire so nicely. I was sure you would go.'

They were to be married in the fall. The glamour was at its height. The plovers won the day – or, rather, the afternoon – over the calf-bound authorities. Littlefield began to put his papers away.

There was a knock at the door. Kilpatrick answered it. A beautiful, dark-eyed girl with a skin tinged with the faintest lemon color walked into the room. A black shawl was thrown over her head and wound once around her neck.

She began to talk in Spanish, a voluble, mournful stream of melancholy music. Littlefield did not understand Spanish. The deputy did, and he translated her talk by portions, at intervals holding up his hands to check the flow of her words.

'She came to see you, Mr Littlefield. Her name's Joya Treviñas. She wants to see you about – well, she's mixed up with that Rafael Ortiz. She's his – she's his girl. She says he's innocent. She says she made the money and got him to pass it. Don't you believe her, Mr Littlefield. That's the way with these Mexican girls; they'll lie, steal or kill for a fellow when they get stuck on him. Never trust a woman that's in love!'

'Mr Kilpatrick!'

Nancy Derwent's indignant exclamation caused the deputy to flounder for a moment in attempting to explain that he had misquoted his own sentiments, and then he went on with the translation:

'She says she's willing to take his place in the jail if you'll let him out. She says she was down sick with the fever, and the doctor said she'd die if she didn't have medicine. That's why he passed the lead dollar on the drug store. She says it saved her life. This Rafael seems to be her honey, all right; there's a lot of stuff in her talk about love and such things that you don't want to hear.'

It was an old story to the district attorney.

'Tell her,' said he, 'that I can do nothing. The case comes up in the morning, and he will have to make his fight before the court.'

Nancy Derwent was not so hardened. She was looking with sympathetic interest at Joya Treviñas and at Littlefield alternately. The deputy repeated the district attorney's words to the girl. She spoke a sentence or two in a low voice, pulled her shawl closely about her face, and left the room.

'What did she say then?' asked the district attorney.

'Nothing special,' said the deputy. 'She said: "If the life of the one" – let's see how it went – "*Si la vida de ella a quien tu amas* – if the life of the girl you love is ever in danger, remember Rafael Ortiz."'

Kilpatrick strolled out through the corridor in the direction of the marshal's office.

'Can't you do anything for them, Bob?' asked Nancy. 'It's such a little thing – just one counterfeit dollar – to ruin the happiness of two lives! She was in danger of death, and he did it to save her. Doesn't the law know the feeling of pity?'

'It hasn't a place in jurisprudence, Nan,' said Littlefield, 'especially *in re* the district attorney's duty. I'll promise you that the prosecution will not be vindictive; but the man is as good as convicted when the case is called. Witnesses will swear to his passing the bad dollar which I have in my pocket at this moment as "Exhibit A." There are no Mexicans on the jury, and it will vote Mr Greaser guilty without leaving the box.'

The plover-shooting was fine that afternoon, and in the excitement of the sport the case of Rafael and the grief of Joya Treviñas was forgotten. The district attorney and Nancy Derwent drove out from the town three miles along a smooth, grassy road, and then struck across a rolling prairie toward a heavy line of timber on Piedra Creek. Beyond this creek lay Long Prairie, the favorite haunt of the plover. As they were nearing the creek they heard the galloping of a horse to their right, and saw a man with black hair and a swarthy face riding toward the woods at a tangent, as if he had come up behind them.

'I've seen that fellow somewhere,' said Littlefield, who had a memory for faces, 'but I can't exactly place him. Some ranchman, I suppose, taking a short cut home.'

They spent an hour on Long Prairie, shooting from the buckboard. Nancy Derwent, an active, outdoor Western girl, was pleased with her twelve-bore. She had bagged within two brace of her companion's score.

They started homeward at a gentle trot. When within a hundred yards of Piedra Creek a man rode out of the timber directly toward them.

'It looks like the man we saw coming over,' remarked Miss Derwent.

As the distance between them lessened, the district attorney suddenly pulled up his team sharply, with his eyes fixed upon the advancing horseman. That individual had drawn a Winchester from its scabbard on his saddle and thrown it over his arm.

'Now I know you, Mexico Sam!' muttered Littlefield to himself. 'It *was* you who shook your rattles in that gentle epistle.'

Mexico Sam did not leave things long in doubt. He had a nice eye in matters relating to firearms, so when he was within good rifle range, but outside of danger from No. 8 shot, he threw up his Winchester and opened fire upon the occupants of the buckboard.

The first shot cracked the back of the seat within the two-inch space between the shoulders of Littlefield and Miss Derwent. The next went through the dashboard and Littlefield's trouser leg.

The district attorney hustled Nancy out of the buckboard to the ground. She was a little pale, but asked no questions. She had the frontier instinct that accepts conditions in an emergency without superfluous argument. They kept their guns in hand, and Littlefield hastily gathered some handfuls of cartridges from the pasteboard box on the seat and crowded them into his pockets.

'Keep behind the horses, Nan,' he commanded. 'That fellow is a ruffian I sent to prison once. He's trying to get even. He knows our shot won't hurt him at that distance.'

'All right, Bob,' said Nancy, steadily. 'I'm not afraid. But you come close, too. Whoa, Bess; stand still, now!'

She stroked Bess's mane. Littlefield stood with his gun ready, praying that the desperado would come within range.

But Mexico Sam was playing his vendetta along safe lines. He was a bird of different feather from the plover. His accurate eye drew an imaginary line of circumference around the area of danger from the birdshot, and upon this line he rode. His horse wheeled to the right, and as his victims rounded to the safe side of their equine breastwork he sent a ball through the district attorney's hat. Once he miscalculated in making a detour, and overstepped his margin. Littlefield's gun flashed, and Mexico Sam ducked his head to the harmless pattern of the shot. A few of them stung his horse, which pranced promptly back to the safety line.

The desperado fired again. A little cry came from Nancy Derwent. Littlefield whirled, with blazing eyes, and saw the blood trickling down her cheek.

'I'm not hurt, Bob – only a splinter struck me, I think he hit one of the wheel-spokes.'

'Lord!' groaned Littlefield. 'If I only had a charge of buckshot!'

The ruffian got his horse still, and took careful aim. Fly gave a snort and fell in the harness, struck in the neck. Bess, now dis_ abused of the idea that plover were being fired at, broke her traces and galloped wildly away. Mexico Sam sent a ball neatly through the fullness of Nancy Derwent's shooting jacket.

'Lie down – lie down!' snapped Littlefield. 'Close to the horse – flat on the ground – so.' He almost threw her upon the grass against the back of the recumbent Fly. Oddly enough, at that moment the words of the Mexican girl returned to his mind:

'If the life of the girl you love is ever in danger, remember Rafael Ortiz.'

Littlefield uttered an exclamation.

'Open fire on him, Nan, across the horse's back! Fire as fast as you can! You can't hurt him, but keep him dodging shot for one minute while I try to work a little scheme.'

Nancy gave a quick glance at Littlefield and saw him take out his pocket-knife and open it. Then she turned her face to obey orders, keeping up a rapid fire at the enemy.

Mexico Sam waited patiently until this innocuous fusillade ceased. He had plenty of time, and he did not care to risk the chance of a bird-shot in his eye if it could be avoided by a little caution. He pulled his heavy Stetson low down over his face until the shots ceased. Then he drew a little nearer, and fired with careful aim at what he could see of his victims above the fallen horse.

Neither of them moved. He urged his horse a few steps nearer. He saw the district attorney rise to one knee, and deliberately level his shotgun. He pulled his hat down and awaited the harmless rattle of the tiny pellets.

The shotgun blazed with a heavy report. Mexico Sam sighed, turned limp all over, and slowly fell from his horse – a dead rattlesnake.

*

At ten o'clock the next morning court opened, and the case of the United States *versus* Rafael Ortiz was called. The district attorney, with his arm in a sling, rose and addressed the court.

'May it please your honor,' he said, 'I desire to enter a *nolle pros.* in this case. Even though the defendant should be guilty, there is not sufficient evidence in the hands of the government to secure a conviction. The piece of counterfeit coin upon the identity of which the case was built is not now available as evidence. I ask, therefore, that the case be stricken off.'

At the noon recess, Kilpatrick strolled into the district attorney's office.

'I've just been down to take a squint at old Mexico Sam,' said the deputy. 'They've got him laid out. Old Mexico was a tough outfit, I reckon. The boys was wonderin' down there what you shot him with. Some said it must have been nails. I never see a gun carry anything to make holes like he had.'

'I shot him,' said the district attorney, 'with Exhibit A of your counterfeiting case. Lucky thing for me – and somebody else – that it was as bad money as it was! It sliced up into slugs very nicely. Say, Kil, can't you go down to the jacals and find where that Mexican girl lives? Miss Derwent wants to know.'

# A Chaparral Christmas Gift

The original cause of the trouble was about twenty years in growing. At the end of that time it was worth it.

Had you lived anywhere within fifty miles of Sundown Ranch you would have heard of it. It possessed a quantity of jet-black hair, a pair of extremely frank, deep-brown eyes and a laugh that rippled across the prairie like the sound of a hidden brook. The name of it was Rosita McMullen; and she was the daughter of old man McMullen of the Sundown Sheep Ranch.

There came riding on red roan steeds or, to be more explicit, on a paint and a flea-bitten sorrel – two wooers. One was Madison Lane, and the other was the Frio Kid. But at that time they did not call him the Frio Kid, for he had not earned the honours of special nomenclature. His name was simply Johnny McRoy.

It must not be supposed that these two were the sum of the agreeable Rosita's admirers. The broncos of a dozen others champed their bits at the long hitching rack of the Sundown Ranch. Many were the sheeps'-eyes that were cast in those savannas that did not belong to the flocks of Dan McMullen. But of all the cavaliers, Madison Lane and Johnny McRoy galloped far ahead, wherefore they are to be chronicled.

Madison Lane, a young cattleman from the Nueces country, won the race. He and Rosita were married one Christmas Day. Armed, hilarious, vociferous, magnanimous, the cowmen and the sheepmen, laying aside their hereditary hatred, joined forces to celebrate the occasion.

Sundown Ranch was sonorous with the cracking of jokes and sixshooters, the shine of buckles and bright eyes, the outspoken congratulations of the herders of kine.

But while the wedding feast was at its liveliest there descended upon it Johnny McRoy, bitten by jealousy, like one possessed.

'I'll give you a Christmas present,' he yelled, shrilly, at the door, with his .45 in his hand. Even then he had some reputation as an offhand shot.

His first bullet cut a neat underbit in Madison Lane's right ear. The barrel of his gun moved an inch. The next shot would have been the bride's had not Carson, a sheepman, possessed a mind with triggers somewhat well oiled and in repair. The guns of the wedding party had been hung, in their belts, upon nails in the wall when they sat at table, as a concession to good taste. But Carson, with great promptness, hurled his plate of roast venison and frijoles at McRoy, spoiling his aim. The second bullet, then, only shattered the white petals of a Spanish dagger flower suspended two feet above Rosita's head.

The guests spurned their chairs and jumped for their weapons. It was considered an improper act to shoot the bride and groom at a wedding. In about six seconds there were twenty or so bullets due to be whizzing in the direction of Mr McRoy.

'I'll shoot better next time,' yelled Johnny; 'and there'll be a next time.' He backed rapidly out the door.

Carson, the sheepman, spurred on to attempt further exploits by the success of his plate-throwing, was first to reach the door. McRoy's bullet from the darkness laid him low.

The cattlemen then swept out upon him, calling for vengeance, for, while the slaughter of a sheepman has not always lacked condonement, it was a decided misdemeanour in this instance. Carson was innocent; he was no accomplice at the matrimonial proceedings; nor had any one heard him quote the line 'Christmas comes but once a year' to the guests.

But the sortie failed in its vengeance. McRoy was on his horse and away, shouting back curses and threats as he galloped into the concealing chaparral.

That night was the birthnight of the Frio Kid. He became the 'bad man' of that portion of the State. The rejection of his suit by Miss McMullen turned him to a dangerous man. When officers went after him for the shooting of Carson, he killed two of them, and entered upon the life of an outlaw. He became a marvellous shot with either hand. He would turn up in towns and settlements, raise a quarrel at the slightest opportunity, pick off his man and laugh at the officers of the law. He was so cool, so deadly, so rapid, so inhumanly blood-thirsty that none but faint attempts were ever made to capture him. When he was at last shot and killed by a little one-armed Mexican who was nearly dead himself from fright, the Frio Kid had the deaths of eighteen men on his head. About half of these were killed in fair duds depending upon the quickness of the draw. The other half were men whom he assassinated from absolute wantonness and cruelty.

Many tales are told along the border of his impudent courage and daring. But he was not one of the breed of desperadoes who have seasons of generosity and even of softness. They say he never had mercy on the object of his anger. Yet at this and every Christmastide it is well to give each one credit, if it can be done, for whatever speck of good he may have possessed. If the Frio Kid ever did a kindly act or felt a throb of generosity in his heart it was once at such a time and season, and this is the way it happened.

One who has been crossed in love should never breathe the odour from the blossoms of the ratama tree. It stirs the memory to a dangerous degree.

One December in the Frio country there was a ratama tree in full bloom, for the winter had been as warm as springtime. That way rode the Frio Kid and his satellite and co-murderer, Mexican Frank. The Kid reined in his mustang, and sat in his saddle, thoughtful and grim, with dangerously narrowing eyes. The rich, sweet scent touched him somewhere beneath his ice and iron.

'I don't know what I've been thinking about, Mex,' he remarked in his usual mild drawl, 'to have forgot all about a Christmas present I got to give. I'm going to ride over tomorrow night and shoot Madison Lane in his own house. He got my girl Rosita would have had me if he hadn't cut into the game. I wonder why I happened to overlook it up to now?' 'Ah, shucks, Kid,' said Mexican, 'don't talk foolishness. You know you can't get within a mile of Mad Lane's house tomorrow night. I see old man Allen day before yesterday, and he says Mad is going to have Christmas doings at his house. You remember how you shot up the festivities when Mad was married, and about the threats you made? Don't you suppose Mad Lane'll kind of keep his eye open for a certain Mr Kid? You plumb make me tired, Kid, with such remarks.'

'I'm going,' repeated the Frio Kid, without heat, 'to go to Madison Lane's Christmas doings, and kill him. I ought to have done it a long time ago. Why, Mex, just two weeks ago I dreamed me and Rosita was married instead of her and him: and we was living in a house, and I could see her smiling at me, and – oh! h—l, Mex, he got her: and I'll get him – yes, sir, on Christmas Eve he got her, and then's when I'll get him.'

'There's other ways of committing suicide,' advised the Mexican. 'Why don't you go and surrender to the sheriff?'

'I'll get him,' said the Kid.

Christmas Eve fell as balmy as April. Perhaps there was a hint of faraway frostiness in the air, but it tingled like seltzer, perfumed faintly with late prairie blossoms and the mesquite grass.

When night came the five or six rooms of the ranch-house were brightly lit. In one room was a Christmas tree, for the Lanes had a boy of three, and a dozen or more guests were expected from the nearer ranches.

At nightfall Madison Lane called aside Jim Belcher and three other cowboys employed on his ranch.

'Now, boys,' said Lane, 'keep your eyes open. Walk around the house and watch the road well. All of you know the "Frio Kid", as they call him now, and if you see him, open fire on him without asking any questions. I'm not afraid of his coming around, but Rosita is. She's been afraid he'd come in on us every Christmas since we were married.'

The guests had arrived in buckboards and on horseback, and were making themselves comfortable inside.

The evening went along pleasantly. The guests enjoyed and praised Rosita's excellent supper, and afterward the men scattered in groups about the rooms or on the broad 'gallery', smoking and chatting.

The Christmas tree, of course, delighted the youngsters, and above all were they pleased when Santa Claus himself in magnificent white beard and furs appeared and began to distribute the toys.

'It's my papa,' announced Billy Sampson, aged six. 'I've seen him wear 'em before.'

Berkly, a sheepman, an old friend of Lane, stopped Rosita as she was passing by him on the gallery, where he was sitting smoking.

'Well, Mrs Lane,' said he, 'I suppose by this Christmas you've gotten over being afraid of that fellow McRoy, haven't you? Madison and I have talked about it, you know.'

'Very nearly,' said Rosita, smiling, 'but I am still nervous sometimes. I shall never forget that awful time when he came so near to killing us.'

'He's the most cold-hearted villain in the world,' said Berkly. 'The citizens all along the border ought to turn out and hunt him down like a wolf.'

'He has committed awful crimes,' said Rosita, 'but – I – don't – know. I think there is a spot of good somewhere in everybody. He was not always bad – that I know.'

Rosita turned into the hallway between the rooms. Santa Claus, in muffling whiskers and furs, was just coming through.

'I heard what you said through the window, Mrs Lane,' he said.

'I was just going down in my pocket for a Christmas present for your husband. But I've left one for you, instead. It's in the room to your right.'

'Oh, thank you, kind Santa Claus,' said Rosita, brightly.

Rosita went into the room, while Santa Claus stepped into the cooler air of the yard.

She found no one in the room but Madison.

'Where is my present that Santa said he left for me in here?' she asked.

'Haven't seen anything in the way of a present,' said her husband, laughing, 'unless he could have meant me.'

The next day Gabriel Radd, the foreman of the XO Ranch, dropped into the post-office at Loma Alta.

'Well, the Frio Kid's got his dose of lead at last,' he remarked to the postmaster.

'That so? How'd it happen?'

'One of old Sanchez's Mexican sheep herders did it! – think of it! the Frio Kid killed by a sheep herder! The Greaser saw him riding along past his camp about twelve o'clock last night, and was so skeered that he up with a Winchester and let him have it. Funniest part of it was that the Kid was dressed all up with white Angora-skin whiskers and a regular Santy Claus rig-out from head to foot. Think of the Frio Kid playing Santy!'

# Out of Nazareth

Okochee, in Georgia, had a boom, and J. Pinkney Bloom came out of it with a 'wad.' Okochee came out of it with a half-million-dollar debt, a two and a half per cent city property tax, and a city council that showed a propensity for traveling the back streets of the town. These things came about through a fatal resemblance of the river Cooloosa to the Hudson, as set forth and expounded by a Northern tourist. Okochee felt that New York should not be allowed to consider itself the only alligator in the swamp, so to speak. And then that harmless, but persistent, individual so numerous in the South – the man who is always clamoring for more cotton mills, and is ready to take a dollar's worth of stock, provided he can borrow the dollar – that man added his deadly work to the tourist's innocent praise, and Okochee fell.

The Cooloosa River winds through a range of small mountains, passes Okochee, and then blends its waters trippingly, as fall the mellifluous Indian syllables, with the Chattahoochee.

Okochee rose, as it were, from its sunny seat on the post-office stoop, hitched up its suspender, and threw a granite dam two hundred and forty feet long and sixty feet high across the Cooloosa one mile above the town. Thereupon, a dimpling, sparkling lake backed up twenty miles among the little mountains. Thus in the great game of municipal rivalry did Okochee match that famous drawing card, the Hudson. It was conceded that nowhere could the Palisades be judged superior in the way of scenery and grandeur. Following the picture card was played the ace of commercial importance. Fourteen thousand horsepower would this dam furnish. Cotton mills, factories, and manufacturing plants would rise up as the green corn after a shower. The spindle and the flywheel and turbine would sing the shrewd glory of Okochee. Along the picturesque heights above the lake would rise in beauty the costly villas and the splendid summer residences of capital. The naphtha launch of the millionaire would spit among the romantic coves; the verdured hills would take formal shapes of terrace, lawn, and park. Money would be spent like water in Okochee, and water would be turned into money.

The fate of the good town is quickly told. Capital decided not to invest. Of all the great things promised, the scenery alone came to fulfilment. The wooded peaks, the impressive promontories of solemn granite, the beautiful green slants of bank and ravine did all they could to reconcile Okochee to the delinquency of miserly gold. The sunsets gilded the dreamy draws and coves with a minting that should charm away heart-burning. Okochee, true to the instinct of its blood and clime, was lulled by the spell. It climbed out of the arena, loosed its suspender, sat down again on the post-office stoop, and took a chew. It consoled itself by drawling sarcasms at the city council which was not to blame, causing the fathers, as has been said, to seek back streets and figure perspiringly on the sinking fund and the appropriation for interest due.

The youth of Okochee – they who were to carry into the rosy future the burden of the debt – accepted failure with youth's uncalculating joy. For, here was sport, aquatic and nautical, added to the meagre round of life's pleasures. In yachting caps and flowing neckties they pervaded the lake to its limits. Girls wore silk waists embroidered with anchors in blue and pink. The trousers of the young men widened at the bottom, and their hands were proudly calloused by the oft-plied oar. Fishermen were under the spell of a deep and tolerant joy. Sailboats and rowboats furrowed the lenient waves, popcorn and ice-cream booths sprang up about the little wooden pier. Two small excursion steamboats were built, and plied the delectable waters. Okochee philosphically gave up the hope of eating turtle soup with a gold spoon, and settled back, not ill content, to its regular diet of lotus and fried hominy. And out of this slow wreck of great expectations rose up J. Pinkney Bloom with his 'wad' and his prosperous, cheery smile.

Needless to say J. Pinkney was no product of Georgia soil. He came out of that flushed and capable region known as the 'North.' He called himself a 'promoter'; his enemies had spoken of him as a 'grafter'; Okochee took a middle course, and held him to be no better or no worse than a 'Yank.'

Far up the lake – eighteen miles above the town – the eye of this cheerful camp-follower of booms had spied out a graft. He purchased there a precipitous tract of five hundred acres at forty-five cents per acre; and this he laid out and subdivided as the city of Skyland – the Queen City of the Switzerland of the South. Streets and avenues were surveyed; parks designed; corners of central squares reserved for the 'proposed' opera house, board of trade, lyceum, market, public schools, and 'Exposition Hall.' The price of lots ranged from five to five hundred dollars. Positively, no lot would be priced higher than five hundred dollars.

While the boom was growing in Okochee, J. Pinkney's circulars, maps, and prospectuses were flying through the mails to every part of the country. Investors sent in their money by post, and the Skyland Real Estate Company (J. Pinkney Bloom) returned to each a deed, duly placed on record, to the best lot, at a price, on hand that day. All this time the catamount screeched upon the reserved lot of the Skyland Board of Trade, the opossum swung by his tail over the site of the exposition hall, and the owl hooted a melancholy recitative to his audience of young squirrels in opera house square. Later, when the money was coming in fast, J. Pinkney caused to be erected in the coming city half a dozen cheap box houses, and persuaded a contingent of indigent natives to occupy them, thereby assuming the rôle of 'population' in subsequent prospectuses, which became, accordingly, more seductive and remunerative.

So, when the dream faded and Okochee dropped back to digging bait and nursing its two and a half per cent tax, J. Pinkney

Bloom (unloving of checks and the cold interrogatories of bankers) strapped about his fifty-two-inch waist a soft leather belt containing eight thousand dollars in big bills, and said that all was very good.

One last trip he was making to Skyland before departing to other salad fields. Skyland was a regular post-office, and the steamboat, *Dixie Belle*, under contract, delivered the mail bag (generally empty) twice a week. There was a little business there to be settled – the postmaster was to be paid off for his light but lonely services, and the 'inhabitants' had to be furnished with another month's homely rations, as per agreement. And then Skyland would know J. Pinkney Bloom no more. The owners of these precipitous, barren, useless lots might come and view the scene of their invested credulity, or they might leave them to their fit tenants, the wild hog and the browsing deer. The work of the Skyland Real Estate Company was finished.

The little steamboat *Dixie Belle* was about to shove off on her regular up-the-lake trip, when a rickety hired carriage rattled up to the pier, and a tall, elderly gentleman, in black, stepped out, signaling courteously but vivaciously for the boat to wait. Time was of the least importance in the schedule of the *Dixie Belle*; Captain MacFarland gave the order, and the boat received its ultimate two passengers. For, upon the arm of the tall, elderly gentleman, as he crossed the gangway, was a little elderly lady, with a gray curl depending quaintly forward of her left ear.

Captain MacFarland was at the wheel; therefore it seemed to J. Pinkney Bloom, who was the only other passenger, that it should be his to play the part of host to the boat's new guests, who were, doubtless, on a scenery-viewing expedition. He stepped forward, with that translucent, child-candid smile upon his fresh, pink countenance, with that air of unaffected sincerity that was redeemed from bluffness only by its exquisite calculation, with that promptitude and masterly decision of manner that so well suited his calling – with all his stock in trade well to the front, he stepped forward to receive Colonel and Mrs Peyton Blaylock. With the grace of a grand marshal or a wedding usher, he escorted the two passengers to the side of the upper deck, from which the scenery was supposed to present itself to the observer in increased quantity and quality. There, in comfortable steamer chairs, they sat and began to piece together the random lines that were to form an intelligent paragraph in the big history of little events.

'Our home, sir,' said Colonel Blaylock, removing his wide-brimmed, rather shapeless black felt hat, 'is in Holly Springs – Holly Springs, Georgia. I am very proud to make your acquaintance, Mr Bloom. Mrs Blaylock and myself have just arrived in Okochee this morning, sir, on business – business of importance in connection with the recent rapid march of progress in this section of our state.'

The Colonel smoothed back, with a sweeping gesture, his long, smooth, gray locks. His dark eyes, still fiery under the heavy black brows, seemed inappropriate to the face of a business man. He looked rather to be an old courtier handed down from the reign of Charles, and re-attired in a modern suit of fine, but raveling and seam-worn, broadcloth.

'Yes, sir,' said Mr Bloom, in his heartiest prospectus voice, 'things have been whizzing around Okochee. Biggest industrial revival and waking up to natural resources Georgia ever had. Did you happen to squeeze in on the ground floor in any of the gilt-edged grafts, Colonel?'

'Well, sir,' said the Colonel, hesitating in courteous doubt, 'if I understand your question, I may say that I took the opportunity to make an investment that I believe will prove quite advantageous – yes, sir, I believe it will result in both pecuniary profit and agreeable occupation.'

'Colonel Blaylock,' said the little elderly lady, shaking her gray curl and smiling indulgent explanation at J. Pinkney Bloom, 'is so devoted to business. He has such a talent for financiering and markets and investments and those kinds of thing. I think myself extremely fortunate in having secured him for a partner on life's journey – I am so unversed in those formidable but very useful branches of learning.'

Colonel Blaylock rose and made a bow – a bow that belonged with silk stockings and lace ruffles and velvet.

'Practical affairs,' he said, with a wave of his hand toward the promoter, 'are, if I may use the comparison, the garden walks upon which we tread through life, viewing upon either side of us the flowers which brighten that journey. It is my pleasure to be able to lay out a walk or two. Mrs Blaylock, sir, is one of those fortunate higher spirits whose mission it is to make the flowers grow. Perhaps, Mr Bloom, you have perused the lines of Lorella, the Southern poetess. That is the name above which Mrs Blaylock has contributed to the press of the South for many years.'

'Unfortunately,' said Mr Bloom, with a sense of the loss clearly written upon his frank face, 'I'm like the Colonel – in the walk-making business myself – and I haven't had time to even take a sniff at the flowers. Poetry is a line I never dealt in. It must be nice, though – quite nice.'

'It is the region,' smiled Mrs Blaylock, 'in which my soul dwells. My shawl, Peyton, if you please – the breeze comes a little chilly from yon verdured hills.'

The Colonel drew from the tail pocket of his coat a small shawl of knitted silk and laid it solicitously about the shoulders of the lady. Mrs Blaylock sighed contentedly, and turned her expressive eyes – still as clear and unworldly as a child's – upon the steep slopes that were slowly slipping past. Very fair and stately they looked in the clear morning air. They seemed to speak in familiar terms to the responsive spirit of Lorella. 'My native hills!' she murmured, dreamily. 'See how the foliage drinks the sunlight from the hollows and dells.'

'Mrs Blaylock's maiden days,' said the Colonel, interpreting her mood to J. Pinkney Bloom, 'were spent among the mountains of northern Georgia. Mountain air and mountain scenery recall to her those days. Holly Springs, where we have lived for twenty years, is low and flat. I fear that she may have suffered in health and spirits by so long a residence there. That is one potent reason for the change we are making. My dear, can you not recall those lines you wrote – entitled, I think, "The Georgia Hills" – the poem that was so extensively copied by the Southern press and praised so highly by the Atlanta critics?'

Mrs Blaylock turned a glance of speaking tenderness upon the Colonel, fingered for a moment the silvery curl that drooped upon her bosom, then looked again toward the mountains. Without preliminary or affection or demurral she began, in rather thrilling and more deeply pitched tones, to recite these lines:

> 'The Georgia hills, the Georgia hills! –
> Oh, heart, why dost thou pine?
> Are not these sheltered lowlands fair
> With mead and bloom and vine?
>
> Ah! as the slow-paced river here
> Broods on its natal rills
> My spirit drifts, in longing sweet,
> Back to the Georgia hills.
>
> 'And through the close-drawn, curtained night I steal on
> sleep's slow wings
> Back to my heart's ease – slopes of pine –
> Where end my wanderings.
>
> Oh, heaven seems nearer from their tops –
> And farther earthly ills –
> Even in dreams, if I may but
> Dream of my Georgia hills.
>
> 'The grass upon their orchard sides
> Is a fine couch to me;

> *The common note of each small bird*
> *Passes all minstrelsy.*
>
> *It would not seem so dread a thing*
> *If, when the Reaper wills,*
> *He might come there and take my hand*
> *Up in the Georgia hills.'*

'That's great stuff, ma'am,' said J. Pinkney Bloom, enthusiastically, when the poetess had concluded. 'I wish I had looked up poetry more than I have. I was raised in the pine hills myself.'

'The mountains ever call to their children,' murmured Mrs Blaylock. 'I feel that life will take on the rosy hue of hope again in among these beautiful hills. Peyton – a little taste of the currant wine, if you will be so good. The journey, though delightful in the extreme, slightly fatigues me.'

Colonel Blaylock again visited the depths of his prolific coat, and produced a tightly corked, rough, black bottle. Mr Bloom was on his feet in an instant. 'Let me bring a glass, ma'am. You come along, Colonel – there's a little table we can bring, too. Maybe we can scare up some fruit or a cup of tea on board. I'll ask Mac.'

Mrs Blaylock reclined at ease. Few royal ladies have held their royal prerogative with the serene grace of the petted Southern woman. The Colonel, with an air as gallant and assiduous as in the days of his courtship, and J. Pinkney Bloom, with a ponderous agility half professional and half directed by some resurrected, unnamed, long-forgotten sentiment, formed a diversified but attentive court. The currant wine – wine home-made from the Holly Springs fruit – went round; and then J. Pinkney began to hear something of Holly Springs life.

It seemed (from the conversation of the Blaylocks) that the Springs was decadent. A third of the population had moved away. Business – and the Colonel was an authority on business – had dwindled to nothing. After carefully studying the field of opportunities open to capital he had sold his little property there for eight hundred dollars and invested it in one of the enterprises opened up by the book in Okochee.

'Might I inquire, sir,' said Mr Bloom, 'in what particular line of business you inserted your coin? I know that town as well as I know the regulations for illegal use of the mails. I might give you a hunch as to whether you can make the game go or not.'

J. Pinkney, somehow, had a kindly feeling toward these unsophisticated representatives of by-gone days. They were so simple, impractical, and unsuspecting. He was glad that he happened not to have a gold brick or a block of that western Bad Boy Silver Mine stock along with him. He would have disliked to unload on people he liked so well as he did these; but there are some temptations too enticing to be resisted.

'No, sir,' said Colonel Blaylock, pausing to arrange the queen's wrap. 'I did not invest in Okochee. I have made an exhaustive study of business conditions, and I regard old settled towns as unfavorable fields in which to place capital that is limited in amount. Some months ago, through the kindness of a friend, there came into my hands a map and description of this new town of Skyland that has been built upon the lake. The description was so pleasing, the future of the town set forth in such an attractive style that I decided to take advantage of the opportunity it offered. I carefully selected a lot in the center of the business district, although its price was the highest in the schedule – five hundred dollars – and made the purchase at once.'

'Are you the man – I mean, did you pay five hundred dollars for a lot in Skyland?' asked J. Pinkney Bloom.

'I did, sir,' answered the Colonel, with the air of a modest millionaire explaining his successes; 'a lot most excellently situated on the same square with the opera house, and only two squares from the board of trade. I consider the purchase a most fortuitous one. It is my intention to erect a small building upon it at once, and open a modest book and stationery store. During past years I have met with many pecuniary reverses, and I now find it necessary to engage in some commercial occupation that will furnish me with a livelihood. The book and stationery business, though an humble one, seems to me not inapt nor altogether uncongenial. I am a graduate of the University of Virginia; and Mrs Blaylock's really wonderful acquaintance with belles-lettres and poetic literature should go far toward insuring success. Of course, Mrs Blaylock would not personally serve behind the counter. With the nearly three hundred dollars I have remaining I can manage the building of a house, by giving a lien on the lot. I have an old friend in Atlanta who is a partner in a large book store, and he has agreed to furnish me with a stock of goods on credit, on extremely easy terms. I am pleased to hope, sir, that Mrs Blaylock's health and happiness will be increased by the change of locality. Already I fancy I can perceive the return of those roses that were once the hope and despair of Georgia cavaliers.'

Again followed that wonderful bow, as the Colonel lightly touched the pale cheek of the poetess. Mrs Blaylock, blushing like a girl, shook her curl and gave the Colonel an arch, reproving tap. Secret of eternal youth – where art thou? Every second the answer comes – 'Here, here, here.' Listen to thine own heart-beats, O weary seeker after external miracles.

'Those years,' said Mrs Blaylock, 'in Holly Springs were long, long, long. But now is the promised land in sight. Skyland! – a lovely name.'

'Doubtless,' said the Colonel, 'we shall be able to secure comfortable accommodations at some modest hotel at reasonable rates. Our trunks are in Okochee, to be forwarded when we shall have made permanent arrangements.'

J. Pinkney Bloom excused himself, went forward, and stood by the captain at the wheel.

'Mac,' said he, 'do you remember my telling you once that I sold one of those five-hundred-dollar lots in Skyland?'

'Seems I do,' grinned Captain MacFarland.

'I'm not a coward, as a general rule,' went on the promoter, 'but I always said that if I ever met the sucker that bought that lot I'd run like a turkey. Now, you see that old babe-in-the-wood over there? Well, he's the boy that drew the prize. That was the only five-hundred-dollar lot that went. The rest ranged from ten dollars to two hundred. His wife writes poetry. She's invented one about the high grounds of Georgia, that's way up in G. They're going to Skyland to open a book store.'

'Well,' said MacFarland with another grin, 'it's a good thing you are along, J.P.; you can show 'em around town until they begin to feel at home.'

'He's got three hundred dollars left to build a house and store with,' went on J. Pinkney, as if he were talking to himself. 'And he thinks there's an opera house up there.'

Captain MacFarland released the wheel long enough to give his leg a roguish slap.

'You old fat rascal!' he chuckled, with a wink.

'Mac, you're a fool,' said J. Pinkney Bloom, coldly. He went back and joined the Blaylocks, where he sat, less talkative, with that straight furrow between his brows that always stood as a signal of schemes being shaped within.

'There's a good many swindles connected with these booms,' he said presently. 'What if this Skyland should turn out to be one – that is, suppose business should be sort of dull there, and no special sale for books?'

'My dear sir,' said Colonel Blaylock, resting his hand upon the back of his wife's chair, 'three times I have been reduced almost to penury by the duplicity of others, but I have not yet lost faith in humanity. If I have been deceived again, still we may glean health and content, if not worldly profit. I am aware that there are dishonest schemers in the world who set traps for the unwary, but even they are not altogether bad. My dear, can you recall those verses entitled, "He Giveth the

Increase," that you composed for the choir of our church in Holly Springs?'

'That was four years ago,' said Mrs Blaylock; 'perhaps I can repeat a verse or two.'

> *'The lily springs from the rotting mould;*
> *Pearls from the deep sea slime;*
> *Good will come out of Nazareth*
> *All in God's own time.*
>
> *'To the hardest heart the softening grace*
> *Cometh, at last, to bless;*
> *Guiding it right to help and cheer*
> *And succor in distress.*

'I cannot remember the rest. The lines were not ambitious. They were written to the music composed by a dear friend.'

'It's a fine rhyme, just the same,' declared Mr Bloom. 'It seems to ring the bell, all right. I guess I gather the sense of it. It means that the rankest kind of a phony will give you the best end of it once in a while.'

Mr Bloom strayed thoughtfully back to the captain, and stood meditating.

'Ought to be in sight of the spires and gilded domes of Skyland now in a few minutes,' chirruped MacFarland, shaking with enjoyment.

'Go to the devil,' said Mr Bloom, still pensive.

And now, upon the left bank, they caught a glimpse of a white village, high up on the hills, smothered among green trees. That was Cold Branch – no boom town, but the slow growth of many years. Cold Branch lay on the edge of the grape and corn lands. The big country road ran just back of the heights. Cold Branch had nothing in common with the frisky ambition of Okochee with its impertinent lake.

'Mac,' said J. Pinkney suddenly, 'I want you to stop at Cold Branch. There's a landing there that they made to use sometimes when the river was up.'

'Can't,' said the captain, grinning more broadly. 'I've got the United States mails on board. Right to-day this boat's in the government service. Do you want to have the poor old captain keelhauled by Uncle Sam? And the great city of Skyland all disconsolate, waiting for its mail? I'm ashamed of your extravagance, J.P.'

'Mac,' almost whispered J. Pinkney, in his danger-line voice, 'I looked into the engine room of the *Dixie Belle* a while ago. Don't you know of somebody that needs a new boiler? Cement and black japan can't hide flaws from me. And then, those shares of building and loan that you traded for repairs – they were all yours, of course. I hate to mention these things, but –'

'Oh, come now, J.P.,' said the captain. 'You know I was just fooling. I'll put you off at Cold Branch, if you say so.'

'The other passengers get off there, too,' said Mr Bloom.

Further conversation was held, and in ten minutes the *Dixie Belle* turned her nose toward a little, cranky wooden pier on the left bank, and the captain, relinquishing the wheel to a roustabout, came to the passenger deck and made the remarkable announcement: 'All out for the Skyland.'

The Blaylocks and J. Pinkney Bloom disembarked, and the *Dixie Belle* proceeded on her way up the lake. Guided by the indefatigable promoter, they slowly climbed the steep hillside, pausing often to rest and admire the view. Finally they entered the village of Cold Branch. Warmly both the Colonel and his wife praised it for its homelike and peaceful beauty. Mr Bloom conducted them to a two-story building on a shady street that bore the legend, 'Pinetop Inn.' Here he took his leave, receiving the cordial thanks of the two for his attentions, the Colonel remarking that he thought they would spend the remainder of the day in rest, and take a look at his purchase on the morrow.

J. Pinkney Bloom walked down Cold Branch's main street.

He did not know this town, but he knew towns, and his feet did not falter. Presently he saw a sign over a door: 'Frank E. Cooly, Attorney-At-Law and Notary Public.' A young man was Mr Cooly, and awaiting business.

'Get your hat, son,' said Mr Bloom, in his breezy way, 'and a blank deed and come along. It's a job for you.'

'Now,' he continued, when Mr Cooly had responded with alacrity, 'is there a bookstore in town?'

'One,' said the lawyer. 'Henry Williams's.'

'Get there,' said Mr Bloom. 'We're going to buy it.'

Henry Williams was behind his counter. His store was a small one, containing a mixture of books, stationery, and fancy rubbish. Adjoining it was Henry's home – a decent cottage, vine-embowered and cosy. Henry was lank and soporific, and not inclined to rush his business.

'I want to buy your house and store,' said Mr Bloom. 'I haven't got time to dicker – name your price.'

'It's worth eight hundred,' said Henry, too much dazed to ask more than its value.

'Shut that door,' said Mr Bloom to the lawyer. Then he tore off his coat and vest, and began to unbutton his shirt.

'Wanter fight about it, do yer?' said Henry Williams, jumping up and cracking his heels together twice. 'All right, hunky – sail in and cut yer capers.'

'Keep your clothes on,' said Mr Bloom. 'I'm only going down to the bank.'

He drew eight one-hundred-dollar bills from his money belt and planked them down on the counter. Mr Cooly showed signs of future promise, for he already had the deed spread out, and was reaching across the counter for the ink bottle. Never before or since was such quick action had in Cold Branch.

'Your name, please?' asked the lawyer.

'Make it out to Peyton Blaylock,' said Mr Bloom. 'God knows how to spell it.'

Within thirty minutes Henry Williams was out of business, and Mr Bloom stood on the brick sidewalk with Mr Cooly, who held in his hand the signed and attested deed.

'You'll find the party at the Pinetop Inn,' said J. Pinkney Bloom. 'Get it recorded, and take it down and give it to him. He'll ask you a hell's mint of questions; so here's ten dollars for the trouble you'll have in not being able to answer 'em. Never ran much to poetry, did you, young man?'

'Well,' said the really talented Cooly, who even yet retained his right mind, 'now and then.'

'Dig into it,' said Mr Bloom, 'it'll pay you. Never heard a poem, now, that ran something like this did you? –

> *'A good thing out of Nazareth*
> *Comes up sometimes, I guess*
> *On hand, all right, to help and cheer*
> *A sucker in distress.'*

'I believe not,' said Mr Cooly.

'It's a hymn,' said J. Pinkney Bloom. 'Now, show me the way to a livery stable, son, for I'm going to hit the dirt road back to Okochee.'

# Hearts and Hands

At Denver there was an influx of passengers into the coaches on the eastbound B. & M. express. In one coach there sat a very pretty young woman dressed in elegant taste and surrounded by all the luxurious comforts of an experienced traveler. Among the newcomers were two young men, one of handsome presence with a bold, frank countenance and manner; the other a ruffled, glum-faced person, heavily built and roughly dressed. The two were handcuffed together.

As they passed down the aisle of the coach the only vacant seat offered was a reversed one facing the attractive young woman. Here the linked couple seated themselves. The young woman's glance fell upon them with a distant, swift disinterest; then with a lovely smile brightening her countenance and a tender pink tingeing her rounded cheeks, she held out a little gray-gloved hand. When she spoke her voice, full, sweet, and deliberate, proclaimed that its owner was accustomed to speak and be heard.

'Well, Mr Easton, if you *will* make me speak first, I suppose I must. Don't you ever recognize old friends when you meet them in the West?'

The younger man roused himself sharply at the sound of her voice, seemed to struggle with a slight embarrassment which he threw off instantly, and then clasped her fingers with his left hand.

'It's Miss Fairchild,' he said, with a smile. 'I'll ask you to excuse the other hand; it's otherwise engaged just at present.'

He slightly raised his right hand, bound at the wrist by the shining 'bracelet' to the left one of his companion. The glad look in the girl's eyes slowly changed to a bewildered horror. The glow faded from her cheeks. Her lips parted in a vague, relaxing distress. Easton, with a little laugh, as if amused, was about to speak again when the other forestalled him. The glum-faced man had been watching the girl's countenance with veiled glances from his keen, shrewd eyes.

'You'll excuse me for speaking, miss, but, I see you're acquainted with the marshal here. If you'll ask him to speak a word for me when we get to the pen he'll do it, and it'll make things easier for me there. He's taking me to Leavenworth prison. It's seven years for counterfeiting.'

'Oh!' said the girl, with a deep breath and returning color. 'So that is what you are doing out here? A marshal!'

'My dear Miss Fairchild,' said Easton, calmly, 'I had to do something. Money has a way of taking wings unto itself, and you know it takes money to keep step with our crowd in Washington. I saw this opening in the West, and – well, a marshalship isn't quite as high a position as that of ambassador, but –'

'The ambassador,' said the girl, warmly, 'doesn't call any more. He needn't ever have done so. You ought to know that. And so now you are one of these dashing Western heroes, and you ride and shoot and go into all kinds of dangers. That's different from the Washington life. You have been missed from the old crowd.'

The girl's eyes, fascinated, went back, widening a little, to rest upon the glittering handcuffs.

'Don't you worry about them, miss,' said the other man. 'All marshals handcuff themselves to their prisoners to keep them from getting away. Mr Easton knows his business.'

'Will we see you again soon in Washington?' asked the girl.

'Not soon, I think,' said Easton. 'My butterfly days are over, I fear.'

'I love the West,' said the girl, irrelevantly. Her eyes were shining softly. She looked away out the car window. She began to speak truly and simply, without the gloss of style and manner: 'Mamma and I spent the summer in Denver. She went home a week ago because father was slightly ill. I could live and be happy in the West. I think the air here agrees with me. Money isn't everything. But people always misunderstand things and remain stupid –'

'Say, Mr Marshal,' growled the glum-faced man. 'This isn't quite fair. I'm needin' a drink, and haven't had a smoke all day. Haven't you talked long enough? Take me in the smoker now, won't you? I'm half dead for a pipe.'

The bound travelers rose to their feet, Easton with the same slow smile on his face.

'I can't deny a petition for tobacco,' he said, lightly. 'It's the one friend of the unfortunate. Good-bye, Miss Fairchild. Duty calls, you know.' He held out his hand for a farewell.

'It's too bad you are not going East,' she said, reclothing herself with manner and style. 'But you must go on to Leavenworth, I suppose?'

'Yes,' said Easton, 'I must go on to Leavenworth.'

The two men sidled down the aisle into the smoker.

The two passengers in a seat nearby had heard most of the conversation. Said one of them: 'That marshal's a good sort of chap. Some of these Western fellows are all right.'

'Pretty young to hold an office like that, isn't he?' asked the other.

'Young!' exclaimed the first speaker, 'why – Oh! didn't you catch on? Say – did you ever know an officer to handcuff a prisoner to his *right* hand?'

PENGUIN ENGLISH
LIBRARY

# OTHER TITLES IN THIS SERIES

## Lady Audley's Secret
MARY ELIZABETH BRADDON

**'Lady Audley uttered a long, low, wailing cry, and threw her
arms above her head with a wild gesture of despair'**

In this outlandish, outrageous triumph of scandal fiction, a new Lady Audley
arrives at the manor: young, beautiful – and very mysterious. Why does she
behave so strangely? What, exactly, is the dark secret this seductive outsider
carries with her?

A huge success in the nineteenth century, the book's anti-heroine – with
her good looks and hidden past – embodied perfectly the concerns of the
Victorian age with morality and madness.

PENGUIN ENGLISH
LIBRARY

## OTHER TITLES IN THIS SERIES

### The Scarlet Letter
NATHANIEL HAWTHORNE

**'Shame, Despair, Solitude! These had been her teachers, — stern and wild ones, — and they had made her strong, but taught her much amiss'**

Fiercely romantic and hugely influential, *The Scarlet Letter* is the tale of Hester Prynne, imprisoned, publicly shamed, and forced to wear a scarlet 'A' for committing adultery and bearing an illegitimate child, Pearl. In their small, Puritan village, Hester and her daughter struggle to survive, but in this searing study of the tension between private and public existence, Hester Prynne's inner strength and quiet dignity mean she has frequently been seen as one of the first great heroines of American fiction.

PENGUIN ENGLISH
LIBRARY

# OTHER TITLES IN THIS SERIES

## The Way of All Flesh
SAMUEL BUTLER

> 'The greater part of every family is always odious; if there are one or two good ones in a very large family, it is as much as can be expected'

Written with great humour, irony and honesty, *The Way of All Flesh* exploded perceptions of the Victorian middle-class family in its radical depiction of Ernest Pontifex, a young man who casts off his background and disovers himself.

The akward but likable son of a tyrannical clergyman and a priggish mother, and destined to follow his father into the church, Ernest gleefully rejects his parents' respectability, and chooses instead to find his own way in the world.

PENGUIN ENGLISH
LIBRARY

## OTHER TITLES IN THIS SERIES

### The House of Mirth
EDITH WHARTON

> **'It was characteristic of her that she always roused speculation, that her simplest acts seemed the result of far-reaching intentions'**

A searing, shocking tale of woman as consumer item in a man's world, *The House of Mirth* tells of Lily Bart, beautiful and charming, and living among the wealthy families of New York City but reluctant to finally commit herself to one. In an endless search for freedom and the happiness she feels she deserves, she is ultimately ruined by scandal.

Edith Wharton's shattering novel created controversy on its publication in 1905 with its scathing portrayal of the world's wealthy and the prison that marriage can become.

PENGUIN ENGLISH
LIBRARY

# OTHER TITLES IN THIS SERIES

## Ethan Frome
EDITH WHARTON

> **'He seemed a part of the mute melancholy landscape, an in-
> carnation of its frozen woe, with all that was warm and sen-
> tient in him fast bound below the surface'**

One of American fiction's finest and most intense narratives, *Ethan Frome* tells
a story of ill-starred lovers and their tragic destinies.

Ethan works his unproductive farm and struggles to maintain a bearable existence with his difficult, suspicious and hypochondriac wife, Zeenie. But when
Zeenie's vivacious cousin enters their household as a 'hired girl', Ethan finds
his life changed by her and the possibilities for happiness she comes to rep-
resent.

PENGUIN ENGLISH
LIBRARY

## OTHER TITLES IN THIS SERIES

### Emma
JANE AUSTEN

**"I never have been in love; it is not my way, or my nature; and
I do not think I ever shall"**

Jane Austen's sparkling and flawless comic masterpiece is the story of Emma
Woodhouse: rich, charming, spoilt, obsessed with matchmaking and blind to
everyone's faults – including her own.

Although Austen described Emma as a character 'whom no one but myself
will much like', her wit and her gradual self-realization make her one of the
author's most remarkable, believably imperfect heroines.

PENGUIN ENGLISH
LIBRARY

# OTHER TITLES IN THIS SERIES

### The Confidence-Man *and* Billy Budd, Sailor
HERMAN MELVILLE

**"Life is a pic-nic *en costume*; one must take a part, assume a character, stand ready in a sensible way to play the fool"**

In *The Confidence-Man*, Melville's unnerving and hallucinatory satire on the American dream, a slippery trickster and master of disguise comes to swindle his fellow passengers – who themselves may also be con-men – aboard a Mississippi steamboat.

*Billy Budd, Sailor*, published after Melville's death in 1891, is a gripping allegory of good and evil, as an innocent man, pressed into service on a British man-of-war, is falsely accused of mutiny.

Both these late works are animated with the dark genius of the greatest of American writers.

www.penguin.com

PENGUIN ENGLISH
LIBRARY

# OTHER TITLES IN THIS SERIES

## The Murders in the Rue Morgue
EDGAR ALLAN POE

**'...an agility astounding, a strength superhuman, a ferocity brutal, a butchery without motive, a *grotesquerie* in horror absolutely alien from humanity...'**

Horror, madness, violence and the dark forces hidden in humanity abound in this collection of Poe's brilliant tales, including – among others – the bloody, brutal and baffling murder of a mother and daughter in Paris in 'The Murders in the Rue Morgue', the creeping insanity of 'The Tell-Tale Heart', the Gothic nightmare of 'The Masque of the Red Death', and the terrible doom of 'The Fall of the House of Usher'.

PENGUIN ENGLISH
LIBRARY

# OTHER TITLES IN THIS SERIES

## The Hound of the Baskervilles
ARTHUR CONAN DOYLE

**"Mr Holmes, they were the footprints of a gigantic hound!"**

The terrible spectacle of the beast, the fog of the moor, the discovery of a body: this classic horror story pits detective against dog, rationalism against the supernatural, good against evil. When Sir Charles Baskerville is found dead on the wild Devon moorland with the footprints of a giant hound nearby, the blame is placed on a family curse. It is left to Sherlock Holmes and Doctor Watson to solve the mystery of the legend of the phantom hound before Sir Charles's heir comes to an equally gruesome end. *The Hound of the Baskervilles* gripped readers when it was first serialized and has continued to hold its place in the popular imagination.

PENGUIN ENGLISH
LIBRARY

## OTHER TITLES IN THIS SERIES

### The Invisible Man
H. G. WELLS

'People screamed. People sprang off the pavement ... "The
Invisible Man is coming! The Invisible Man!"'

With his face swaddled in bandages, his eyes hidden behind dark glasses and
his hands covered even indoors, Griffin – the new guest at The Coach and
Horses – is at first assumed to be a shy accident-victim. But the true reason
for his disguise is far more chilling: he has developed a process that has made
him invisible, and is locked in a struggle to discover the antidote. Forced from
the village, and driven to murder, he seeks the aid of an old friend, Kemp. The
horror of his fate has affected his mind, however – and when Kemp refuses to
help, he resolves to wreak his revenge.

PENGUIN ENGLISH
LIBRARY

# OTHER TITLES IN THIS SERIES

## The Invisible Man
H. G. WELLS

**'People screamed. People sprang off the pavement ... "The Invisible Man is coming! The Invisible Man!"'**

With his face swaddled in bandages, his eyes hidden behind dark glasses and his hands covered even indoors, Griffin – the new guest at The Coach and Horses – is at first assumed to be a shy accident-victim. But the true reason for his disguise is far more chilling: he has developed a process that has made him invisible, and is locked in a struggle to discover the antidote. Forced from the village, and driven to murder, he seeks the aid of an old friend, Kemp. The horror of his fate has affected his mind, however – and when Kemp refuses to help, he resolves to wreak his revenge.